Matters of the Heart

ASHLEY FARLEY

ALSO BY ASHLEY FARLEY

Palmetto Island Series

Muddy Bottom

Change of Tides

Lowcountry on My Mind

Sail Away

Hope Springs Series

Dream Big, Stella!

Show Me the Way

Mistletoe and Wedding Bells

Matters of the Heart

Tangled in Ivy

Lies that Bind

Life on Loan

Only One Life

Home for Wounded Hearts

Nell and Lady

Sweet Tea Tuesdays

Saving Ben

Sweeney Sisters Series

Saturdays at Sweeney's

Tangle of Strings

Boots and Bedlam

Lowcountry Stranger

Her Sister's Shoes

Magnolia Series

Beyond the Garden

Magnolia Nights

Scottie's Adventures

Breaking the Story

Merry Mary

1

STELLA

I stand on the stone terrace of my castle, looking out over my kingdom. In my modern-day fairytale, my castle is a restored historic inn and my kingdom the encompassing seventy acres. The new Summer House Wellness Center, which includes a spa and pool complex, is at the bottom of the hill on a natural lake where guests paddleboard, kayak, and fish for small-mouth bass. To the left, nestled amongst the trees by a gentle-flowing stream, is a row of weekly rental guest cottages. Woodlands extend beyond the property lines with hiking trails leading into the Virginia mountains.

I count my blessings every day, thanking my father for trusting me with this jewel. Recently, though, the strings attached to those blessings have been strangling me.

When I came to Hope Springs thirteen months ago, I'd only planned to stay long enough to satisfy the three-year obligation stipulated in my father's will. When that time was up, I had every intention of selling the inn and hightailing it back to my beloved New York. But I fell in love instead. With the charming town. With a handsome contractor who is now my husband,

Jack. With the biological family I never knew about—Opal, my grandmother; Brian, my uncle; and Jazz, my eight-year-old half sister whom I am now raising as my daughter. And the memory of my father, whose presence I feel in the sacred halls of the inn.

Because of his declining health, my father neglected the inn during the last years of his life. I embraced the challenge of overseeing the extensive renovations. But now that all my projects are complete, I find the day-to-day running of the inn mundane. Our nightly rates are high. But our five-star service is unsurpassed. Yet guests still find reason to complain. I spend most of my time putting out fires.

I'm complaining like my pampered guests when I should be grateful for the inn's success. For a brief time after we reopened, I worried the inn wouldn't make it. But thanks to my dedicated staff and talented marketing team, we're booked solid through the end of the year.

Upon opening in the spring, the new wellness center has put us on the map as a hot spot for destination weddings. I notice my event planner, Lia, on the lawn with a long-legged blonde beauty and an elegant middle-aged couple—a bride and her parents coordinating the details for the big day.

Lia spots me and motions for me to join them. I walk down the stone steps to the sidewalk and cut across the grass to where they're standing near my grandmother Opal's favorite dogwood tree.

The daughter is her mother's clone with crystal blue eyes, pearly white teeth, and toned limbs. Mother and daughter are wearing brightly patterned sundresses. The gentleman, in khaki slacks and a navy linen blazer, carries an air of dignity, and I'm not surprised to learn he's a state governor.

Lia sweeps her arm at the family. "Stella, meet Governor Dupree, his wife, Luann, and daughter, Peaches."

"Peaches! What a cute nickname." The words depart my tongue before I notice Lia vigorously shaking her head.

Peaches raises her chin, looking down her nose at me. "It is *not* a nickname."

With an incensed humph, Luann says, "My daddy was also a Georgia governor back in the sixties. As First Lady, his wife, my mama, was much loved by the people of Georgia. Her name was Sarah Jane, but they called her Peaches, because she was as sweet as a Georgia peach. I felt it fitting for my only child to carry on the name."

"Well . . . Welcome to Hope Springs Farm. What brings you to town?" I know the names of all our summer brides, and Dupree does not ring a bell.

"I'm planning my wedding," Peaches says.

Lia, as though sensing my confusion, explains, "Our bride for the fourth weekend in July came down with a case of cold feet and called off her wedding."

"I only got engaged a month ago," Peaches says. "But I had my heart set on a summer wedding. When I found out about the cancellation, I jumped at the chance."

My eyes naturally gravitate toward her midsection.

Peaches huffs out her annoyance. "I'm not pregnant, if that's what you're thinking. My fiancé just moved to London for a new job. I miss him like crazy, and I can't stand the thought of being without him for months on end."

"I'm glad we can accommodate you." I gesture at my event planner. "You're in expert hands with Lia. I'm certain your wedding will be lovely."

I start to walk off, but Lia calls after me. "Stella! Wait! If you have a minute, we could use your input. Peaches has some . . . um, interesting ideas. Things we haven't done before. I'd like to clear them with you."

I turn back toward the group. "Of course. I'd love to hear your ideas. What're you thinking?"

"Well, let's see." Peaches spreads her arms wide at the main building. "The ceremony will be on the terrace with clear Lucite chairs for the guests and a pathway of white rose petals leading to an arbor covered in peach peonies."

Peaches turns around, placing her back to the building. "The reception will be down here on the lawn. I want sailcloth tents, the authentic Sperry Tents, on either side of the sidewalk, one for the band and the other for the food." She taps her chin with a french-manicured fingernail. "We'll have a champagne fountain, lobsters flown in from Maine, Chincoteague Salts oysters from the Eastern Shore, and Wagyu beef from Japan." She glances over at her mother. "What am I missing?"

"We'll release a thousand peach balloons when you're pronounced husband and wife," Luann says.

"Right! And fireworks when we leave the reception. We'll be departing by helicopter." Peaches spins around in a circle. "There's plenty of room here to land it."

"We've blocked off all the rooms for our guests," Luann says. "But the band will need accommodations. Is there another hotel in town?"

Peaches claps her hands and bounces on her sandaled toes. "I forgot the best part! You're never gonna believe who the band is."

Lia, who has been hanging on Peaches's every word while rapidly typing notes on her iPad, says, "Who?"

"Earth, Wind, and Desire!" Peaches says, doing a little victory dance.

Excitement flutters across my chest, and for a brief second, I forget I'm the manager of a five-star resort. "Shut up! *The* Earth, Wind, and Desire?"

Peaches bobs her head. "Daddy is friends with the manager." She flicks her wrist in her father's direction without bothering to look at him.

"My father was a musician. He'll dance on his grave when Earth, Wind, and Desire plays at Hope Springs Farms." I notice Luann glaring at me, and I straighten. "To answer your question, there is no other hotel in town. But we'll figure something out."

"I have some concerns about your ability to pull off our elaborate affair," Luann says in a condescending tone. "We've met the key members of your staff. They are all so young. I worry they lack the experience to give us what we want."

Pink dots appear on Lia's cheeks. She's been on staff only since Christmas, and she's doing an excellent job despite her limited experience. But our guests host enough parties and weddings to keep three event planners busy. As of now, Lia only has our summer intern, Emma, to help her.

I gather my wits. "My staff may be young, but they've proven themselves with their strong work ethic and innovative ideas. I am certain they can deliver on your expectations." I turn my attention to the governor, who hasn't spoken since the introductions. "The wedding your wife and daughter describe will be costly. If you'd like to proceed, I'll draw up a proposal and send it to you."

Peaches presses her hands together under her chin. "Please, Daddy!"

Despite his enormous power and influence, I don't imagine the governor ever wins an argument with his wife and daughter. "Send me the proposal," he says, handing me his business card, which includes his cell number and personal email address.

Taking the card, I turn back to Peaches. "How long are you in town? We should have a sit-down meeting to discuss more details."

Peaches beams, her sun-kissed complexion aglow. "I've rented a cottage on Cottage Row! I'll be here until the wedding!"

I have a sick feeling in the pit of my stomach. This is going to be a long two months with Peaches Dupree underfoot. "Wonderful." I lock eyes with my event planner. "Lia, I'll leave it to you to set up a meeting for early next week."

Relief crosses Lia's face. "Will do."

"Good day, folks. Enjoy your stay. Don't hesitate to contact me if you need anything. You can reach me through the front desk." I wave in parting as I continue on toward the wellness center.

The original summer house was nothing more than an oversized screened porch, but I kept the name to honor the good times enjoyed here by generations of families over the decades. While the building was built to look like an old farmhouse, the new facility sports all the modern conveniences.

The first floor houses a healthy lunch spot and a sporting goods shop where guests can purchase high-end outdoor attire, book hiking and fishing outings, and rent paddleboards, kayaks, and fishing equipment.

A state-of-the art fitness center featuring studios for exercise classes and a lap pool takes up the second floor. And the spa is located on the third. Walls of windows overlook the lake on the front side of the wellness center, and off the back is the pool complex.

The hot springs are located on the side of the building opposite the main entrance. The original hot springs were housed in a run-down hut. We tore down the hut and created an open-air space where guests can view the mountains during the day and the starry skies at night.

It's almost lunchtime and my stomach is growling. Grabbing a blueberry and banana smoothie from Roots, I make my way through the building, stopping to chat with staff members and guests.

Claudia, the desk attendant in the fitness center, informs me Ollie is looking for me. "Last I heard, she was out by the pool," Claudia says.

"Thanks. I'm on my way," I say, and head off to put out another fire.

2

OLLIE

Ollie's eyes are on the small children splashing in the pool, but her mind is a million miles away. She doesn't hear Stella approach until she's standing beside her.

Ollie startles. "I didn't see you there."

"You were lost in thought. What's the crisis du jour?"

Ollie gives her head a solemn shake. "I'm afraid we're facing a crisis of the summer."

"Let's sit down," Stella says, and motions Ollie to an umbrellaed table.

Ollie chooses a chair that gives her a view of the pool. "We have a cohabitation problem. The parents of young children"— she gestures at the children in the pool—"are complaining our adult guests are too rowdy. And the adults, mostly young single people, criticize the kids for being too rambunctious."

"What do they expect? Kids are supposed to be loud and unruly. As long as they are not being dangerous. Are they misbehaving?"

Ollie thinks before answering. "Not really. The guests are pretty responsible about not letting their kids swim without adult supervision. But kids splash a lot, and some of these divas are worried about getting their hair wet."

"For goodness' sake," Stella says. "Why get in the pool if they're afraid of getting wet?"

"Right." Ollie nods, her dark ponytail dancing around her shoulders. "If you ask me, these young adults are more of a problem than the kids. These weddings are bringing in a lot of single people. A group of them arrived early for this weekend's wedding. They apparently had a raging pool party last night. I've been hearing about it from parents all morning."

"Hmm." Stella drums her fingers on the table. "I can see where that would be a problem. Parents don't want to subject their innocent children to that kind of behavior."

Mischief tugs at Ollie's lips. "You should build another pool, one designated just for families, closer to the main building."

Stella raises an eyebrow. "I just finished building this pool."

Ollie slumps down in her chair. "I've been wracking my brain, and I can't come up with another solution. If we stop serving alcoholic beverages, these young adults will find somewhere else to party. And the pool bar is currently bringing in a lot of revenue."

"What time were these shenanigans going on last night?"

Ollie thumbs through the text messages on her phone. "I got the first complaint around ten."

Stella scowls. "In my opinion, that's entirely too late for children to be swimming. Let's restrict the hours to allow only ages eighteen and above after dark. I've been putting off hiring lifeguards, hoping we wouldn't need them. Clearly, we do."

Ollie grunts. "Good luck finding them. I don't imagine a small town like Hope Springs has a surplus of out-of-work lifeguards."

Stella snickers. "True. But I'm sure there are summer school students at Jefferson College looking for work."

Ollie's aqua eyes are like the crystal clear Caribbean Sea. "I didn't think of that. Great idea!"

Stella stands to go. "I'll put out some feelers, and let you know what I find out."

Ollie watches Stella exit the pool area and stroll up the sidewalk toward the main building. She's beautiful in a natural way with unruly shoulder-length cinnamon-brown hair. And she's accomplished so much for someone so young. She manages the inn with graceful authority, treating every member of her team with respect. Although Ollie grew up working her family's vineyard, on paper, she is grossly underqualified to be in charge of the wellness center. But Stella gave her a chance, and Ollie is grateful for the opportunity. She had nowhere else to go. She was sinking, and Stella threw her a life jacket. Ollie hopes she doesn't disappoint her.

Ollie leaves the pool and returns to her office on the spa level. She's passing through the relaxation room when she hears a woman arguing with Wanda, the receptionist. "But I'm a guest in the hotel. Please! I'm begging you. Can't you fit me in? I can stay until Monday if necessary."

Ollie joins them at the reception desk. "Is there a problem?"

The woman gives Ollie the once-over, her eyes lingering on the name tag that identifies Ollie's position. She extends her hand to Ollie. "Hi! I'm Rosemarie Cross from Knoxville, Tennessee."

Ollie shakes the woman's hand. "I'm Olivia Hendrix, Wellness Center Manager. What can I do for you?"

"I'm trying to book an appointment for a soak in the mineral tubs," Rosemarie says. "This woman says you're full all weekend."

Stella's genius contractor husband, Jack, concocted a system to pump mineral water from the natural hot springs up to the third floor. Their most popular spa treatment is a fifty-minute soak in one of two private claw-footed tubs.

"We're hosting a wedding this weekend," Ollie explains. "All spa treatments have been booked solid for weeks."

"You don't understand. I've had eczema since I was a baby. I had a treatment when I was here two weeks ago, and now the eczema is gone. It's a pluperfect miracle. See!" Rosemarie holds her arms out straight, showing Ollie the tender white skin on the underside.

Ollie studies the crooks of the woman's elbows, which she knows firsthand is a common problem area for eczema.

"I drove all the way here, six hours door-to-door, for the sole purpose of getting another mineral water treatment. Can't you please fit me in? I'm flexible. I'll even come at midnight if necessary."

"We can work something out." Ollie pulls the woman aside, out of the way of another guest who is waiting to check in for her treatment. "You have two choices. We can see if there is a spot available in the outdoor hot tubs. The mineral water is the same. We pump it up to the spa from the hot springs. Or I'll personally oversee your soaking room treatment after we close at seven tonight."

Rosemarie narrows her green eyes as she considers her options. "How long can I soak outside?"

"Only eight guests are allowed in the hot springs at a time," Ollie says. "And we reserve those spots for ninety-minutes."

Rosemarie slaps her thigh. "Let's do it."

"You'll need to change into your swimsuit," Ollie says.

Rosemarie lifts up her polo shirt, revealing a black one-piece bathing suit.

"All right then. Let's go see what's available." With Rosemarie on her heels, Ollie retraces her steps to the elevator.

When they reach the first floor, they exit the back door and pass through the pool area to the side of the building where a privacy fence prohibits access to the hot springs. The attendant confirms space available, hands Rosemarie a towel, and unlocks the gate for them.

"I'll show you around," Ollie says as they enter the hot springs. "Looks like you have the place to yourself. At least for a while." They approach a kidney-shaped natural pool with rock bottom and sides and steam floating from the surface of teal-colored water.

"How do you use it?" Rosemarie asks, staring into the pool, providing a romantic and mysterious ambiance.

"Sit down and slide in. The water is five feet at the deepest, but some areas are as shallow as three feet. Large rocks jut out from certain places along the sides for seating."

"But it's so small," Rosemarie says in a skeptical tone.

"We prefer to think of it as intimate. Hence the reason we limited the number of occupants to eight at a time."

Rosemarie lowers herself to the edge of the pool and slips into the water. "Ah, this is heavenly, like liquid butter."

Ollie smiles down at her. "I'll leave you to relax. Enjoy yourself, now."

When she starts off, Rosemarie calls after her. "Can I soak in the hot springs tomorrow?"

"As long as space is available. Speak with the attendant on your way out," she says and keeps walking.

Ollie is on her way back inside when she spots Stella's grandmother at her easel under the dogwood tree everyone refers to as Opal's. Ollie and Opal became fast friends when they met at the wellness center opening back in April. Opal is a quirky hipster who paints like Vincent van Gogh. Her landscape scenes of the farm adorn the walls in the main building. And she's the resident historian. Opal would know if there was anything special about the mineral water.

Opal sees her coming and waves. "Good afternoon, sweet girl. You look like a woman on a mission. What's up?"

"I'm a bit stumped, and I could use your help. A guest who was here two weeks ago claims the mineral water cured her eczema. Is that even possible?"

Opal doesn't hesitate. "Not only is it possible. It's probable." She takes Ollie by the arm. "Let's sit a spell. My old bones are tired." She leads Ollie over to a nearby park bench.

There are several park benches on this stretch of lawn, but Stella has designated this one as Opal's. She even had a brass plate made for the back of the seat that says Opal's Bench.

Once seated, Opal says, "The mineral water contains hydrogen sulfide, identified by the smell of rotten eggs. Our bodies contain sulfur in the form of keratin, a protein that makes up our skin, nails, and hair. So yes, the hot springs have special healing powers. Although, I've never known anyone who has experienced such. Then again, Billy, Stella's father, kept the hot springs under lock and key for the past two decades."

Lines appear in Ollie's forehead. "Why would he do that?"

"Same reason everything else went to hell in a hand basket around here. The support structure surrounding the hot springs needed work, and he wasn't well enough to deal with it. The first documented settlers to the area built a lodge where the main building now stands. The farm came first and then the town. The townsfolk view the springs as a symbol of hope. Hence the name Hope Springs."

"Wow! Can you imagine what this could mean for the spa and the farm if the water does have healing powers? What if it cures cancer?"

Opal laughs. "That's a bit of a stretch. But you never know. If you're curious to learn more, a section in the inn's library houses history books of the farm and the town." Opal's face lights up, as though struck with an idea. "Stella recently discovered her great-grandmother's diaries in a warehouse where some of her ancestors' possessions are stored. You should check with Stella. Her great-grandmother may have written something about the hot springs."

"Cool. I'll do that. Thanks Opal," Ollie says, suddenly curious to know more about this place she's beginning to think of as home.

3

PRESLEY

Presley is overcome with emotion as she drives up the hill to the inn's main entrance. Her throat thickens and tears threaten at the sight of the three-story building with cupolas and dormer windows, green awnings, and sweeping verandas. Even though she only spent a brief three months here last fall, she feels as though she's returning home after a long journey. She attributes much of these warm fuzzies to her newfound family.

Presley had been eager to leave Hope Springs after Christmas. Originally from Nashville, she'd found small town living stifling. She felt destined for bigger and better things. Turns out, her husband is the one bound for success as a country music star. Everett's manager hired Presley to help organize his inaugural tour. She'd been the tagalong. Everett's shadow. The wife who always seemed to be in the way.

Elton, the bell captain who's been greeting guests at the inn for over sixty years, opens her car door and flashes a toothy grin. He's carried luggage for some of the inn's most prestigious guests. Whitney Houston. Margaret Thatcher. Even Jackie and

John Kennedy stayed here once, the summer before a gunman took the president's life in Dallas the following November.

"Welcome back, Miss Presley. According to this"—he waves a reservation card—"you're booked in a cottage on Cottage Row. After you get checked in, I'll have one of my men follow you down to help you get settled."

"Thank you, Elton." Presley hands him her car key and a five-dollar bill. "I may be awhile. I have a few people I want to see."

He bends slightly at the waist. "That's perfectly okay. Take your time. We'll be right here whenever you're ready."

A bellman opens one of a pair of wood-and-glass paned doors for Presley. The smell of beeswax and old memories greets her inside. Large bouquets of assorted roses grace the priceless antique chests flanking the wide entryway. Ahead, at the marble reservations counter, Stella, the general manager, and Presley's aunt Rita, the reservations manager, are deep in conversation with their heads pressed together.

When Stella spots Presley, she lets out a squeal and rushes toward her, engulfing her in a hug. "I've missed you so much." She holds her at arm's length. "You look fabulous. Marriage and pregnancy agree with you."

Stella's being kind. Presley has studied her reflection in the mirror. She's aware of the dark circles and hollow cheeks. Her obstetrician warned her she needed to start gaining weight instead of losing it. At twenty weeks, her desired weigh is way below what it should be. "You're the one who looks amazing," Presley says. "Marriage agrees with you."

"I've gained five pounds, but I can't blame it on pregnancy." Stella chuckles, but there's a sadness in her eyes that wasn't there before. Is she trying to get pregnant? Or is she having trouble in her marriage, too?

Stella looks over at Rita. "Did you know Presley was coming?"

Rita drags an imaginary zipper across her lips. "Presley swore me to secrecy. She wanted to surprise you," she says, and steps away to assist an older couple with information about tourist spots in the area.

"How long are you staying?" Stella asks.

"I booked a cottage for the summer. Everett is still on tour, and there's nothing keeping me in Nashville."

Stella looks heavenward. "There is a God."

Presley laughs. "I'm afraid to ask what that means."

"We're hosting the wedding of the century in July." She leans in close to Presley. "Don't tell anyone. But Earth, Wind, and Desire is the band."

It's Presley's turn to squeal. "That's amazing."

"Problem is, the bride is a Southern belle diva from Georgia. I'll comp your stay and pay you whatever you want if you'll collaborate on the planning."

"What happened to Amelia?"

"Amelia's doing a tremendous job. And Emma is an enormous asset, but she's only an intern. This wedding will require all hands on deck. Really and truly, Presley. You're the best event planner on the East Coast. You're wasting your talents organizing snacks and drinks for Everett's tour." Stella's blue eyes grow wide. "Speaking of the tour. Jack and I have been following his schedule. Why aren't you with him in Los Angeles?"

Presley looks away. "The tour, the late nights, and long road trips proved to be too much for someone in my condition. I'm working on a project this summer, but I can carve out some time to consult on your wedding."

Stella's expression morphs from concern to gratitude. "Excellent. I'll make it worth your while."

Presley aims her thumb toward the lounge. "I'm headed down to Jameson's to see Cecily. Wanna come with?"

"I wish I could. But I have to get started on the proposal for the governor."

Presley's auburn brows meet in the middle. "What governor?"

"The father of the Southern Belle Bride is Georgia's governor, Marcus Dupree."

Presley rubs her palms together. "Ooh. Now, I'm totally Intrigued. This could be fun."

"Reserve your opinion until you meet the bride." Stella hugs her again. "Come to the manor for dinner tomorrow night. Jack and Jazz will be thrilled to see you. And Angel. Wait until you see her. She's grown and into everything."

Presley smiles at the mention of the golden retriever puppy Stella and her husband surprised Jazz with at Christmas. "Dinner sounds lovely. Thanks."

As Stella heads off, Rita finishes with the couple and returns to Presley's end of the counter. "You look tired, sweetheart. Is everything okay?"

The lump in Presley's throat returns. What's up with all these emotions? Must be hormones. She forces a smile. "Everything is fine. I just need a rest. Which is why I'm here. What's new with you and the girls?"

At the mention of her teenage daughters, Presley's cousin, Rita's oldest, Emma, comes flying through the front door. "I saw your car out front. I'm so glad you're here. We're gonna have the best summer ever." She almost knocks Presley down with her hug.

Presley cuts her eyes at her aunt. "You told her I was coming."

Rita coughs up a *ha*. "You know Emma. There's no keeping secrets from her."

Pulling away, Emma's eyes travel to Presley's belly. "Aww, look. How cute. You have a baby bump. Please say you'll stay in town until the baby comes."

"That's not until October. You'll be settled into your freshman year at Cornell by then, anyway."

Emma drapes her lanky body over the check-in counter toward her mother. "I know. But Mom needs you now that Aunt Lucy is out of rehab and back at work."

A grim expression crosses Rita's face. "Lower your voice, honey. I'd hate for Lucy to hear you."

Lines appear in Presley's forehead. "I don't understand. You've been attending the weekly family therapy sessions in Richmond. Wasn't the goal to improve your relationship?"

Rita's shoulders sag. "That was my hope. But Lucy resented my presence at the sessions. She's still so bitter. We're constantly at each other's throats. It's not healthy for us to work together."

"She's not using drugs again, is she?" Presley asks, alarmed.

Rita shakes her head. "She's clean. Thank goodness."

"Lucy is just a bitch," Emma says.

Rita gives her daughter a scolding look. "Don't you have work to do?"

"But—"

"Shoo," Rita says, waving her daughter away.

"Ugh! Okay." Emma gives Presley a hip bump. "Let's hang out soon," she says and slinks off down the hall toward the event office.

Rita moves to the computer and stabs at the keyboard. "Your cottage isn't quite ready. But it shouldn't be too much longer."

"That's fine. I'll be down at Jameson's. Will you text me when the cottage is ready?"

"Sure thing," Rita says, giving Presley a thumbs-up.

Presley leaves the reception hall with a heavy heart. The prospect of seeing her biological mother again is the only hesitation she has in spending the summer in Hope Springs. Lucy has made it abundantly clear she wants nothing to do with Presley. Having Presley around is a constant reminder of the fraternity boy who date-raped Lucy in college. On the bright side, Presley loves her aunt and cousins and half brother Chris. She's looking forward to getting to know them better this summer.

Her spirits lift as she enters the grand lobby where comfortable furnishings and a wall of windows offer guests a relaxing place to look out over the mountains. As she passes through the lobby, her heart skips a beat at the tall guy with broad shoulders and wavy dark hair behind the bar in the adjacent lounge. She's used to seeing Everett behind the bar. But this guy isn't Everett. Her husband is on tour in California.

She sticks her head into Billy's Bar, named after Stella's late father, rock legend Billy Jameson. Nothing much has changed here. To the right is a marble-topped bar with glass shelves housing an enormous selection of liquor bottles. Opposite it, a high-gloss indigo blue wall showcases Billy's prize collection of rock and roll memorabilia.

Continuing on to Jameson's, Presley makes her way through the crowded dining room to the kitchen where servers and cooks are winding down after the lunch rush. Cecily is standing with her back to Presley, adding seasonings to a concoction in a stainless mixing bowl. Her honey-blonde hair is piled on top of her head in a messy bun, and she wears her white chef's coat with houndstooth britches. While they've had their share of differences in the past, Presley considers her a friend.

Presley sneaks up behind her, and taps Cecily's shoulder.

Cecily spins around and her jaw hits the floor. "Girlfriend! What are you doing here? How long are you staying? And where's Everett?"

Presley can see the questions spinning in Cecily's head, and she's not in the mood to answer them. Ignoring her, she circles the room. "The kitchen looks great. What's different about it?"

Cecily gestures at the row of rollout windows above the counter where she's working. "I convinced Stella a view of the mountains would inspire me to create. An artist needs her studio."

"And so, she just knocked out a brick wall and put in windows for you?"

"What can I say?" Cecily spreads her arms wide. "I'm the main attraction around here."

Presley rolls her eyes. "I'd forgotten how your ego sucks all the air out of the room."

"Don't lie. You've missed me. And I've missed you. Look at this." Cecily places a hand on Presley's baby bump but quickly jerks it away. "It kicked me."

Presley laughs. "This baby is an active little bugger. We've decided not to find out the sex, but I have a hunch it's a boy."

"Interesting. Your instincts about people are usually spot-on. Come. Check this out." Taking Presley by the hand, she leads her to the back door, swinging it open to reveal a new covered porch.

They step out onto the porch and round the corner to the back of the kitchen. "Look! We planted a garden." Off the porch, surrounded by a white picket fence, is a lush garden with flowers and herbs. "Not only do we have every herb imaginable, but we're also growing flowers for our table arrangements. We even have a wide assortment of edible flowers. Parker, our new bartender, is a phenomenal mixologist."

Presley cuts her gray eyes at Cecily. "Better than Everett?"

"Way better than Everett. And that's saying a lot because Everett was good. Parker's easier on the eyes than Everett too."

Presley sends an elbow to Cecily's ribs. "Wait a minute. Are you saying you don't think Everett is hot?"

Cecily curls up her lip. "Eww. No." Presley's face falls, and Cecily laughs. "Just kidding. Everett is adorable. I just never thought of him that way. He was always my buddy."

Presley raises an eyebrow. "Are you saying Parker is more than your buddy?"

"No, Presley. Duh! I'm engaged to Lyle."

"How are things between you and Lyle?"

Cecily hangs her head. "Nothing's changed. Even though we're living together, we hardly ever see each other. I'm always working, and he's always complaining about me always working."

"I'm sorry to hear that, Cecily. He must be busy with his lacrosse team."

"Oh, he is. Plenty busy. But he seems to think it's okay for him to be committed to his job and not me." Cecily tosses her hands in the air. "Anyway, enough about Lyle."

The women return to the kitchen. "Would you like some tea?" Cecily asks. "Parker has formulated a blend of blueberry honey iced tea which we have adopted as our signature blend. Wait until you try it. The combination of flavors is to die for."

"Parker again. I hope you don't talk about Parker this much around Lyle."

"I'm not stupid, Presley. And I don't have a thing for Parker."

Cecily pours two glasses of tea and hands one to Presley. She takes a tentative sip and then a longer gulp. "This is seriously good."

"I told you. Let's go out to the porch," Cecily says, and Presley follows her back through the dining room to the porch where a table is opening up on the railing.

Presley gazes out at the mountain range. The beauty and tranquility of the landscape provide a calming effect, and she settles back in her chair. Why had she been so eager to escape all this? "So, what else is going on around here? Who else is new besides Parker?"

"Stella hired a whole new staff to run the wellness center. I don't really know any of them except Ollie, the manager."

"Ollie? Is that short for Olivia?"

"Yep." Cecily gulps some tea and slams down her glass. "Olivia Hendrix is her name. She's originally from California. She's the healthiest, most outdoorsy person I've ever met. And she's supercool. You're gonna love her."

"California?" Presley says, tilting her head to the side. "How did she end up in Hope Springs, Virginia?"

"The same way everyone else does. She's either searching, running, or hiding. Who knows which is the case with Ollie? She doesn't like to talk about herself. But she's definitely carrying some baggage."

"Aren't we all. Can't wait to meet her."

An attractive blonde in a peach shorts set makes her way onto the porch. "Yoo-hoo!" She waves as she approaches their table. "Are you Chef Cecily?"

Cecily looks up at her. "I am. And you are?"

"I'm Peaches Dupree. I'm getting married here in July." Without being invited, Peaches drags a chair over from another table and sits down. "I met with Stella this morning. She's now in charge of planning my wedding. Amelia was over her head."

Cecily glares at Peaches. "Amelia's my cousin."

Peaches sits up ramrod straight. "And she's a perfectly lovely girl. But my wedding isn't your average wedding."

"Is that so?" A wicked smirk tugs on Cecily's lips. "You don't need Stella. You need Presley."

Peaches appears confused. "Who's Presley?"

Presley's hand shoots up. "I am. I'm Presley Baldwin."

"Never heard of you," Peaches says, dismissively.

"Presley's husband is Everett Baldwin, the hot new country music star," Cecily says, her eyes shining with mischief.

"Shut up!" Peaches brings her hands crashing down on the table. "I'm from Georgia. I've been a fan of Everett's since forever." She surveys the guests at the other tables. "Is Everett here with you?"

"No. He's currently in Los Angeles on tour." Presley is used to women throwing themselves at her husband. Now that she's left the tour, she doesn't have to watch the fawning in action.

"Presley was our event planner before she got married. She actually planned Stella's wedding last Christmas. You should've seen it. Rustic by choice, but so elegant." Cecily is digging Presley's grave. Any moment, she's going to push Presley in.

"Will you help plan my wedding, Presley?" Peaches steeples her fingers. "Pretty please."

Presley already committed to Stella. While she didn't come to Hope Springs to get her old job back, a governor's daughter's lavish wedding will look awesome on her resume.

"Actually, I already am," Presley says. "I ran into Stella when I was checking in, and since I'll be spending the summer in Hope Springs, she asked me to consult with her on your wedding."

"Oh, goody." Peaches turns to Cecily. "About the food . . . My bestie since childhood just graduated from culinary school. She'll be in charge of the food and drinks."

Cecily, who has her glass raised to her lips, spits out a mouthful of tea. She wipes her lips on her coat sleeve. "What did you just say?"

Peaches levels her gaze at Cecily. "I'm pretty sure you heard me the first time. My best friend, Fiona, will be in charge of the catering."

Cecily leans across the table toward Peaches. "In order for

that to happen, Fiona would need to be a member of my kitchen staff, and we're not hiring. Sorry."

Peaches plants her hands on the table, fingers splayed. "Then make room for her. It'll only be for a couple of months."

Cecily's face beams red. "No one, especially some pipsqueak nobody like you, is going to tell me how to run my kitchen."

Peaches shoots out of her chair like a rocket. "For your information, my daddy is the governor of Georgia. And what I say goes."

Cecily stands to face her. "Oh, yeah? We'll see about that."

"Indeed we will." Spinning on her heels, Peaches storms off the porch.

Presley shifts in her chair to watch Peaches's exit.

Dropping back down to her chair, Cecily says, "What just happened here?"

"I have no clue," Presley says with a bewildered expression. "But I'm tempted to cancel my reservation and get the heck out of here."

Cecily's messy bun flops about as she vehemently shakes her head. "No way, girlfriend. You're not leaving me alone to cope with Bridezilla."

4

CECILY

The exchange with Bridezilla plagues Cecily's thoughts throughout the dinner rush. Peaches has gotten under her skin, and Cecily can't seem to shake off her irritation. She snaps at her staff and bangs around pots and pans until her head server, Elsa, asks her to please stop. "You're giving me a migraine."

A few minutes before nine, Stella enters the kitchen and drags Cecily into the office. Cecily collapses in her desk chair. "What's up?" she asks, even though she already knows why Stella is here.

Stella eases into the folding metal chair opposite her. "I understand you've met Peaches Dupree. We need to buckle our seat belts. We're in for a wild ride these next few weeks."

Cecily can't help but smile. Stella is letting her know they are on the same side.

Stella goes on. "I spent an hour on the phone with Governor Dupree this evening. We discussed the preliminary proposal for his daughter's wedding. I threw in everything. Including that fancy farmhouse sink you asked for."

Cecily smiles again. Stella would never charge the governor

for the sink. She's offering a bribe. If Cecily makes nice to the governor's daughter, Cecily gets a new sink.

Stella tucks a stray curl behind her ear. "I expected the governor to balk at the estimated expenses. But he didn't miss a beat. He was more upset about the phone call he received from his daughter, complaining about you. I explained how we do things around here, and we compromised. There's no way around it. We have to work with Peaches's friend, Fiona Fortnanny."

Cecily laughs out loud. "Are you kidding me? Her last name is Fortnanny."

Stella bites on her lip, as though trying not to laugh. "It's unfortunate."

"What's wrong with her parents? When your last name is Fortnanny, why would you name your child Fiona?"

Stella snaps her fingers. "Stay focused, Cecily. This is serious. I don't want to lose this wedding. This bride's father is Georgia's governor. I'm certain the guest list will include some of the wealthiest socialites in the Southeast. Which means excellent publicity for the resort. Not to mention, Earth, Wind, and Desire is the band."

Cecily's jaw goes slack. "You're joking?"

Stella shakes her head. "I'm not."

"I love Earth, Wind, and Desire." Cecily leans back in her chair, her thoughts overcome with images of her partying late night with the band.

Stella slides a computer printout across the desk to Cecily. "About Fiona. She looks good on paper."

Cecily snatches up the resume. Fiona recently graduated from Auguste Escoffier School of Culinary Arts in Colorado, one of the best culinary schools in the country. "What kind of deal did you make with the governor? Do we have to hire this person?"

"The governor will pay her salary. Fiona will only be here until the wedding. Her sole responsibility will be planning the wedding menu. Although, you retain final authority over everything relating to food and beverage. The governor understands this is nonnegotiable."

"Good—"

Stella holds up a finger. "But there's a catch. You have to put forth your best effort, Cecily. You must find a way to get along with both Peaches and Fiona."

Not only is Stella her boss, but she's also Cecily's best friend. So far, they've managed to separate business from pleasure. She's good to Cecily, supporting her in all her endeavors and rarely interfering with her decisions. Cecily can see this is important to Stella. And she won't let her down.

Cecily rights her chair, letting the resume float down to the desk. "All right. I'll make nice."

Stella stands to go. "There's one other thing."

Cecily looks up at her boss. "Ugh. I'm afraid to ask what."

"I'm hosting a small dinner party tomorrow night to welcome Presley back to town, and I want you to come."

"But tomorrow is Thursday—"

Stella holds up a hand, silencing her. "This party is also nonnegotiable. You can get away for a couple of hours. Your kitchen won't fall apart in your absence. I expect to see you at the manor around seven."

Cecily presses her cheek against Stella's. "I'll be there. Promise."

From the doorway, Cecily watches Stella circle the kitchen, speaking to each of her staff in turn. Stella leaves the kitchen, and Cecily envisions her making her way around the dining room greeting guests. She insists on being an active participant in every aspect of managing the inn. But Cecily worries the responsibilities may be taking a toll on her best friend.

Cecily doesn't like to be backed into a corner. Especially by a pampered princess. But Earth, Wind, and Desire is huge. The governor of Georgia is a pretty big deal as well. She'll make nice. But she'll politely show Fiona and Peaches who's in charge.

As she winds down from dinner, Cecily daydreams about the social media opportunities a wedding like this could present. After resetting the kitchen for breakfast, she locks the back door and walks around the building to the main entrance.

She thinks about her fiancé, Lyle, a lacrosse coach at Jefferson College, and the house on campus they rent, which is a straight shot up Main Street. Last December, when searching for housing, they had been at odds, both wanting to be near their jobs. They'd been racing against the clock, desperate to sign a lease before their wedding on Christmas Eve. At the last minute, they agreed they were rushing into marriage after dating only a few months and decided to try living together instead. When a faculty house became available, Cecily had been too worn down to argue. But she feels out of place on Lyle's turf.

Weather permitting, Cecily walks the mile and a half to and from work every day. The fresh air clears her head, and she enjoys peeking in the shop windows. This night is no exception. She passes the Dairy Deli, best ice cream in town, and Caffeine on the Corner where she worked as a barista before taking a job at the inn. When she reaches Town Tavern, Cecily pauses to look at the renovated warehouse building across the street. A law firm occupies the downstairs with apartments on the second and third floors. Amelia lives in Presley's old corner unit, which offers stunning views of the mountains.

Laughter from inside Town Tavern catches her attention and she turns toward the window. Stretching down the center of the restaurant, a rectangular table seats about twenty. She recognizes all of Lyle's friends except the striking blonde in deep conversation with Cecily's fiancé at one end of the table. Lyle places his arm on the back of the blonde's chair. Cecily knows this possessive gesture all too well. When the blonde says something to Lyle, he leans in closer to listen, and then tilts his head back in laughter. Who is this woman? And why, instead of anger or jealousy, does Cecily feel relief?

Turning away from the window, Cecily continues on her way home. Despite the late hour, she pours a glass of Barboursville Pinot Grigio and takes it out to the porch. She clears a path through Lyle's bikes, lacrosse sticks, and assortment of other sporting gear to the rocking chairs.

The rockers were their first purchase as roommates. One of their few joint purchases. After finding them at a yard sale on a warm Saturday in early March, Lyle and Cecily spent the next day sanding and repainting them a deep Charleston green. They'd dreamed of watching sunsets and sipping margaritas on their porch. But that dream, like so many others, has yet to come true.

Cecily is still sitting in the rocker twenty minutes later when Lyle stumbles up the front walk. He doesn't see her in the dark, and when she asks where he's been, he startles, dropping his keys.

Hand against chest, he says, "Cecily, you scared me. What're you doing here?"

"I live here, remember? I came home early to surprise you." The lie slides too easily off her tongue.

Lyle drops to his knees, crawling around on the porch floor until he finds his keys. He sits down in the empty rocker beside her. "You should've texted me. I was at Town Tavern with some friends. You could've joined us."

"Oh yeah? What friends?" She's met most of the people who were seated at his table. She wants him to identify the blonde.

He shrugs. "You know. The usual crowd."

His friend group is made up of college coaches and professors while her friends are the other staff members at the inn. They have no couple friends, only his and hers. Come to think of it, everything they have is his and hers. Nothing is theirs, aside from the rockers. Cecily and Lyle are on two separate paths in life. Those paths rarely cross. And they'll never merge unless one of them is willing to yield.

The past five months are like a Giphy animation, replaying over and over the same old argument that scared them away from getting married. Lyle blames all their problems on Cecily's job.

"July Fourth falls on a Sunday this year," Lyle says. "One of the coaches for the girls' lacrosse team has invited a bunch of us to spend the weekend at her parents' house at The Homestead."

Cecily wonders if the blonde is the girls' lacrosse coach. "Sounds like fun. You should go."

"I was thinking I could go up with the others on Friday, and since you're off on Sunday, you could drive up for the day."

Irritation crawls across Cecily's skin. Why didn't he suggest she ask for the weekend off? Because he knows she won't get it on a holiday weekend? Or because he wants to be alone with the blonde on Friday and Saturday nights?

She drains the rest of her wine and gets to her feet. "Go ahead and make your plans. I'll come if I can get away."

Cecily's heart aches as she climbs the stairs to their second-floor bedroom. Something is very wrong in their relationship, and she doesn't have a clue how to go about fixing it.

5

PRESLEY

A high-pitched shriek jerks Presley out of a deep slumber on Thursday morning. She glances at the alarm clock. Eight o'clock. She overslept after being awake half the night waiting for a call from Everett. She'd hoped to get some work done before Chris arrives for their hike at ten.

Another scream and Presley is out of the bed and running down the hall, through the kitchen and living room and out the front door.

"Help!" Peaches screams from the front porch next door. She's teetering on a rocking chair. Any second, she could lose her balance and crash to the floor.

Of all the rotten luck. Presley had to get stuck with Bridezilla for a neighbor.

Presley leaves her porch and stands in the small patch of lawn separating their cottages. She calls up to the hysterical bride-to-be. "Calm down, Peaches! Tell me what's wrong."

"There's a rat in my bedroom." Peaches covers her eyes with one hand and points at the cottage door with the other. The movement throws her off balance and she nearly falls.

"Come down off that chair before you break your neck," Presley orders.

Peaches leaps off the rocking chair and darts across the yard to Presley's porch. "Do something!"

Presley climbs the stairs to the porch. "Let me get my phone, and I'll call maintenance."

Peaches is on Presley's heels as she enters the cottage and passes through the living room and kitchen. When she tries to follow her into the bedroom, Presley turns around and glares at her. "Do you mind? Wait for me in the kitchen. I'll be out in a minute. There are no mice in here."

Peaches lets out an incensed breath of air. "It wasn't a mouse. It was a rat," she says, and storms back down the hall.

Throwing her robe on over her shortie pajamas, Presley grabs her phone and punches in the inn's main number as she heads back to the kitchen. When the operator answers, she asks to be connected to maintenance. She's explaining the crisis to the woman in the maintenance department when she notices Peaches helping herself to Presley's Keurig machine.

Presley ends the call. "Maintenance is on the way," she says, popping an English Breakfast tea pod in her Keurig machine.

As the tea brews, she notices the file folders and papers littering every surface in the adjacent living room. She'd spent yesterday evening preparing her materials to begin her project. When she notices Peaches open a folder and thumb through the torn magazine pages, Presley grabs her tea mug and says, "Let's wait for maintenance on the porch."

Seated in rocking chairs, Peaches begins babbling about her wedding, the rat seemingly forgotten. She rambles on about such lavish ideas in such great detail Presley's head begins to spin. She craves a cup of strong black coffee, and for the umpteenth time since learning she was pregnant, she wonders why caffeine is bad for the baby.

When Peaches pauses to breathe, Presley jumps on the opportunity to speak. "You'll need a miracle to pull off the wedding you're describing in seven weeks' time. You don't seem like the slacker type to me, Peaches. Why are you getting such a late start in planning?"

Peaches drops her smile. "I've only been engaged a few weeks. My fiancé lives abroad. All I want is to be with him. This long-distance relationship is killing me."

Presley softens toward Peaches. She's walked in these shoes before. She knows exactly how Peaches feels. "Then why not have a small wedding? *Or,* have you considered eloping?"

Peaches let's out an exaggerated humph. "Seriously?" She jabs her finger at her chest. "I'm Peaches Dupree. My father is governor of the great state of Georgia. I'm American Royalty. Daddy's constituents are counting on a grand event."

Presley works hard to keep a straight face. *American Royalty?* "If your wedding is so important to his constituents, why aren't you getting married in Georgia?"

"All the best venues in the state are booked. I was lucky there was a cancellation at Hope Springs."

Presley notices the maintenance van pulling into the driveway next door. "Your rodent patrol is here."

Peaches looks at the van and back at Presley. "Well?" she asks, as though she expects Presley to deal with the maintenance men. Peaches Dupree is a pampered young woman who's used to others taking care of life's inconveniences.

Presley rises from the rocker. "Sorry. You're on your own. I'm going hiking soon, and I need to get ready."

Peaches curls her upper lip. "Eww. That sounds hot and buggy."

Presley laughs. "Hiking is good exercise. And the view at the overlook is worth the effort."

Getting to her feet, Peaches sucks in a deep breath and leaves the porch. She flags down the maintenance man. "Yoo-hoo! I'm over here. I have a rat in my cottage. My daddy is Marcus Dupree, the governor of Georgia. I don't do rats. Get it out this instant."

So much for my peaceful summer, Presley thinks as she goes inside the cottage.

Presley hasn't taken time to unpack. When rummaging through her suitcase for exercise clothes, she realizes she forgot to pack her hiking shoes. Maybe the sporting goods shop in the wellness center will have something suitable. She dresses in exercise pants, a dry-fit short-sleeved shirt, and a lightweight fleece. The morning air is crisp and the sky clear, and she takes her time in strolling down the curving gravel path to the wellness center.

Mountain Adventures has exactly what Presley is looking for and so much more. The boutique is packed with stylish apparel and the latest equipment for fishing and hiking. She pays for her shoes, making a mental note to come back later when she has more time to shop.

In the cafe next door, she places an order for grain bowls with grilled chicken for her picnic. While the staff is preparing her order, she ventures outside to the pool complex.

"This turned out exactly as I imagined it," Presley says to the staff member collecting used towels from lounge chairs on the pool deck. When the woman straightens, Presley continues. "I'm Presley Baldwin. I was the event planner here for a short time last fall."

The woman extends her hand from beneath an armful of towels. "Nice to meet you, Presley. I'm Olivia Hendrix. But everyone calls me Ollie. Stella invited me to a dinner party in your honor tonight."

Presley furrows her brow. "Stella didn't mention a party. I thought we were just having a low-key dinner."

"She referred to it as a Girls' Night Out," Ollie says. "She sounded super excited about it when she called."

"Oh well. It'll be fun to see everyone." Presley follows Ollie over to the dirty towel bin. "Cecily mentioned you're from California. What brings you to Hope Springs?"

Ollie deposits the towels in the bin. "I needed a change."

Presley waits for her to say more, but she busies herself with picking up empty plastic cups instead. She guesses Ollie to be in her mid-thirties. But she has a youthful air about her, and she's a striking beauty with shiny dark brown hair, a rounded nose, full rosy lips, and crystal clear aqua eyes. Presley's people reader goes into overdrive. She gets the impression Ollie is hiding something. Not something bad. Something sad.

"How're things going?" Presley asks. "Are you liking your new job?"

With a vigorous nod, Ollie says, "Very much so. Everyone's been so nice."

Presley spins in a circle, surveying her surroundings. "Stella outdid herself. The wellness center is fabulous."

"We're working through a few challenges. I need to hire more staff. But overall, things are great. Stella is the best boss ever. She's always so calm. Even in the most trying of circumstances."

Presley knows Stella well. She isn't always calm. She's just an expert at hiding her emotions.

"I'll let you get back to work. I look forward to seeing you tonight," Presley says, waving at Ollie as she heads off.

Chris is waiting on the porch when Presley arrives back at the cottage. "Sorry. I forgot to pack my hiking shoes and had to buy new ones." She raises the bag in her right hand and then the one in her left. "And I picked up some lunch for our picnic from Roots while I was at the wellness center." She holds the cottage door open for him. "Come on in. Let me put on my shoes, and I'll be ready to go."

"Can I help with anything?" Chris asks once they're inside.

Presley sits down on the sofa to lace up her new shoes. "Sure! There's a pink backpack cooler in the kitchen. You can pack our grain bowls in there along with some bottled water from the fridge."

While he loads up the cooler, Chris eyes the file folders spread about the living room. "What's with all the papers?"

"My summer project. I'll tell you about it on our hike."

When he's finished packing the cooler, Chris slips the straps over his shoulders.

Presley finishes tying her shoes and jumps to her feet. "I don't mind carrying that."

He pushes her hand away when she tries to take the cooler. "No way! It's heavy, and you're pregnant."

She raises an eyebrow at him. "You seriously don't mind wearing a pink backpack?"

He shrugs. "Why would I mind?"

"Okay then. Let's hit the trails."

Exiting the cottage, they walk together down the gravel path to the end of Cottage Row. When the gravel turns to dirt and the path narrows, Presley takes the lead.

"I thought we'd hike up to the overlook," Presley calls to him over her shoulder.

"I'm fine with whatever."

Presley appreciates her brother's easygoing nature, and they set out on the forty-minute hike in comfortable silence. When they reach the overlook, they sit down side-by-side on a rock, guzzling down bottles of water.

"Tell me about your summer project," Chris says.

"Well . . ." Presley screws the cap back on the empty bottle. "I'm launching my own event planning firm in Nashville. I'll wait until after the baby comes to go full steam, but I'm laying the groundwork this summer by designing my logo, building my website, and networking with old and new connections in the entertainment industry."

"That's cool. What does Everett think?"

"He's fine with it," Presley says, even though she hasn't told her husband about her plan. Everett's been too busy lately for a serious conversation about anything.

"This view is incredible," Chris says staring down at the bird's-eye view of Hope Springs Farm. "I love the mountains."

She nudges him with her elbow. "Is that why you decided to go to Washington and Lee? Not that it's a bad school. It has an excellent reputation. But I was hoping you'd come to Nashville."

Chris had stayed with Presley and Everett when he visited Vanderbilt last January. They'd had a fun few days of visiting the campus and checking out all the tourist attractions.

Chris's shoulders sag. "Me too. I really liked Vanderbilt. And I got accepted, believe it or not. But I feel like I should be close to my mom."

"I understand that. How *are* things at home?" Presley asks, and watches closely for his reaction.

"They suck." Chris picks up a rock and hurls it down the rocky slope in front of them. "My mom is a straight-up bitch. I liked her better when she was popping pills."

"I'm sorry, Chris. I know this is hard for you. But give her some time. She's adjusting to life without the opioids. I can't imagine what that's like."

"She doesn't have to be so mean. She yells at me about every-thing. I'd move back in with my dad, except he's taking the summer off. He calls it a 'sabbatical.'" Chris uses air quotes. "I think he's having a mid-life crisis. He's hiking some wilderness trail out west. He'll probably get eaten by a bear."

Presley presses her lips thin to keep from smiling. "He's not going to get eaten by a bear."

Chris leans back, propping himself on his elbows and tilting his face to the sun. "Are all grown-ups this screwed up, Presley?"

Presley thinks about her adoptive mother who drank herself to death. And her beloved father who died from cancer. He was the most normal person she's ever known. Then again, she'd been a young child when he died.

"It seems like it sometimes, Chris. We're both lucky to have Rita. Your aunt adores you. And now you have me. Although I don't consider myself an adult. I'm still learning the ways of the world. How about if we try to figure out life together?"

He jerks his head up as he looks over at her. "But you have Everett."

"Everett is experiencing some growing pains too. We're all on a journey, Chris. We need every bit of support we can get." She grins at him. "I, for one, could use a younger brother to keep me in line."

He smiles back. "And I definitely need an older sister."

"Let's make a pact. I propose that, for the rest of the summer, you and I focus on ourselves and not worry so much about the other people in our lives. I'm starting my new company, and you're getting ready to go to college. Do we have a deal?" Presley holds out her hand, and he shakes it.

"Deal! Will you really be here all summer, Presley?" he asks in a hopeful tone that warms her heart.

"Yep. Until Labor Day." Presley removes the grain bowls from her backpack, handing one to him along with a plastic fork and napkin. "Do you have any big plans for the summer?"

Chris removes the plastic lid from his bowl and sets it aside. "I kept my schedule open, so I could support my mom. But she's made it clear she doesn't want me around. I guess I'll find a job. I need to earn some spending money for college."

"Now you're thinking." A thought occurs to Presley. "The wellness center is hiring. You should reach out to Ollie, the manager."

Chris cuts his eyes at Presley. "What would I do?"

"You'd have to ask her which positions are available. Maybe you could be a pool attendant. It's not glamorous, but you could meet some fun people."

Chris considers this while he shovels forkfuls of food into his mouth. "I'm eighteen. I could be a server at the pool cafe. They make good tips. I'll talk to her after our hike."

"I would love having you close. I could pop over in the afternoons, and you could serve me nonalcoholic daiquiris while I dip my swollen ankles in the pool."

Chris looks down at her feet. "Your ankles look fine to me."

"They won't be by the end of the summer," Presley says with a chuckle.

"You look good, Presley. You don't even look pregnant."

"You're lying." Presley leans into him. "But thank you."

He takes another few bites and wipes his mouth. "Will you help me shop for college? I got this sick single room. I wanna fix it up."

"I assume *sick* is a good thing. But why a single? Don't you want a roommate?" Presley thinks back to her freshman year at the University of Alabama. How excited she'd been to meet her new roommate, Alani, a petite Hawaiian girl with shiny dark hair. They were complete opposites. Presley was outgoing and Alani shy. But they ended up being great roommates.

"Graham-Lees is the cool dorm. Most of the rooms are single," Chris explains.

"I see." Presley hands Chris a chocolate macadamia nut cookie for dessert. "In any case, I'd love to help you. We'll have fun. I'll start looking for some ideas."

Presley studies her half brother while they eat. When Presley came to Hope Springs, she wasn't looking for a mother to replace the one she'd recently lost to liver failure. She wanted to see something of herself in the face of another. She and Chris resemble their maternal grandmother, Rita and Lucy's mother. Chris's auburn hair is darker than hers, his gray eyes stormier. But their faces have the same oval shape with pointy noses.

He blots his lips with a napkin, a feminine gesture for a guy. Is it possible Chris is gay? Most masculine guys she knows would refuse to carry a pink backpack. And he's interested in decorating his dorm room. His sexuality doesn't matter to her. But he already has enough problems with his mom without having to struggle with his sexual identity. On the other hand, maybe he's already out of the closet and waiting for the right time to tell Presley. Either way, she's growing to love this kid. She'll be here for him if he needs a shoulder to cry on.

6

STELLA

My dinner guests arrive all at once. They file in through the front door in pairs. Rita and Emma. Cecily and Amelia. Presley and Ollie. And Opal brings up the rear. "Listen up everyone," I call out above the loud chatter in the center hallway. "Make yourselves at home. Cecily allowed me to borrow Maggie from Jameson's for the evening. She's waiting for you on the terrace with a tray of mango mojitos. She even has a special nonalcoholic one for our guest of honor. Welcome back, Presley."

Jazz sprints down the hall from the family room with Angel leaping along behind her. She throws her arms around Presley's waist. "What is it? Boy or girl?"

Presley pats down Jazz's wild hair. "We don't know yet. We want to be surprised. Which means you'll have to wait until October to find out."

When the guests migrate as one to the back of the house, Ollie pulls me aside. "Your home is lovely. Can I have a quick tour?"

"Certainly." I show her the vast rooms downstairs before taking her up the sweeping staircase to the second floor. "My great-grandfather built the inn in 1923 and the manor house shortly thereafter. You may have noticed the manor house is a miniature replica of the inn." I lead her to the master bedroom, and we stand in front of a large window, staring out across the street at the inn.

"I've been researching the inn's history," Ollie says. "The books in the library are fascinating."

This surprises and pleases me. I'm thrilled when my employees take an interest in the inn's celebrated history. "Are you looking for anything specific or just curious?"

"Both. One of our guests, who stayed at the inn a couple of weekends ago, claims the water healed her eczema. *And*, this afternoon, I had a call from a local woman. She spent a day in the spa earlier in the week. She says the arthritis in her hands is gone. She called it a miracle. Although, I wouldn't exactly call it a miracle. I've done some online research. Natural mineral water is known for healing skin issues and alleviating symptoms of arthritis. From what I've read in the history books about the inn, our hot springs have been known to cure matters of the heart, failed marriages, and betrayed lovers."

"You're kidding? That's incredible. I thought I'd read everything there is to know about the inn's history." I pause a beat, staring out the window at the inn. "Come to think of it, I remember Opal once mentioning a legend about the springs having healing powers."

Ollie nods. "Opal told me the same thing. She also said you'd found your great-grandmother's journals. Does your great-grandmother mention the hot springs in her entries?"

"I've been so busy, I've only had time to read a few pages." Leaving the window, I retrieve three leather-bound journals from the top drawer of my night table. I hold the journals out to Ollie. "You're welcome to read them."

Ollie's eyes, the same color as her aqua silk tank, go wide as she stares at the journals. "I couldn't. Your great-grandmother's private thoughts are on those pages."

"She should've destroyed them if she didn't want anyone reading them." I snicker. "Maybe you'll learn some juicy gossip about the inn."

Ollie furrows her brow. "As best I can tell from my research, the hot springs were the focus of activity at the inn until the late fifties. I can't find any mention of them after that."

I consider this for a minute. "When I first came here, until we started construction on the wellness center, the hot springs were housed in a rickety hut. I think Opal was the only one who ever actually soaked in them." I thrust the journals at her. "Please, take them. I want you to read them. Skip over the personal parts if it makes you uncomfortable."

Ollie accepts the journals. "I'll be careful with them. I promise."

"Let me know what you find," I say, and motion her toward the door.

We walk down the stairs and join the others on the terrace. My guests sip fruity cocktails while Jack grills pork tenderloins and Jazz tumbles across the grass in a series of cartwheels and handstands.

I make my way over to Presley who is standing at the edge of the terrace cheering on Jazz.

"She's quite good," Presley says about Jazz. "She told me she quit ballet."

"Gymnastics is her sport du jour. She has posters of Simone Biles all over her walls. Who knows? Swimming might be next. Whatever makes her happy."

Presley smiles. "She definitely seems happy. Does she ever talk about her mom?"

"Rarely. Jack and I insisted she see a therapist. Dr. Grant assures us she's coping well. Jack and I have filed for adoption."

"Oh, Stella! That's wonderful." Presley gives me a half hug. "I'm so happy for y'all."

Unexpected tears fill my eyes "I'd love to give her a little brother or sister. We've been trying for a few months. But so far, nothing."

Presley drops her arm from around me. "You never know how these things will go. Everett and I decided to start trying, thinking it could take a year. And I got pregnant the first month."

"You don't seem very happy about it. Is everything okay?"

"Sure!" she says unconvincingly.

I give her a look that tells her I don't believe her.

"The pregnancy presents a challenge with Everett's concert schedule." Presley juts out a chin in determination. "But we're figuring it out."

Something is bothering Presley, but I don't press her for details. "I'm so busy at the inn, maybe God is telling me now isn't a good time to get pregnant."

"You're a hands-on manager, Stella. Which is why you've made such a success of the resort. Maybe you should be more hands off while you're trying to conceive."

"We'll see," I say, wondering if taking a step back is even possible for someone in my position.

I notice Cecily standing by herself, staring blankly into the backyard. "Excuse me a minute."

I leave Presley and wander over to Cecily. "What's on your mind? You look as though something is bothering you."

Cecily glances over at me and then returns her attention to the yard. "You once offered for me to live in your garage apartment. Any chance that offer is still on the table?"

"But you and Lyle are all settled in your campus house."

"Things aren't great with Lyle. It's a good thing we didn't get married."

"I'm sorry, Cecily.

Cecily presses her lips thin. "I'm sorry too. I've wasted so much time on our relationship. I feel like I need to try and make it work. But I'm not sure I've got it in me. I'm so tired of arguing with him."

"You're looking at it all wrong. You've only been together for a year. Which is nothing in the span of a lifetime. And you've learned a lot about yourself during that time. I don't consider that a waste."

Cecily tilts her head to the side, as though she hasn't thought of this. "That's true, I guess."

"The two of you had only been dating four months when you got engaged. You barely knew each other. I've always worried you were rushing your relationship. Is it possible you were more in love with the idea of getting married and settling down than you were with the guy?"

She hangs her head. "Yes."

"And think how much you've changed this year. How much you've grown as a person. You were working as a barista when you met Lyle. And now you're at the top of the list of the South's most up-and-coming chefs."

Cecily sniffles, and I suspect she's crying.

I lean in close to her. "About the apartment . . . Not only will I rent it to you, Jack and I will help you move. The previous owner updated the kitchen and baths for their live-in nanny. It's one bedroom with hardwood floors and lots of windows offering natural sunlight."

Cecily looks up at me with red-rimmed eyes. "Thanks, Stella. I'm not ready to move just yet. I want to give my relationship a little more time."

My fingers graze her arm. "I'm available for you, if you ever need to talk."

I hear giggling behind me, and I turn to face Amelia, Emma, and Rita. "What's so funny?"

"These two are discussing Parker's rear end," Rita says.

Emma's and Amelia's faces beam red.

I laugh out loud. "I don't blame you. His is a fine specimen of a male backside. If I wasn't married and a few years younger."

The girl's giggle again.

I wag my finger at Emma. "He's way too old for you."

Emma sticks her tongue out at me. "I can look."

"As long as that's all you do." I turn to Amelia. "And he'll break your heart."

Amelia bobs her head, her blonde ponytail bouncing. "That's what I keep telling myself."

I notice Rita's expression is uncharacteristically grim. I've been meaning to have a word with her about her sister. "Girls, why don't you check in with Jack, to see how long before the meat is ready?"

"Yes, ma'am," Emma calls as the two scurry off.

I wait for them to leave before asking Rita, "You seem distracted. Is something on your mind?"

"Everything's fine," Rita says. "I was just wondering why Lucy didn't come."

"She declined my invitation. She didn't give a reason. I've noticed things are tense between you two. Is there anything you want to talk about? Or anything I should know?"

Rita hesitates, as though considering what to say. The warm smile I count on to greet me from behind the check-in desk every morning spreads across her lips and dimples appear, transforming her face into the lovely middle-aged woman she is. "It's nothing really," Rita says with a flick of her wrist. "Just silly sister stuff."

What Lucy is going through is anything but silly. But Rita is a master at smoothing things over, giving the appearance that everything is normal when it's anything but. Which makes her a highly effective front desk manager. "Then I won't worry. But I'm counting on you to tell me if there's a problem."

"I will. I promise," Rita says, drawing an imaginary *X* over her heart.

Emma returns. "Jack says meat's ready. I'll help Maggie get the other dishes on the buffet," she says and disappears into the kitchen.

"That kid is amazing," I say, watching her go. "You've done a fabulous job with her. She's going to set the world on fire."

"That she will," Rita says, shaking her head as though in amazement.

"Well then. Let's get this crowd fed."

I cross the terrace to the rectangular teak table, which I've set with my grandmother's blue-and-white damask linens, my Herend Fortuna Blue wedding china and cobalt handblown wineglasses, also a wedding gift from my mothers. I light the candles in the hurricane lanterns and call my guests to the kitchen to load their plates with slices of juicy pork tenderloin, squares of moist cornbread, cheese grits casserole, and a mixed green salad.

Back outside on the terrace, everyone gathers around the table with me at one end and Jazz at the other.

Seated beside me, Presley asks, "Isn't Jack eating with us?"

"I offered for him to join us. But he refused." I laugh at the image of my manly husband seated at the table with all these women. "He's actually going back to the office for a while. He's working on a big proposal."

"For a project here in town?" Presley asks.

"Actually, the proposal is for me, for a project I'm considering."

Ignoring her curious gaze, I clink my fork against my glass to get everyone's attention. "I'm thrilled you all could come tonight.

This seemed like an opportune time to get together, not only to welcome Presley back to town but to thank you in advance for all the hard work you'll be doing this summer. The next three months promise to be busy ones. But I have faith in each and every one of you. If we work together, we can accomplish any obstacles that come our way."

"Even Peaches Dupree?" Amelia calls from the opposite end of the table and everyone laughs.

"Especially Peaches Dupree." My gaze travels to my grandmother, who is seated in the center of the table on my right. "Opal, will you please say grace?"

Opal bows her head and offers a brief prayer, thanking God for the food and the friendship.

Amen has no sooner left Opal's lips when she looks across the table at Ollie and says, "Tell us what you've learned about the hot springs' miraculous healing powers."

I cast a gaze upward. My grandmother loves to stir up mischief.

The table buzzes with curiosity, and Ollie fills the others in on what she's learned about the hot springs so far. "Two recent guests report having made miraculous recoveries, one from eczema and one from arthritis. But there's still much we don't know about the mysterious hot springs. According to ancient rumor, the hot springs have helped many recover from broken hearts." Ollie is an excellent storyteller. She holds everyone spellbound with her intoxicating tone of voice and mesmerizing aqua eyes.

While we eat, a discussion about what this could mean for the farm takes place. I let them have their fun, but during dessert—a coconut lemon ice cream cake Cecily made herself— I clink my glass again for their attention. "In all seriousness, talk of healing waters must not leave this table. We could have a riot on our hands if word gets out to the general public. We must put our paying guests first. We can't afford to have opportunity-seekers interfering with their relaxation."

A sense of doom overcomes me. There's a reason my Jameson parents and grandparents kept the hot springs under lock and key all these years. I'm afraid of the secrets Ollie will discover about the mysterious hot springs.

7

CECILY

Cecily arrives at work early Friday morning to find her new intern seated on the floor behind Cecily's desk, going through the inn's prize collection of cookbooks. When Cecily clears her throat, Fiona Fortnanny jumps to her feet.

"I'm sorry. A server told me to wait for you in here." She inclines her head at the bookshelves. "I hope you don't mind. I'm a magnet for cookbooks."

Her young intern is far different than what Cecily anticipated. Peaches is tall, lean, and graceful. Fiona has a boyish figure and a sandy pixie cut. Behind her petite frame, however, Cecily senses a powerhouse personality.

"The books belong to the inn. The collection chronicles the inn's culinary history. You're welcome to borrow them, as long as you return them."

Fiona runs her hand across the worn leather cover of the book she's holding. "I did a report on Hugo Perez when I was in culinary school. I can't believe I'm holding the handwritten journal of one of the country's most notable chefs."

Cecily stares with appreciation at the girl whose face shines with enthusiasm. "Any fan of Hugo Perez is a friend of mine."

Fiona looks up from gazing at the journal. "I've been following the progress of the inn's renovations. When Peaches was desperately searching for a wedding venue, I told her to check here."

"Gee thanks," Cecily says in a teasing tone.

Fiona barks out a laugh. "Peaches isn't so bad, once you get to know her." She returns the journal to the bookcase. "You're making quite a name for yourself, Cecily. I'm honored to have the opportunity to learn from a true rising star in the industry."

Cecily's lips curve into a smile. "You can start by getting us both some coffee."

"Sure thing." Fiona comes from behind the desk. "Cream and sugar?"

"Black is fine." Cecily waits until the girl leaves her office before claiming her chair behind the desk.

Fiona is only gone a few minutes. When she returns with the coffee, she sits down in the empty chair opposite the desk.

Cecily takes a coffee from her. "Your primary responsibility will be developing the menu for Peaches's wedding. After all, the governor's paying you."

"Actually, I refused the governor's offer of a salary. I'm staying with Peaches in her cottage. And he's picking up the bill for my meals and incidentals. I consider that payment enough."

"He should be paying you to keep Peaches in line."

Fiona snorts coffee through her nose when she laughs. "Peaches has a big heart," she says, wiping her nose with a napkin. "Her problem is, she's been spoiled rotten all her life. Moving to London will be good for her. She needs to get away from her doting parents."

Cecily leans back in her chair. "You're not what I expected, Fiona Fortnanny. You're so laid back compared to your best friend."

"When you have a name like Fiona Fortnanny, you learn at

an early age to let things roll off your back." Fiona crosses her legs. "You're not what I expected either. I like your sarcastic sense of humor. Although I'm not sure I want that sarcasm directed at me."

It's Cecily's turn to laugh. "Something tells me we're going to get along fine. We're all about hard work at Hope Springs Farm. If you do a good job, I'll give you a glowing recommendation."

Fiona moves to the edge of her seat. "That would be incredible. I'm at your beck and call. Just tell me what you need."

"We have a busy weekend ahead. The inn is booked to capacity, and we're hosting a wedding tomorrow afternoon. Why don't you shadow me for a couple of days to see how we prepare for the wedding."

"That sounds like a plan," Fiona says with exuberant enthusiasm.

Fiona turns out to be an enormous asset. Not only is she full of fresh ideas, she's an artist at creating food displays. She quickly becomes Cecily's second set of hands.

During the lunch rush on Saturday, Cecily receives a text from Lyle asking if she can attend his boss's birthday dinner with him tonight. She has no interest in spending her evening with a bunch of lacrosse coaches. She texts back. *Sorry. We have a big wedding tonight.*

Guilt plagues her as the hours wear on. The wedding is late afternoon. She could easily make the birthday dinner. Their relationship will never survive if they don't try. Around four o'clock, she calls Lyle. When he doesn't answer, she texts him. *I'm leaving work early tonight. Text me the address, and I'll meet you for the dinner.*

But she never hears back from Lyle. And ends up staying at

the inn until closing. She arrives home to a dark house just before midnight. She changes into her nightgown and crawls into bed with her iPad. She downloads her favorite mystery author's hot new release and reads the first paragraph of the first chapter a dozen times before giving up and turning out the light.

Cecily drifts off to sleep sometime around two, and when she wakes at eight on Sunday morning, Lyle's side of the bed is empty. She checks her phone. There are no voice or text messages from him. Getting out of bed, she sticks her head into the guest bedroom before going downstairs. There is no sign of Lyle in the kitchen or living room, and his truck is not parked on the curb out front.

She's both worried and angry. What if he was in an accident? She considers reaching out to his friends, to see if any of them know his whereabouts. On the other hand, if Lyle hooked up with the blonde and his friends know about it, Cecily will look like a desperate fool.

Dressing in cutoffs and a cropped T-shirt, she brews coffee and takes the mug outside to the front porch. The weather is ideal with blue skies and cool temperatures. When Cecily and Lyle first started dating, Sundays had been their special day. They slept late, had morning sex, and went to Caffeine on the Corner for coffee. They spent the early afternoons doing chores —cleaning and laundry and grocery shopping. Late afternoons were reserved for hiking or biking or watching football. But their Sunday time together had come to an end during lacrosse season when Lyle was either out of town at an away game or coaching a team practice. And he blames her career for the problems in their relationship.

When Cecily can sit still no longer, she goes to the backyard and drags the lawn mower out of the shed. Her anger mounts with each strip of grass she cuts. She starts in the back, and she's nearly finished with the front when Lyle arrives home in his truck. He's scurrying up the front walk, as though trying to sneak around her, when she turns off the mower. "Where have you been?"

Lyle stops in his tracks. "I spent the night at Todd's house."

Cecily marches over to him. She can smell the booze on him as she approaches. "Didn't you get my messages? I left work early to attend the party."

Fumbling in his pocket, he removes his phone. "My phone died. See." He flashes a black screen.

She glares at him. "I texted you yesterday afternoon. Are you saying it's been dead all this time?"

He shakes the phone, as though a good jolt will make it come alive. "I need to get a new one. This one's been acting up lately."

"Cut the crap, Lyle. There's nothing wrong with your phone."

"Come on, Cecily baby. Why are you so angry?" Lyle asks, with a dimpled grin. His little boy act ceased to work on her a long time ago.

"I'm not angry, Lyle. I'm furious." Cecily stomps her foot. "You stayed out all night. You didn't even have the decency to let me know you were alive." She waves a hand in front of her nose. "And you reek of alcohol. You shouldn't even be driving."

"I'm fine. You don't know what you're talking about."

"I'm the one who's fine. I'm the one who's sober. I'm cutting the grass. It's Sunday morning. The only day we have to spend together."

"Whose fault is that?"

Cecily tosses up her hands. "Here we go again! Well, I have a newsflash for you. My job isn't the source of all our problems. You've been missing in action since early January." She finger-stabs his chest. "You're the one who wanted to rent a house instead of an apartment. You promised you'd be in charge of the yard. Have you cut the grass once since we've lived here?"

"Geez, Cecily. I don't remember. I'm sure I have."

Cecily punches his arm with all her strength. "You haven't. And you know it. I've been picking up the slack for months. Why is it okay for you to work all the time but not me?"

"Because you're the woman. You're supposed to take care of the house."

Cecily's body goes rigid. "You mean, like your mom did? Like your mom gave up the opportunity to have a career so she could stay home and take care of you?"

A flush creeps up Lyle's neck. "What're you talking about? Mom never wanted a career."

She stares him down. "Are you sure? Have you ever asked her?"

He lowers his gaze to the ground. "No," he says in a meek voice.

"So, let me get this straight. You want me to give up the success I've busted my butt to achieve, and a career that gives my life purpose, so I can take care of your house and kids. Instead of being a chef at a five-star restaurant, you want me to change diapers, pack lunches, and be a team mom for our kids' sports teams." Cecily is aware she's yelling, but she doesn't care if the neighbors hear.

Looking up, Lyle hunches his shoulders. "What's so wrong with that?"

"Because it's not who I am." Cecily gets up in his face. "Here's another newsflash for you, you male chauvinist ass. You don't earn enough money to support a wife and kids." She's being intentionally cruel. His income is a sore subject. But she doesn't care. He needs to know she's pulling more than her share of the weight in this relationship.

Lyle appears wounded. "I will one day. When I'm head coach at a big SEC school."

"Ha. You don't know if that *one day* will ever come. And,

since you have no career to fall back on, you'd better get used to the demands of my job."

His head snaps back as though she hit him. "Are you suggesting I get another career? You always said my salary doesn't matter as long as I enjoy my job."

"Your salary *doesn't* matter, as long as we have mine." Cecily stomps off into the house, banging the door shut behind her.

8

OLLIE

O llie wakes with a start from a terrifying nightmare during the wee hours of Tuesday morning. She sits bolt upright in bed as snippets of the dream come back to her. She can smell the pungent smoke. Hear the voices screaming for help. Feel her brother's icy glare. Her gown is soaked through with perspiration. Her tongue is swollen with the remnants of wine. She'd drunk so much wine that night.

She hasn't had a nightmare since she came to Hope Springs months ago. Is it possible the past is catching up with her?

She plods in bare feet across the living room to the kitchenette. The studio apartment—located above Caffeine on the Corner with a picture window overlooking Main Street—is the ideal size. Small enough to offer a sense of security while big enough to accommodate her meager belongings. She brews a cup of the calming lavender tea blend she orders from California and curls up at one end of her teal-colored velvet sofa with the last of Stella's great-grandmother's diaries.

Imogen's pages are filled with fascinating details of life at Hope Springs Farms during the forties and fifties. She describes elaborate balls in the lounge with men dressed in white tie and women in elegant gowns with white kid elbow-length gloves. She talks of fox hunting parties and guided fly-fishing trips, bingo nights in the summer house and Fourth of July picnics. And she mentions the many famous people who frequented the inn, such as Doris Day, Elvis Presley, Ernest Hemingway.

Imogen writes of the guests who soaked for long spans of time in the hot springs tub. The women whose gynecological problems were healed, and the men whose dangerously high blood pressures were lowered. Ollie believes nature heals. She has faith in homeopathic remedies. It stands to reason mineral water from deep within the earth would improve physical ailments. As for matters of the heart, she's more inclined to believe couples resolved their marital problems and lovers' spats by spending a weekend alone together, rekindling their feelings for each other surrounded by the beauty of the farm and mountains.

Ollie stays awake for the rest of the night reading. The first rays of sunlight bathe her living room in a pale yellow when she reads the tragic tale that prompted Imogen's husband, William Jameson, to prohibit guest use of the hot springs for the next two decades.

Ollie arrives at work early. She's traumatized from Imogen's journals and exhausted from lack of sleep. She drinks too much coffee, which sets her on edge. She pours over the latest batch of employment applications, some of which show promise, before moving on to social media. She's posting an image of the spa's serene lap pool to Instagram when she receives a text from her brother.

She drops the phone as though she's been burned, and it falls screen down on the desk with a thud. Ollie hasn't heard from her brother in ten months and fourteen days. Why is he texting her now?

She flips the phone over on the desk and reads his text. *We need to talk.* Three dots appear followed by another message. *I can come to you. Where are you living now?*

She blocks the number from her phone without responding.

Her chest tightens as she's transported back ten and a half months. Her eyes and nose burn. She can hear voices calling for her, but she can't find her way to them through the smoke. She can hear Murphy, the family's golden retriever, barking his head off in a distant part of the house.

No! Please no! Ollie shakes her head, bringing herself back to the present. Her heart is racing, and her armpits are damp with sweat. When the walls begin to close in on her, she jumps up and jerks open the door to the cabinet where she keeps a supply of clean workout clothes.

Tilting the blinds closed for privacy, she strips out of her work clothes and pulls on her sports bra, jogging shorts, and a tank top. She stuffs her feet into running shoes, grabs her phone, and leaves her office. Bypassing the elevator, she hurries down the stairs and out the front door, hitting the nearest hiking trail at a run.

Her therapist in California encouraged Ollie to take an anti-anxiety medicine to control the panic attacks. But Ollie prefers to deal with the crippling fear the natural way. She circles the farm three times, an equivalent of nine miles, before returning to the wellness center.

After a long hot shower in the locker room, she feels calm enough to focus on her work. She spends the late-morning and early afternoon-hours in her office, catching up on paperwork and reaching out to the potential job candidates. Around two o'clock, she begins her daily tour of the wellness center, starting in the spa and ending by the pool.

She's at the check-in gate, handing out towels to guests, when Jazz hobbles in on crutches. She's wearing white shorts and a pink top with her hair smoothed off her face by a yellow headband.

"Ollie! I've been looking all over for you. Why are you working here?"

"We're short staffed. I'm filling in for a pool attendant who needed a break. If you were a little older, I'd hire you on the spot."

"Hire me now! What's so hard about handing out towels?"

"Hmm." Ollie considers the menial duties associated with the position. "Nothing, now that I think about it. Get Stella's permission, and you've got the job." Her gaze shifts to Jazz's ankle, which is bound by an elastic bandage. "What happened to you?"

Jazz crosses her eyes. "I sprained my ankle doing an aerial cartwheel."

"Ouch," Ollie says with a shiver. "Does it hurt much?"

"Sorta. But I landed the cartwheel."

"Thatta girl," Ollie says, offering her a high five.

"If it's not better by the weekend, Stella won't let me go to gymnastics camp next week." Jazz leans in close. "I heard you talking the other night at dinner, and I was wondering if I could soak my foot in the hot springs."

"Ah, the magic cure. Technically, you're supposed to be over eighteen. But as long as I'm with you, I don't imagine soaking your foot a few minutes would be a problem." Ollie spots the gate attendant heading their way. "And here comes Lindsay now."

Grabbing two bottles of water from the cooler, Ollie leads Jazz around the pool to the far side of the building. She's relieved to find no one is soaking in the hot springs. She'd hate for a guest to complain about a child being in a restricted area.

Ollie directs Jazz to a stone bench. "Sit down, and I'll take off your bandage." She gently unwraps the bandage, revealing a tiny bruised and swollen ankle. "This doesn't look good, Jazz. Have you been to see the doctor?"

Jazz bobs her head, her crown of frizzy hair flopping up and down. "She took an X-ray. It's not broken."

"All right then. Let's see the magic." Ollie scoops Jazz up and places her on the rocky side of the pool. "Remember, feet only. I don't want to get in trouble with Stella."

"I understand," Jazz says in a disappointed tone.

Ollie lowers herself down beside the child, and they sit in silence for a few minutes. As the warm water massages her feet, Ollie wonders if the mineral water cures panic attacks.

"Ollie . . . why do you always seem so sad?"

Taken aback, Ollie asks, "What do you mean?"

"You hide it really well. My therapist says the same about me. I'm sad, because I'm not sad. That doesn't make any sense to anyone but me. My mom died, back in December. But she had a lot of problems. She was an alcoholic and mentally unstable."

The kid sounds like a grown-up. She's obviously learned a lot from listening to adult conversations. "I'm so sorry, Jazz. I didn't know."

"I loved my mom, because she was my mom. But I was scared a lot of the time when I was living with her. And I like living with Stella and Jack *so* much better." Jazz hunches her small shoulders. "That's why I'm sad, because I'm not sad."

"In other words, you feel guilty for not feeling sad."

Jazz scrunches up her forehead. "Something like that. I'm supposed to feel sad, but I don't."

Ollie rests a hand on Jazz's shoulder. "You're a kid, Jazz. Kids are resilient. They're forgiving and trusting, which helps them recover quickly from bad stuff. But you can't help how you feel. It's okay to not feel sad."

"That's what Stella says! Are you not forgiving and trusting?"

The person Ollie needs to forgive is herself. And the only people she ever truly trusted are gone. "My situation is more complicated. My mom died too. And my dad."

Jazz's amber eyes get big. "At the same time?"

Ollie nods. "In a fire."

Jazz places her hand in Ollie's. "I'm sorry, Ollie. If you want, I know the name of a really good therapist."

Ollie bursts out laughing. "How old are you?"

Mischief twinkles in her golden eyes. "Seven, going on twenty. That's what Stella says. Can I have the job?"

Ollie laughs again. "We'll see. Now, let's take a look at that foot."

Jazz slowly removes her foot from the water. "Look! It's better."

Ollie stares at her foot in utter amazement. In the fifteen minutes she's been soaking her ankle, the swelling has gone down considerably, and the bruise has transitioned from blue to yellow. "That's incredible."

"Let's see if I can walk on it." Jazz spins on her bottom as she swings her legs out of the pool.

When she tries to stand up, Ollie grabs hold of her arm to support her. "Take it easy. You might still feel some pain."

Gripping Ollie's arm, Jazz gingerly bears weight on her foot. "It doesn't hurt. I don't believe it."

When Stella comes through the gate, Jazz cartwheels over to her. "Look, Stella. The hot springs fixed my ankle. I can go to gymnastics camp now."

Stella kneels down to examine the foot. After a long minute, she looks up at Ollie with an expression of utter amazement. "I don't believe this."

Ollie considers her words. "Crazy, isn't it?"

She considers whether to tell Stella what she learned in her great-grandmother's journals about the beautiful debutante from Charleston. But decides now is not the time for the tragic tale. Stella let the genie out of the bottle by opening the hot springs to the guests. If word gets out, they will all have to work together to tame it.

9

PRESLEY

P resley is working at her makeshift desk in the cottage late on Tuesday night when Everett finally calls. She answers with a curt, "Hello."

"You're still angry," Everett says.

Presley hears loud voices in the background. He's performing in Seattle tonight. Based on the three-hour time difference, he's likely in his dressing room, preparing to go onstage. "Of course, I'm still angry, Everett. I'm even angrier it's taken you a week to call me."

"I thought you needed a chance to cool off. Besides, you walked out on me. You should've been the one to call me."

"How could I stay after the things you said?" Pushing back from her desk, Presley makes certain the lights are out in the cottage next door before going outside to the porch.

"I'm not the only one at fault. You said some hurtful things too, Presley."

"I stated the truth. The tour was wearing on me. I wasn't getting enough sleep or exercise. But what you said was unforgivable. You accused me of intentionally destroying your career by getting pregnant."

Everett sighs. "Do you blame me? I've been trapped before."

Anger surges through Presley. "Trapped? Are you kidding me right now? Stop comparing me to Carla! *She* got pregnant on purpose, to *trap* you into marrying her. But I'm your wife. You and I decided *together* to start a family."

Everett pauses, and the sound of female laughter fills the line. "I realize that, and I'm sorry. I was out of line. I miss you, babe. I'll be in Nashville on business the week of July 19th. I have that weekend free. We can spend some time together then."

That's more than six weeks away. Can she go that long without seeing her husband? "I'm not in Nashville, Everett."

"What do you mean? Where are you?"

"In Hope Springs. I've rented a cottage at the inn for the summer."

"I don't understand," Everett says, and Presley imagines him running his hands through his reddish-brown hair. "What're you doing there?"

Presley's been asking herself the same question. But the answer suddenly comes to her. "I need to be around people who care about me right now."

"I'm glad you have your family and friends to take care of you."

A voice calls out in the background. "Hey, Ev! Ten minutes until showtime."

"I gotta run, babe. Plan on me coming to Hope Springs that weekend in July. I'll check the schedule. Maybe I can get a few extra days off. We can have a second honeymoon."

"We never had our first honeymoon," Presley mutters. "FYI, I have to work that weekend. We have a huge wedding. Earth, Wind, and Desire is the band."

"Heck, yes! Now, I know I'm coming."

Warmth spreads throughout her body at the thought of spending time alone with her husband. "You'll have to be incognito. I can't have you upstaging the bride. Her father is Georgia's governor."

"I'll wear a disguise." He pauses a beat. "I seriously have to go, Presley. But we'll talk again soon," he says, and hangs up without expressing his love for her.

Presley remains on the porch for a long time listening to the cicadas chirping. She never imagined life as a country music star's wife would be so complicated. Everett is committed to being a hands-on father to his son, Carla's three-month-old baby. Everett will be pressed thin between traveling to Atlanta to see Lee and carving out time for Presley and their child. They can make it work as long as they remain faithful to each other. Can't they?

———

Late afternoon on Wednesday, Presley puts on her bathing suit and heads over to the wellness center. She signs in at the gate, strips off her cover-up, and sits down on the edge of the pool with her feet dangling in the water. It's midweek and only a few guests are lounging around the pool and seated at tables in the Poolside Cafe.

Chris sees her and hurries over. "Afternoon, ma'am. Can I offer you a beverage or a healthy snack?"

Presley smiles up at him. "I'll have a virgin daiquiri, please."

"Certainly. Mango is the flavor of the day. I highly recommend it. But we have summer berry and pineapple as well."

"Hmm." Presley pauses to consider her options. "I'll have mango."

Chris peers into the water. "I'll have to check your ankles first."

She flutter-kicks her feet, causing a gentle splash.

Chris shakes his head. "I'm sorry. Swollen ankles are required to drink nonalcoholic beverages."

She sticks her tongue out at him. "Go get my daiquiri, before I report you to management."

He salutes her and scurries off. While he's gone, she drapes a towel over a lounge chair and stretches out. Presley can't remember the last time she enjoyed a relaxing afternoon by the pool.

Chris returns with her drink, a frozen yellow concoction in a tulip-shaped glass. He pulls up a chair beside her. "We're not busy right now. I can talk for a minute."

"I'm impressed with your professionalism. Do you like working here?"

"Yes! Ollie wanted to hire me as a pool attendant, but I talked her into giving me a chance on the waitstaff. I've made a few mistakes, but Kyle, the cafe manager, is supercool and very forgiving."

"Keep up the good work," Presley says, giving him a high five. "How are things with your mom?"

"Worse. If that's even possible. She gets meaner by the day. I'm lucky to have this job. It keeps me out of the house." Chris dips his chin to his chest and stares over the top of his wraparound sunglasses. "See that girl over there?"

Presley's gaze follows his to a young woman with long tanned legs and a mop of golden flyaway curls. "She's cute. What about her?"

"Her name is Amy, and she digs me."

Presley removes her sunglasses and studies her brother's love-struck expression. So, he's not gay after all. "Looks to me like she's not the only one with a crush."

A grin spreads across his lips, revealing dimples she's never noticed before. "And guess what else? She's a sophomore at W and L. She's originally from Charlotte. But she's living with her grandparents this summer. They have a vacation home in Hope Springs."

Presley returns her sunglasses to her face. "You certainly know a lot about this girl. Have you asked her out yet?"

"No, but I'm going to soon."

As Chris babbles on about how cool Amy is, Presley senses someone watching them. She casually repositions herself on the lounge chair and surveys their surroundings. Peeking at them from around the corner of the cafe is Lucy.

Chris drags his eyes away from Amy back to Presley. "So, how's the daiquiri?"

Presley has been holding her glass, but she has yet to take a sip. She sucks on the straw. "It's delicious."

"I told you." Chris slowly gets to his feet. "I should get back to work."

Presley stands and stretches. "I'm feeling kind of sleepy anyway. I think I'll go back to my cottage for a nap." She lifts the glass. "Can I get a to-go cup?"

Chris flicks his wrist. "Take the glass. Housekeeping will get it when they clean," he says, handing her a black leather folder with the check.

She adds a generous tip, writes in her cottage number, and signs her name. "Here you go," she says, handing him back the folder. "Thanks for the excellent service."

He bows. "Any time, ma'am. Come back soon. We have different daiquiri specials every day. Jalapeño is tomorrow's flavor."

"That sounds disgusting." Leaning in close, Presley whispers, "Amy's a cutie. Ask her out soon before someone else does."

"I heard that," he says, and laughs as he walks away.

Presley slips on her cover-up and leaves the pool. She's exiting the gates when she notices Lucy striding up the sidewalk toward the main building. She hurries to catch up with her.

"Why were you spying on us?" Presley asks, stepping in line beside Lucy.

Lucy gives her a sideways glance. "I wasn't spying on *you*. I was checking on my son. His job is beneath him. Being a poolside burger boy is so common."

Presley tenses. "This is Chris's first job. He'll learn a lot about responsibility and respect. Plus, he'll earn good money in tips."

Lucy stops walking and faces Presley. "Were *you* ever a waitress?"

Her biological mother has lost weight since the last time Presley saw her at Christmas. And she seems on edge, wringing her hands and darting her eyes. Is this a side effect of withdrawing from the drugs?

"As a matter of fact, I waited tables all throughout college. My mother insisted I earn my own spending money."

The color drains from Lucy's face at the mention of Presley's adoptive mother. "Why did you come back to Hope Springs? If you're here because of me, you're wasting your time. I can't be the mother you want me to be."

Heat flushes through Presley's body. "My return to Hope Springs has nothing to do with you. There are other people at this resort who care about me. Everett's on tour, and I prefer not to be alone in Nashville while I'm pregnant."

Lucy's gaze falls to Presley's stomach. "You're pregnant? I didn't know." She seems genuinely surprised. Presley is twenty-one weeks pregnant. How could Lucy not notice her obvious baby bump? Is she that oblivious? Or too self-absorbed?

Presley yearns to give Lucy a piece of her mind. She has much to get off her chest. She opens her mouth to rip into her and thinks better of it for fear she'll make things worse for Chris. She takes a few seconds to compose herself before speaking. "We were friends once, Lucy, before we figured out you were my biological mother. For Chris's sake, why don't we forget about the DNA and go back to being friends?"

"I can't be friends with you. Stay away from my son. And butt out of my life." Lucy spins on her heels and storms off.

Presley feels both relief and sadness as she strolls back to her cottage. She's been dreading the confrontation with Lucy. She was unsure of how the *sober* Lucy feels about her. And now she knows.

10

STELLA

I look up from my desk, surprised to see Lucy standing in the doorway. "I'm early for the meeting," Lucy says. "I can come back in a few minutes."

"No need." I wave for her to enter. "Come in. Have a seat."

Lucy approaches my desk and sits down in one of a pair of comfortable armchairs.

"This gives us a chance to discuss your schedule of wine tastings," I say.

Lucy appears dazed, as though she has no clue what I'm talking about.

"The summer's wine tastings. You promised you'd have the schedule ready for me today."

A flush creeps up Lucy's neck. "I'm sorry. I haven't finished with it yet. I've been busy."

I frown. "Lucy, we agreed we'd have tastings on the weekends for our guests. The first was to be tomorrow."

Pink splotches appear on Lucy's cheeks. "I can throw something together for tomorrow."

I purse my lips. "Our guests expect five-star service. We don't throw things together at Hope Springs Farm."

A kitchen worker appears, pushing a cart loaded with refreshments for our meeting. She busies herself with placing the coffee carafes and trays of baked goods on the conference table.

I lean into my desk and lower my voice. "I'm sympathetic to your situation, Lucy. I realize you've been through a lot. But I have a business to run."

I wait for Lucy to respond, but she remains silent.

"One of Parker's barbacks is really into wine. Why don't I pull her out of Billy's Bar for a couple of weeks to assist you until you get your feet back on the ground?"

Lucy looks past me, staring out the window instead of meeting my gaze. "I don't need an assistant, Stella. I'm perfectly capable of managing things on my own. We'll have the wine tasting tomorrow. I've been saving a few bottles of assorted South African Chenin Blanc."

I sit back in my chair. "That sounds festive. Perhaps, our schedule of tastings should have a theme. Wines from around the world, featuring different countries. I'll leave it up to you to decide. Regardless, I'm asking Holly to come in early a few days a week to help you."

My other key staff members arrive for the meeting in a chorus of chatter and laughter. I get to my feet, signaling to Lucy that I'm finished with our conversation.

The others gather around the table, taking their seats. When Lucy joins them, a hush settles over the group. Lucy glares at her sister, Rita, who is sitting opposite her. Lucy's dark eyes are cold enough to give everyone in the room frostbite. My temper flares. Whatever's going on between these two is affecting my entire staff.

"Good morning, everybody," I say in a chipper voice as I take my seat at the head of the table and pass around a stack of printed agendas. "Presley, since rentals are our most pressing issue, I'll ask you to go first. Were you able to track down any tents?"

Presley straightens in her chair. "Yes! We got lucky. We found a rental company in West Virginia that books a lot of events for the Greenbrier. They have two enormous sailcloth tents available for our dates."

"That's a relief." I glance over at the bride, whose expression remains impassive. Peaches has no idea the effort Presley and Amelia have put into locating tents.

Presley continues, "As for the rest of the rentals. Because we're booking at the last minute, we had a difficult time finding one company that fits all our needs. Some had tables and not chairs. Others had no tablecloths. We determined our best bet is a rental company out of Charlottesville. The only thing they don't have are the clear Chiavari chairs."

"But I want the clear Chiavari chairs," Peaches says, her bottom lip stuck out like a pouting child.

Presley slides a printed photograph across the table to Peaches who is seated next to her. "Amelia and I think gold chairs would be pretty with your peach peonies."

Peaches levels her gaze at Presley. "I want the clear chairs."

Amelia says, "We can order the clear chairs from a different rental company, but you'll have to pay two delivery fees."

"That's fine," Peaches says. "Order them."

"Got it." Presley types a note into her iPad. "As for the flowers . . . I've spoken with Claire who, as you know, is handling the inn's floral arrangements while Katherine is on maternity leave. Claire assures me she has a reliable source for peach peonies, which are hard to come by especially this time of year."

Peaches says under her breath but loud enough for the table to hear, "She'd better."

Fiona elbows Bridezilla hard in the ribs. "Shush!"

The bride certainly looks the part, tanned and toned in a

white sundress with her blonde hair blown out. But the angry scowl she wears suggests trouble in her world. Although I can't imagine what could possibly be wrong on the pampered princess's planet.

"Outstanding work, Presley and Amelia." I shift my gaze to Cecily who has a faraway look on her face. "Cecily, will you give us a catering report?"

Cecily moves forward in her chair. "Fiona is doing an outstanding job of pulling the menu together. Fiona and Peaches plan to meet with Parker soon to create a signature cocktail. The only thing I'm hesitant about is the wine. If we need to place a special order, we should do so soon."

Lucy cuts her eyes at Cecily. "You don't need to worry about the wine, Cecily. That's my job. I sent a list of our offerings to the bride's father. I haven't heard back from him."

"My father, the governor, is a very busy man," Peaches says. "He'll get back to you when he can."

Fiona places a reassuring hand on Peaches's forearm. Locking eyes with Lucy, she says, "Your list is extensive. I'm familiar with the governor's taste in wines. Why don't we narrow his choices down to a few to make it easier for him to decide?"

"Excellent solution. Go for it." I'm quite fond of this young woman. She's enthusiastic, capable of solving problems, and has a calming influence on Peaches. If we survive this wedding, I may insist Cecily offer her a job. "Moving on to the wellness center. Ollie, how are things shaping up in the spa for the wedding?"

Ollie, too, appears distracted. "Well, let's see. I have a couple of questions." She pulls out her phone. "I've reserved the spa on Friday and Saturday. So far, no one has booked treatments. It's still early, but you might want to include the spa brochure when you correspond with your guests. Are you planning a private party with just your bridesmaids on Saturday morning?"

"Of course. And we'll need a hair stylist and makeup artist as well," Peaches says, as though she expects Ollie to arrange both services.

I look over at Amelia. "Amelia, will you ask concierge to forward Peaches a list of the inn's recommended local hair salons?"

"Yes ma'am," Amelia says, typing away on her iPad.

I return my gaze to Peaches. "The stylist you choose can recommend a makeup artist." I continue before she can object. "And while we're on the subject of spa treatments. Governor Dupree gave me strict instructions. He's only paying for the bridesmaids' rooms and their spa treatments the morning of the wedding."

Rita and Ollie simultaneously nod their understanding.

"Rita, what are room reservations looking like for the weekend?" I ask.

"The inn is booked solid with a long waiting list." Rita opens a file folder in front of her. "In order to accommodate the band's excessive demands, I had to put them in the carriage house with overflow on Cottage Row."

Peaches's jaw hits the table. "But my parents booked the carriage house for themselves and my future in-laws."

"I've already worked it out with your mother," Rita says. "They'll be staying in our best two suites on the third floor with stunning views of the mountain range."

Feeling a migraine brewing behind my left eyeball, I push back from the table. "You've made excellent progress in a short amount of time. Keep things rolling along and advise me of any issues that arise."

I return to my desk while the group gathers their belongings and exits my office. I quickly scroll through my emails, and when I look up again, Ollie is studying a picture of Nancy and Ronald Reagan on my wall of fame—my family's collection of black-and-white photographs featuring famous guests from years past.

I walk over and stand beside her. "Can you believe all these people once stayed in our inn? If only we could travel back in time."

Ollie looks at me with sad aqua eyes, and I realize my mistake. "Jazz told me about your parents. She was quite concerned about you. As am I. If you ever need to talk."

"Thank you. That means a lot," Ollie says in a tight voice.

"Did you need to see me about something?" I ask, eyeing the familiar leather-bound journals in her hand.

"Oh. Yes. Here." She hands me the journals. "They make for fascinating reading. You really should take the time."

"I will." I place the journals on my desk. "How are things at the wellness center?"

"Actually, there's something I need to talk to you about. Do you have a few minutes?"

I glance at my watch. "I'm meeting Jack and my architect at the carriage house in ten minutes." I motion her to the door. "Walk with me, and we can talk on the way."

"Ooh! Are you renovating the carriage house?"

"I'm considering it." Leaving my office, we walk past reception and out the back door. "I'd like to build a separate family wing. To maintain the authenticity and charm of the property, we'll build around the carriage house. The old section will feature a dining room and game room. All the accommodations will be identical—a king room connecting to a queen room via a small sitting room with sofa pullout."

"And you'll build a pool at the carriage house just for families?" Ollie says, her face bright.

I chuckle. "That's the plan."

Ollie's shoulders slump, as though relieved. "The sooner the better. Last weekend, we had a full-on war between some parents of young children and the single set."

"Is that what you wanted to talk to me about?"

"We're managing the pool," Ollie says. "The hot springs, on the other hand, are becoming a problem. I'm afraid the cat's outta the bag about the miracle cures. Security is having a problem with locals sneaking into the outdoor hot springs at night. *And*, with the exception of Peaches's wedding weekend, the indoor soaking tubs are booked through the summer."

I let out a sigh. "I'll speak with security. We'll add more guards if necessary. Instruct the spa staff to ask our guests to use discretion when discussing their 'cures,'" I say, hooking my fingers in air quotes.

"Okay," Ollie says, and bites down on her lower lip.

"What aren't you telling me, Ollie?"

"There's something you should know about the hot springs." Jack's pickup pulls up beside the carriage house. She glances at his truck and back at me. "Maybe it's better if you find out for yourself."

"Find out what?" I ask, fear prickling the hairs on the back of my neck.

"The reason your great-grandfather shut down the hot springs. Your great-grandmother explains everything in the last pages of her third journal."

11

CECILY

Midday on Friday and Jameson's is buzzing with weekend guests checking in early and locals and passersby stopping in for lunch and a stroll around the property. The lunch rush is winding down, and Cecily is headed to her office when she hears voices coming from within. She flattens herself against the wall, listening.

"Seriously, Peaches. What is wrong with you today? You were a straight-up bitch at the meeting earlier."

Cecily smiles to herself. Only Fiona can get away with calling Peaches out.

Peaches says, "I don't know what's wrong with me, honestly. Maybe I'm having cold feet. Not about marrying Nathan. But about leaving my parents. I'm their only child, the light of their lives. They'll be lost without me."

Peaches's voice has a genuine quality Cecily hasn't heard before. She truly believes her parents will be devastated when she moves to England. Perhaps they will. But as the governor and first lady of Georgia, Cecily imagines, they'll find plenty to occupy their time.

"Your parents will survive without you," Fiona says, expressing Cecily's thoughts. "Knowing your mama, she'll be bopping over to London every few months."

"That's true," Peaches says.

Cecily doesn't see Parker sneak up beside her, and she nearly jumps out of her skin when he grabs her arm.

"What're you doing?" he asks.

She touches a finger to her lips. "Shh! Spying."

"Ooh!" Parker leans in closer. He's tall and muscular, and his body pressed against hers sparks a desire she shouldn't be feeling. She inches away. What is wrong with her? She's in a relationship. She shakes off the unwelcome longings and returns her attention to the conversation taking place inside her office.

Peaches says, "What will I do with my time? I don't know anyone in London. How will I spend my days while Nathan's at work? And nights too? His banking job is challenging. He rarely comes home before midnight."

"You could get a job," Fiona suggests.

"Doing what? I majored in fashion design. What am I supposed to do with that?"

"Work in a stylish boutique that caters to the wealthy," Fiona says. "You'll meet a ton of people."

"I shop in boutiques like that, Fi. I don't work in them. Besides, why would I need a job when I have a trust fund?"

Parker trembles beside Cecily, as though holding back laughter.

"You'll be miserable, Peaches, if you don't have a life of your own. Haven't you ever wanted a career?"

"Mmm. Nope. I wanna be like my mama. Have two or three children, hire a nanny, and spend my days at the country club, playing tennis and having boozy lunches and getting massaged. Do they even have country clubs in England?"

Unable to contain her laughter, Cecily drags Parker away from the office door and over to the window counter.

"What a piece of work," Parker says when they finish laughing. "I feel sorry for her husband."

Cecily doesn't admit it to Parker, but she feels sorry for Peaches. The bridezilla sounded so lost.

She looks up at Parker, into his sultry blue eyes. "Did you need to see me about something?"

Parker's handsome face lights up. "Yes! Herbs. Stella asked me to fashion a summer welcome cocktail for our guests. I'm getting close, but it needs a little something extra."

"I love the idea of a signature welcome beverage," Cecily says. "What do you have so far?"

"Stella wants something light and crisp. I'm thinking Prosecco and blackberries with a taste of lime, a sprinkle of sugar, and a splash of crème de cassis."

"That sounds yummy. Let's go outside to the garden." Cecily opens the back door and motions for him to go ahead of her. Removing scissors from her apron pocket, she wanders around the herb section of the garden cutting snippets. "If you want to muddle, I would try rosemary and thyme. If you're looking for a sprig, lavender would be nice."

"I'm thinking muddled." He takes the small bouquet of herbs from her. "Can you spare a minute to critique my sample?"

Cecily has a million things she should be doing in the kitchen, but she's always willing to help a fellow staff member. "Sure!"

She follows Parker around to the porch and through the lobby to Billy's Bar. Several tables and barstools are occupied, but Parker's underling, Kathy, appears to have things under control.

Sliding onto the stool at the end of the bar, Cecily replays

Peaches's conversation in her mind while she watches Parker muddle the herbs. "Did you mean what you said, Parker? Do you really feel sorry for Peaches's fiancé? I would think a guy like you would be looking for a girl like her."

He looks up from his task. "What do you mean, 'a guy like me'?"

A guy like Lyle who earns an average living doing a job he loves, she thinks and says, "Not just you. Any guy. Peaches is beautiful. She has a trust fund. And her father is influential."

"That's exactly her problem. She's been given everything on a silver platter. I bet she can't even tie her own shoes. Her husband will come home at the end of a hard day to her whining and complaining about being bored. No thanks to that." Parker adds a bit of rosemary to one champagne flute and a bit of thyme to another, handing both to Cecily.

Cecily sips from both glasses. "Thyme gets my vote. Hands down."

"Let me taste." Parker takes the flutes from her. One glass at a time, he presses his lips to the rims opposite her lipstick smudge and drains the remaining liquid. "Yup. Thyme it is."

Cecily slides back on her barstool. "The country club life Peaches describes doesn't sound boring to me."

"Ha. I know you, Cecily. You'd be pulling your hair out day one. And that's what I admire about you. You know what you want, and you're not afraid to work your butt off to get it. It's a mighty shapely butt I might add."

Cecily flips him the bird. Parker flirts with everyone. She's used to it. At least he noticed her butt, which is more than Lyle has done lately.

"Too bad Lyle doesn't feel the same way about my ambition," she mumbles.

He cocks an eyebrow at her. "Trouble in the love nest?"

"Something like that."

Parker fills a flute with his thyme concoction and hands it to her. "This might help."

Cecily eyes the glass. "I shouldn't. I never drink on the job. But what the heck," she says, taking the drink from him. Maybe she can wash away the empty feeling inside of her.

———

The next days and weeks pass in a blur of activity. The inn is filled to capacity nearly every night. Cecily is in her element, creating lunch and dinner specials guests rave about. And her hard work pays off when *Virginia Living Magazine* wants to do an article about her success at Jameson's in their upcoming August issue.

Cecily calls Lyle to share the news. But he doesn't answer.

Their troubled relationship is dragging her down. Lyle is asleep when Cecily leaves for work in the mornings, and he's out most nights when she comes home. On Sundays, he's either playing pickup lacrosse or helping a friend work on a home-improvement project, leaving Cecily to clean the house and mow the grass alone.

Cecily is slowly coming to terms with the inevitable. The obvious has been glaring at her since she met Lyle's parents at Christmas. She and Lyle are all wrong for each other. Lyle needs a Peaches in his life, a woman with a trust fund who aspires for nothing greater than to birth his babies and promote his coaching career.

On the last Sunday of June, when she gets up during the night to pee, Cecily hears Lyle's phone vibrate on the night-stand. She stops in her tracks. *Who is texting him at three in the morning?* she wonders. She glances over at Lyle, who is snoring softly with his mouth wide open. She tiptoes over to the nightstand and picks up the phone. He has three unread texts from Whitney Doyle.

Are you awake?

Can you talk?

Call me!

Who is Whitney Doyle? Is she the blonde Lyle was with at Town Tavern? Does she have a trust fund?

Cecily places the phone, screen down, on the nightstand and continues to the bathroom. She's been waiting for a sign, a signal prompting her to move on with her life. And now she's got it.

The next morning, she catches up with Stella as Stella is making her morning tour of the property. "About your garage apartment. I'm ready to move in if you'll still have me. Please, don't feel obligated. I can easily find something else."

Stella stops walking and turns to Cecily. "Did you break up with Lyle?"

"Not yet. But I'm going to." Cecily then launches into how bad things have gotten between them, including the texts from Whitney Doyle. "Lyle's going out of town with friends for the holiday weekend. I'll move out while he's gone."

Normally Stella wouldn't condone such underhanded behavior, but her soft smile lets Cecily know she approves. "The apartment is all yours for as long as you like. Although." Stella spins around, facing the main building and gesturing toward the caretaker's cottage to her left. "The cottage is available, if you want something bigger."

Cecily considers this option. "I love the cottage. But two bedrooms is too big. And the proximity is too close to Jameson's."

"I understand. The garage apartment it is." Stella loops her arm through Cecily's as they start walking again. "I'm sorry you're going through this, Cecily. At this stage, I think taking a break from your relationship is the right move. You'll either discover you can't live without each other. Or you'll move on with your lives.

Cecily doesn't feel like she's *taking a break* from her relationship. This feels permanent.

She moves through the week in slow motion. Her home is a hostile environment. Whenever Cecily and Lyle are in the house at the same time, which isn't very often, they barely speak to each other. Cecily is partially to blame for this. She's livid about the texts from Whitney, and she desperately wants to confront Lyle. But she knows he'll deny her accusation, and she wants to avoid second-guessing herself. Leaving him is hard enough.

Cecily waits for Lyle to say something about the upcoming holiday weekend. He hasn't mentioned the trip to The Homestead since he first told her about it at the beginning of June. He's definitely still planning to go. She saw his packing list on a notepad in the kitchen. Clearly, he doesn't want her around. Further evidence he's having an affair.

When Cecily's at home alone, like a bank bandit masterminding a heist, she mentally catalogues what she'll take with her when she moves. Most items are her own possessions from her previous life. But what about the few things she and Lyle purchased together? The cappuccino machine. A pair of decorative throw pillows with the teal geometric design that perfectly match her sofa. The set of gray Egyptian cotton sheets. She considers the sheets hers anyway, since Lyle gave them to her for her birthday.

When Stella shows her the apartment on Thursday afternoon, Cecily becomes more convinced than ever she's making the right decision. The apartment is small—one bedroom and an updated kitchen adjacent to a living room/dining room combo—but cozy with creamy walls, warm pine floors, and windows that overlook Stella's expansive lawn. The apartment is an extension of the manor house, which is an extension of the inn. She felt like an outsider living on Lyle's turf, on Jefferson College's campus. But this is her territory. Without a shadow of a doubt, Cecily knows she belongs at Hope Springs Farm. Now, and maybe forever.

12

OLLIE

Panic attacks plague Ollie during the day and nightmares torment her at night. She hikes and swims and cycles. The exercise temporarily relieves the symptoms. Until something triggers another, most often an email from her brother. Because she blocked Alexander's number from her phone, he's resorted to emailing her. He's anxious to speak with her about their parents' estate. Ollie imagines the painful conversation. Maybe she'll let Alexander have everything. After what happened, Ollie doesn't deserve to be a beneficiary.

Exhausted from the physical exertion, she falls into a deep sleep when her head hits the pillow at night. But she manages to sleep only a few hours before a nightmare jerks her awake. She's thousands of miles from California, but she's reliving the hell of that tragic night over and over again.

The lack of sleep makes Ollie short-tempered during the day, as if her job isn't stressful enough. She's constantly fielding complaints from guests. And not just about the pool. Word has begun to spread about the hot springs. And people are desperate for a chance to soak in the tubs, which are currently booked through the end of the year. The spa phone rings off the hook with people on waitlists checking to see if any appointments have opened up.

Ollie wonders if the mineral water might lessen the severity of her panic attacks. Maybe even chase away the nightmares. On Thursday night before July Fourth weekend, she waits until the pool complex closes at ten, grabs a chilled bottle of Chardonnay from the spa refrigerator, and lets herself into the hot springs area.

The warm water loosens her muscles, and the wine buzzes her brain. Almost immediately, she feels more relaxed than she has in a year. She's been soaking for about twenty minutes when Cecily and Presley appear.

"What brings you two here?" she asks.

"Matters of the heart," Cecily says, holding up a bottle of champagne. "What about you?"

"Same," Ollie says. Truth be told, her panic attacks and nightmares stem from matters of the heart.

"Then we're in good company." Cecily strips off her cover-up and slips into the water.

Presley lowers herself to the edge of the pool, dangling her legs in the water. "For the baby's safety, my doctor advised me not to soak."

"That makes sense." Ollie pours more wine into her empty stemless glass. "Are you seeing an obstetrician in Hope Springs?"

"I am," Presley says, raking her long auburn hair into a ponytail. "I haven't decided yet, but I may stay in town until after the baby comes."

Ollie sips her wine. "I'm being nosy, and you don't have to talk about it if you don't want to, but is your matter of the heart the reason you're hiding out in Hope Springs?"

"Maybe talking about it will help." Presley stares into the teal water. "My husband and I had an awful fight when I left his tour.

The few times we've talked since, things have been awkward between us." She places her hand on her belly and smiles. "Don't get me wrong. I'm excited about the baby. But we may have jumped the gun on getting pregnant. We're having some growing pains. I trust Everett, and I have faith we'll work things out. For the time being, with Everett away on tour, I feel more comfortable here surrounded by my friends."

Cecily leans into Presley. "And we're grateful to have you to help with Bridezilla's wedding."

Ollie snickers. "Isn't that the truth?" She looks over at Cecily. "What's ailing your heart, Cecily?"

"My situation is a little more complicated." Cecily pops the cork on the champagne and takes a swig out of the bottle. "Lyle is going to The Homestead this weekend with friends. I'm moving out while he's gone."

Ollie says, "I'm so sorry, Cecily. I didn't realize things had gotten so bad between you and Lyle. Does he know you're moving out?"

Cecily takes another pull on the champagne bottle. "Nope. I don't trust myself to talk to him about it. I'm worried I won't have the strength to refuse him if he tries to talk me into staying. Not that he would. I'm pretty sure he's sleeping with someone else."

Ollie grimaces. "Bastard. What makes you think that?"

"I'd rather not get into it. But I have my reasons." Cecily hunches a shoulder. "It's fine. Knowing he's cheating on me makes it easier for me to leave."

Ollie considers this. "That makes sense. Where are you moving?"

"Into Stella's garage apartment. Which I'm super excited about." Cecily takes another swig of champagne and sets the bottle down. "What about you, Ollie? What's troubling your heart?"

Ollie slides deeper into the water, resting her head against the edge of the pool as she stares up at the starry sky. "Our family winery, which has been in my family for many generations, burned last year in the Napa Valley fires."

Presley's hand flies to her mouth and Cecily gasps.

Ollie continues in a tight voice, "My parents were killed in the fire."

Cecily's brow knits. "I don't know what to say, Ollie. I'm so sorry."

Presley's eyes glisten with unshed tears. "That's awful, Ollie. I lost my mother recently. I understand what you're going through if you ever want to talk."

Cecily and Presley are sympathetic listeners. She's tempted to confess the rest of her sad story. But she doesn't know them well enough yet, and she's afraid she'll scare them off.

Ollie is spared from having to say more when Stella comes through the gate.

"I'm hurt. You didn't invite me to the party." Stella pretends to make light of it, but her expression is wounded.

Cecily holds up her champagne bottle. "This is an impromptu party, the best kind."

"Join us," Ollie says. "We're confessing our matters of the heart."

"Ironically, a matter of the heart is the reason I'm here. Not my matter. But another young woman's." Stella kicks off her flip-flops and sits down on the side of the tub next to Ollie. "I finally read my great-grandmother's journals. What I learned has been weighing heavily on my mind. I was out taking a walk, and I found myself here. I guess I'm searching for answers."

"What answers?" Presley asks. "What's in the journals?"

Stella shakes her head. "The story is so sad. You don't want to hear it."

"Yes, we do." Cecily holds out the champagne bottle to Stella. "Liquid courage."

Stella takes a swig and licks her lips. "My great-grandmother wrote about a young woman who was the debutante of the season from Charleston, South Carolina, back in 1958. Anna's father had fallen on hard times, financially. He arranged a marriage between Anna and an older gentleman, a wealthy man with a reputation of being a womanizer and a tyrant. But Anna fell in love with a man her own age, a man from a less desirable family. She begged her father to allow her to marry him. But her father refused. Torn between her beloved father and the love of her life, Anna ran away. She hitchhiked to Hope Springs, to soak in the famous hot springs. Her lover followed her here. But so did the man she was betrothed to."

Stella's expression is pained as she drinks again from the bottle. "The fiancé caught Anna and her lover together in the hot tubs. And he drowned them both."

"What?" Cecily says, and Presley adds, "You're joking."

Stella gives a solemn nod. "That's why my great-grandfather closed the hot springs to his guests."

"That's the most tragic thing I've ever heard," Cecily says.

Presley swings her legs out of the pool, tucking her knees beneath her chin. "I don't understand, Stella. You've studied the inn's history. How did you not know about this until now?"

"There was no mention of it in any of the materials I've read," Stella says. "For the past two days, I've been researching the story online and combing through the microfiche at the public library. I found no information about the tragic deaths anywhere."

Presley asks, "What about Opal? Does she know anything about the deaths?"

Stella shakes her head. "This happened before she started vacationing here." She takes one last gulp from the bottle and hands it back to Cecily. "Word is spreading about the hot springs."

"People have already gone a little nutty," Ollie adds, her lips pressed thin.

"I'm worried the promise of miracle cures will attract the wrong sort of people," Stella says. "We can't afford to let this interfere with our paying guests."

"The miracle water isn't working on me. The springs are a sham! "I'm still sad." Cecily's touches the tip of the bottle to her chest and then points it at Ollie. "Are you still sad?"

Ollie thinks about it. "Yep." She feels less anxious. But that's probably because of the wine.

Cecily aims the bottle's tip at Presley. "Are you still sad?"

"A little," Presley says.

Cecily waves the bottle in the air. "See! Problem solved. No reason for the undesirables to come, because the springs don't cure matters of the heart."

"I hope you're right," Stella says under her breath.

Cecily brings the bottle to her lips, but there's no champagne left.

Ollie snatches the bottle away from Cecily. "Give me that before you break it."

With words slurred, Cecily says, "I'm too drunk to walk myself home. And I don't wanna be there anyway. Tonight's my last night with Lyle. What if I start crying? What if I break bad and tell him I'm moving out?" She lays her head on Presley's shoulder. "Can I sleep on your sofa?"

Presley smooths back Cecily's honey-colored hair. "I can do better than a sofa. My cottage has two bedrooms. You can have your own bed. But you have to text Lyle, to tell him where you are."

"You do it," Cecily says, her eyelids drooping.

Presley picks up her phone, her thumbs flying across the screen.

Less than a minute passes before Cecily asks, "Did he respond yet?"

Presley glances down at her phone. "Not yet."

Cecily bursts into tears. "See! He doesn't love me anymore."

"Okay. That's it. We need to get you to bed." Presley stands and helps Cecily to her feet.

"Do you want me to call security to help you?" Stella asks.

Presley dismisses them with a wave. "We're good. We don't have far to walk. The fresh air will help clear her head."

Ollie and Stella watch them exit the gate. "She's a mess," Ollie says.

Stella shakes her head in sadness. "I've never seen her out of control like that. She really loves Lyle. Unfortunately, I don't think he's the right guy for her."

Ollie gets out of the water and grabs two towels, tossing one to Stella. "She's going to need her friends these next few weeks."

"Yes, she will." Drying her feet and legs, Stella tosses the towel into the used towel bin. "If you're headed out, I'll walk with you."

"Sounds good," Ollie says, pulling on a cover-up.

Locking the gate behind them, the women head back up toward the main building in silence, bidding each other goodnight when they part at the front entrance.

Ollie's step is lighter as she strolls down Main Street toward her apartment. California seems like a long way away, and for the first time since coming to Virginia, she feels like she may have found a new home. Maybe the hot springs mend broken hearts after all.

13

PRESLEY

Clusters of locals and guests gather on the lawn for the inn's annual Fourth of July picnic. Red-and-white checkered banquet tables boast chafing dishes bearing hot dogs and hamburgers, baked beans, and watermelon wedges. Children chase each other around while adults mingle, sipping cocktails from clear plastic cups.

Presley and Stella set up camp near the lake on a large picnic blanket with a cooler chilling a bottle of rosé for Stella, craft beer for Jack, and fruity popsicles for Presley and Jazz, who is off with Angel making friends with the other guests.

Today is Stella's birthday, and Presley has arranged a special surprise for her. She can hardly contain her excitement. She's being extra careful, watching what she says, to avoid spilling the beans.

"How is Cecily?" Presley asks.

Stella flaps her hand in a so-so gesture. "Cecily is an expert at hiding her emotions. But she's a survivor. She just needs some time."

"Did she get moved in okay?"

Stella smiles up at her husband who is standing near them

talking with a small group of locals. "Jack recruited a couple of his workers to help her move the heavy stuff. She has an eclectic mixture of furnishings. The apartment is very Cecily."

Grabbing a beer from the cooler, Jack sits down on the blanket beside his wife. "So, Presley, did Stella tell you about her latest project?"

"Someone mentioned the possibility of a new family wing," Presley says. "Are you going through with it?"

Stella sweeps an arm at the crowd. "We don't have much choice. We're busting at the seams. We can't host weddings if we don't have adequate accommodations for the bride's and groom's guests. Besides, we're discovering families with young children and partying singles don't play well together."

"I heard that. I've noticed some rowdy activity on the weekends at the wellness center," Presley says. "How long will it take to build the wing?"

Stella nudges Jack. "If we start right after Labor Day, my contractor assures me he'll be finished by next May." She gets to her feet and offers Jack a hand. "I need to make the rounds. And you're coming with me."

Jack pulls a face. "Seriously? I just sat down."

"Seriously," she says, hauling him to his feet.

Presley watches them mosey off hand in hand. Their relationship seems so solid. Do they ever argue?

She checks her phone for messages. Earlier this morning, she texted Everett a Bitmoji, wishing him a happy Fourth of July. She hasn't yet heard back from him. He performed in Bozeman, Montana, yesterday. His next concert is tomorrow in Madison, Wisconsin. Where is he today? How is he spending his holiday? Are his plans too important, his agenda too busy, to call his pregnant wife?

Looking up from her phone, Presley spots Chris and Amy heading toward her. They're adorable in their matching uniforms—khaki shorts and pale blue polos bearing the well-ness center logo. His right arm is draped casually around her shoulder, and he's holding a clear plastic cup with a beverage Presley suspects is alcoholic in his left hand. He's going to college in two months. She doesn't mind if her brother drinks as long as he does it responsibly.

"What's up, sis?" Chris drops to his knees onto Presley's blanket, pulling Amy down with him.

"Just hanging out. Are you two finished at the cafe?"

Presley has gotten to know her brother and his girlfriend better these past few weeks. She even took them to dinner at Town Tavern one night. Chris is experiencing his first love. And Amy, who appears to be a genuinely kind person, is equally into him.

"We closed early," Chris explains.

"Stella wants all guests and staff at the picnic." Amy spots someone off in the distance and waves. "There's my friend Kate. I'm gonna go speak to her. I'll be right back." She gets to her feet and scurries off.

"You two are getting along well," Presley says, watching her brother watch his girlfriend go.

With a dreamy expression, Chris says, "Yeah. Amy's great. She really gets me."

"It's comforting to have someone to confide in who's on the same page as you." Presley has that with Everett. At least she thinks she does. "What does your mom think of Amy?"

Chris returns his attention to Presley. "She thinks Amy's not good enough for me."

"Are you kidding me? Amy is attractive and intelligent, and comes from a good family. What's not to like?"

"I'm her only child. No one will ever be good enough for me. Speaking of Mom. Tomorrow is her birthday. Do you have any ideas of what I can give her?"

Presley taps her chin while she thinks. "What about giving her a gift certificate for the spa?"

Chris's face lights up. "That's a great idea. I'll suggest she use it for the soaking tubs. Maybe the spring water will improve her bad mood."

Presley drops her chin to her chest. "You mean, you've heard the rumors about the healing waters?"

"Ye-ah! All the guests are talking about it," he says, and tells Presley some of the same things she's been hearing about the miracle spring water.

When the bluegrass band begins to play on the dock, Amy returns for Chris. "Let's go listen to the band."

They've no sooner left when Cecily appears beside her. "Can I join you?" She collapses onto the blanket before Presley can respond. "Thanks for letting me crash the other night. Sorry if I was out of control. I don't know what got into me."

"No worries. You're dealing with a lot right now. Are you feeling any better after moving out?"

"A part of me feels like an elephant stepped off my shoulders. But the other part of me is depressed. The sadness is like a Pacman chasing me around, trying to swallow me whole." Cecily uses her fingers to mimic the yellow video game character. "But I refuse to let it get me."

"That's the fighting spirit," Presley says. "It'll get easier over time."

Cecily stretches her tanned legs out on the blanket in front of her. She's changed out of her work clothes into a yellow sundress. She looks like a summer flower with her golden hair pulled back in a ponytail. "I love my new apartment," she says. "Being so close to the inn is awesome. I took a couple of hours off this afternoon and went home to unpack boxes and hang pictures. The apartment is really coming together. You'll have to come see it soon."

"I'd love that. Have you talked to Lyle at all?"

"Nope. He'd already left for The Homestead when I got home on Friday morning." She furrows her brow. "The end of the night is kinda blurry. You texted him, right? You told him I wasn't coming home."

Presley nods. "I assume he got the message. He never texted back."

"He was probably with his girlfriend," Cecily says, her facial muscles tight. "I'm so glad I moved out."

"You did the right thing, Cecily. I know it wasn't easy for you. But I'm proud of you."

Cecily gives her a sidelong glance. "That means a lot. Thanks. Look! There's Ollie," she says and waves her over.

Ollie is stunning in cutoff denim shorts and an oversized white blouse with her dark hair falling in layers around her face. She accepts Cecily's high five as she gracefully sinks to the blanket. "How is everyone feeling after Thursday night's hot springs therapy session?"

"I feel the same." Presley doesn't need healing water. She needs her husband to call.

"I'm better," Cecily says. "But that's more about me leaving Lyle than the mineral water. What about you, Ollie?"

Ollie shrugs. "The jury is still out. I've been going back every night for more."

An awkward silence falls over them. Ollie is mourning the loss of both her parents. She needs the healing waters more than any of them.

Cecily lets out a groan. "Don't look now. Here comes Bridezilla."

Presley follows her gaze to see Peaches and Fiona walking toward them. "Be nice."

"I don't mind Fiona," Cecily says. "In fact, I like her a lot. But I can't figure out why she hangs out with Peaches."

Presley invites them to sit down. "So, Ollie, I'm getting tennis elbow from rolling out pastry," Fiona says, rubbing her right arm. "Can you arrange for me to soak in the hot springs?"

Peaches's hand shoots up. "Ooh! Me too. Does the spring water cure anxiety?"

Presley notices the color draining from Ollie's face. The newest staff member is a mystery. Presley wonders if whatever she's hiding has something to do with her parents' deaths.

"Depends on the person," Ollie says. "But I'm going over to the hot springs after the fireworks if you want to come with me."

"Yes!" Fiona and Peaches say in unison.

Presley checks her watch and says to Cecily, "Are you ready? It's almost time for Stella's surprise."

Cecily jumps to her feet. "Let's do it!"

Cecily and Presley cross the lawn to the band's makeshift stage where, off to the side, several of Cecily's servers wait with an enormous layered birthday cake.

When the band finishes their song, Cecily directs Presley to the microphone. "This was your idea. You do the honors."

Presley steps up to the microphone and clears her throat. "Can I have your attention? If everyone would please gather around the stage . . . We're celebrating a special birthday this evening."

The guests migrate toward the stage.

"Stella, will you please come forward."

The crowd parts and Stella, her face beaming red, emerges. She gawks when she sees the cake. "You didn't."

"We did." Presley gives the guitarist the signal, and he strums the first notes of "Happy Birthday to You." A chorus of voices break into song, their voices echoing throughout the mountains.

On Monday morning, Presley drives over to the local farmer's market and purchases a gorgeous bouquet of the summer's colorful wildflowers, which she leaves on Lucy's desk along with a birthday card. Leaving the basement wine shop, she heads up to reception to talk to Rita about a block of rooms for an August wedding she's coordinating. Rita's office door is closed. Presley knocks once and opens the door without waiting to be invited in.

"Rita—" She stops in her tracks at the sight of Rita and Brian locked in an embrace with their lips glued together.

The lovers jump apart. "Presley! What're you doing here?" Rita asks, smoothing out her mussed hair.

Spinning on her heels, Presley hurries down the hall and out the back door. Rita runs after her. "Wait! Presley, you don't understand."

"What's not to understand?" Presley increases her pace. "How could you do this to your own sister?"

Rita grabs her elbow. "Stop! Brian and I didn't mean for this to happen. Give me a chance to explain. Let me buy you lunch at Roots."

Presley hesitates, but curiosity gets the best of her. "Fine," she says, and allows Rita to lead her down to the wellness center. They order Mexican bowls with grilled chicken, brown rice, beans, and avocado. They score a table by the window and sit down opposite each other.

"Does Lucy know about you and Brian?" Presley asks.

"No! And please don't tell her. We're trying to figure things out." Rita stares out the window at two little boys fishing on the pier. "This is all so complicated. Brian realized early on in their relationship that his feelings for Lucy weren't lasting. But he sensed she was having emotional problems and was waiting for the right time to let her down easy. He should've broken up with her while she was in rehab, so the therapists could help her cope. He knows that now. But it's too late."

Rita smiles up at the server when she delivers their salad bowls.

Presley's stomach is in knots. She can't think about eating. "Go on," she says.

"Brian was distraught after Lucy committed herself to rehab. As was I. We turned to each other for comfort. We were just friends for months. And then one night in late April, after too many glasses of wine, he kissed me. And things developed from there."

Presley sits back in her chair with her arms folded over her chest.

Rita lifts her fork, digs around in her bowl, and sets the fork down again. "We feel terribly guilty, but we're crazy about each other. As you know, Brian never married. He was waiting for the right person. He claims I'm that person."

Presley doesn't know what to think. Rita and Brian deserve to be happy. At the same time, Lucy is so volatile. "Can you live with yourselves if Lucy starts using drugs again because of you?"

A wounded expression crosses Rita's face. But there's a tinge of anger there as well. "I'm so tired of everything in my life being about my sister. The years since my divorce have been difficult. But I kept my chin up. I never wallowed in self-pity. I never resorted to using drugs. I shouldn't have to sacrifice a relationship with a man I care about for a sister who won't even speak to me."

Exhaling a gush of air, Presley says, "That's fair. What're you going to do?"

Rita appears bewildered. "I have no clue. For now, Brian and I are keeping our relationship a secret."

"You're not doing a very good job of it. Anyone could've

walked in on you a few minutes ago. You're lucky it was me and not Lucy."

"I know. And you're right. We need to be more careful. Brian was comforting me. Lucy and I had a fight this morning. I took her a birthday gift, a pair of earrings I found in a boutique that reminded me or her. She wouldn't accept them."

Presley scrunches up her face. "Why not?"

"Your guess is as good as mine. I've tried everything. I've supported her through thick and thin. Her divorce. Her cancer. Her depression. For whatever reason, she can't stand the sight of me." A sob catches in Rita's throat, and she presses her balled fist to her mouth. "I can't take it anymore, Presley. I can't go on like this, pretending her anger toward me doesn't hurt."

Presley reaches for Rita's hand. "I'm so sorry, Rita. You're a devoted sister. You deserve better from her. If it makes you feel any better, you're not the only one Lucy is alienating. If she's not careful, she'll lose Chris."

Sniffling, Rita reaches for a napkin to wipe her nose. "He told me. I don't understand why Lucy is turning everyone away."

"Is there any chance Lucy already knows about you and Brian?"

"No. Lucy would tell me if she did. But she suspects something's up with Brian. She's been shamelessly throwing herself at him since she got out of rehab. It's been really hard on him. He keeps giving her the cold shoulder, but she won't take the hint."

"Sounds like Brian needs to be more direct with her."

"He's worried the rejection will send her off the cliff."

Presley picks up her fork and stabs a chunk of chicken. "What a mess."

"Yep. A giant one. But it's mine and Brian's mess to figure out. Promise me, you won't say anything. Especially to Stella. Lucy and I are already treading on thin ice with her."

Presley drops her fork and reaches for Rita's hand. "You can count on me not to say anything to anybody. But Lucy will eventually find out. When she does, I hope Chris doesn't get caught in the crossfire."

———

Two hours later, Presley is dozing on the sofa with the current issue of *Garden and Gun* open on her mounded belly, when Brian comes to her door. She's struck, as always, by his dignified good looks. The crinkles around his piercing blue eyes soften his serious demeanor.

"I'm sorry to bother you," he says. "I wanted to follow up on your conversation with Rita from earlier."

Presley doesn't think he owes her an explanation, but his pained expression tells her how important this is to him. He steps back, and she follows him onto the porch. When she gestures at the rockers, he shakes his head. "I'll only take a minute of your time."

"Rita explained the situation, Brian. And I understand how difficult this has all been for you."

His shoulders cave in on his lanky frame. "I handled things poorly. And I take full responsibility." He chuckles. "There's a reason I'm still a bachelor at age fifty-seven. As an attorney, I consider myself a shrewd negotiator. When it comes to women, I'm at a total loss. Keeping our relationship a secret is unfair to Rita. However, until Lucy gets stronger, I see no other way." He moves to the porch railing. "I care about Rita a great deal, more than I've ever cared about a woman. I only wish we'd met years ago."

The sadness in his voice pulls at Presley's heartstrings. She joins him at the railing, leaning slightly against him for comfort. "Have you considered talking to Stella about the situation?"

"I wish I could talk to Stella. I hate keeping this from her. According to Rita, she and Lucy are already on shaky ground with her. And she worries it'll make matters worse."

Presley says, "Stella is more understanding than they give her credit for. On the other hand, if I were in their shoes, I might feel the same way."

Brian turns to face Presley. "Rita and I have agreed to give it until the end of the summer. If things aren't better by then, we'll come out of the closet," he says with a smile.

"That's a good plan." Presley stands on her tiptoes to kiss his cheek. "Hang in there. Lucy is a ticking time bomb. For better or worse, I have a sneaking suspicion things will come to a head sooner rather than later."

14

CECILY

Late Monday afternoon, Cecily is standing at the window counter, dicing garlic while staring out at the mountains, when Lyle knocks on the back door. She's not surprised. She's been expecting him.

He beckons her outside, and she joins him on the back stoop.

"Seriously, Cecily. You just up and moved out with no warning?" He digs the note she left him out of his shorts pocket, her monogrammed stationery now crumpled. "What is this pitiful excuse for an explanation?"

"I've been trying to get your attention for weeks, Lyle. I invited you to dinner countless times." Cecily dips her head at the note. "That explains enough. Our relationship is over." Moving to the porch railing, she looks down at her garden. She wills herself to be strong, to stand up to him. She belongs at Hope Springs Farm. Not with Lyle.

He comes to stand beside her at the railing. "I admit we've grown apart these past few months. But we were engaged to be married."

She angles her body toward him. "Who's Whitney?" she asks, watching closely for his response.

His shoulders slump as the breath leaves his body. "How'd you know?"

Cecily's heart rate quickens. Even though she suspected his affair, hearing him acknowledge it cuts deeply. "I saw a text from her on your phone."

His jaw clenches. "You were snooping on my phone?"

She glares at him. "I got up to go to the bathroom and heard your phone vibrate. It was late at night. I thought something might be wrong. What difference does it make how I found out?"

He throws his hands in the air. "I admit it. Whitney and I had a thing. A fling. Things were so bad between you and me. And Whitney . . . well, she made herself available to me. But I ended it with Whitney. You're the one I love, Cecily."

"You had to sleep with someone else to realize that?" He doesn't respond, and she continues. "We may love each other, Lyle, but we're not compatible. We want different things out of life. We'd end up making each other miserable. Better to figure that out now instead of after we're married."

Lyle's eyes are wet, as though he might cry. "But I can't afford to live in the house alone."

Her body tenses. He's worried about the *rent*? "Then get a roommate," she snarls and storms past him.

Instead of returning to the kitchen, she heads across the lawn and down toward the wellness center. When she's certain he's not following her, she collapses onto a bench. She's still sitting there fuming ten minutes later when Fiona plops down beside her.

"You look like you could use a friend," Fiona says. "Was that your fiancé I saw peeling out of the parking lot in a gray pickup truck?" Fiona has never met Lyle, but Cecily has told her about their breakup.

"Ex-fiancé. He admitted to sleeping with Whitney. He claims he loves me, and that it's over between him and Whitney. Do you know what he's worried about the most? Who's going to pay my share of the rent."

"What a jerk," Fiona says with curled lip. "You're better off without him, Cecily. What you really need is a soak in the hot springs. We formed the Girls Only Wounded Hearts Soaking Club. No boys or booze allowed. We're getting together again after work tonight. You have to come."

Cecily had planned to finish unpacking. But she'll have plenty of time for that later. Right now, she needs her friends. "I'll be there."

As they return to the kitchen together, Fiona quizzes Cecily about the evening's special. Cecily is grateful for the distraction. She chose work over the man she loves. Her career is the primary focus of her life, the obstacle in their relationship that drove Lyle into the arms of another woman. But he showed his true colors today. His self-centeredness assures her she's made the right decision.

Later that evening, Cecily goes to Billy's Bar for a chocolate martini, a special dessert order for a VIP guest. As Parker pours the ingredients in a martini shaker, he says, "I ran into Lyle in the parking lot earlier. He told me y'all broke up."

She gives him a thumbs-up. "I moved out." Call her vain, but she wants people to know she's the one who ended the relationship.

"So, what happened?" Parker asks, as he shakes the shaker.

"Growing pains," she says in a bored tone. "Turns out we were ill-suited."

"Duh. I never liked that guy. He's a punk. An adolescent lax bro."

Cecily winces. "Ouch. That's harsh."

"But true. You can do so much better, Cecily. You're a badass chef who doesn't take shit off anyone. Why were you taking it from him?"

She feigns nonchalance despite her pounding heart. "Who says I was taking anything off him?"

Parker places the martini glass on a round tray and carries it around from behind the bar. "I'd hate for you to spill it. I'll walk with you back to Jameson's."

"That's not necessary." When she moves to take the tray, he holds it out of her reach.

"Humor me," he says with a smile. "I could use a break."

"Fine," she says, and they wend their way through the crowd.

Parker pauses in the lobby. "I heard Lyle was sleeping around."

Her neck snaps as she looks up at him. "And you didn't tell me?"

He offers her a sympathetic smile. "I don't listen to gossip until it's proven true."

"That's smart." She drops her eyes. "Truth is, our relation-ship was doomed from the beginning. We should've realized it in December when we called off the wedding."

"I'm sorry, Cecily. I'm here for you if you need to talk. Or if you just wanna hang out."

"I appreciate it. But I'm fine. Better than fine. The worst is over. It's full speed ahead. I have plenty to keep me busy at work." Cecily wonders who she's trying to convince, Parker or herself.

Cecily takes the tray from him and returns to the kitchen.

For the rest of the evening, she rides an emotional roller coaster. Parker's words ring out in her ears. *A punk. An adolescent lax bro.* Does everyone feel this way about Lyle? Cecily considers herself a good judge of character. Why didn't she see it?

Eager for fresh air, Cecily leaves her sous chef to lock up and hurries home to change into her bathing suit. She pauses to admire her new digs. The apartment has a fresh vibe. She's made the right choice. She'll miss Lyle. She will undoubtedly have down times. But she'll survive.

The scene at the hot springs takes Cecily's breath. Lit candles are scattered about the deck for ambience, and in the background, the full moon casts a golden glow over the mountains. The air is clean and crisp. And Cecily suddenly feels more alive than she has in months. If ever. She's rocking her career. And she now has the freedom to do whatever she wants, whenever she wants.

Cecily takes off her cover-up and slips into the mineral water next to Ollie, opposite Fiona and Peaches. "What an incredible evening. The candles add a nice touch."

Ollie's aquamarine eyes are like sparkling gemstones in the moonlight. "Thanks! I wanted to do something special for our first official meeting of The Soaking Club."

"Is membership closed, or can we invite Presley to join?" Cecily asks.

"All female staff members are welcome," Ollie says.

"As long as they have a broken heart story to tell," Fiona adds.

"Oh really? Do *you* have a story to tell?" Cecily has never heard Fiona mention a boyfriend or significant other.

"I do." Fiona sinks to her chin in the water. "I started dating Tyler my senior year at Georgia. I was certain he was the one. But he got real possessive, really quick. When I broke up with him, he began stalking me. He made my life a living hell. Fortunately, my professors let me finish my last month of classes remotely. But I missed graduation."

"Is that why you went to culinary school in Colorado?" Cecily asks.

"Exactly." Fiona sits up. "After everything that happened, getting away from Georgia seemed like a good idea. I never told Tyler I was considering culinary school. So, he had no clue where to look for me."

"She basically fell off the planet," Peaches says. "She's not on social media anymore, if you can believe that. Other than her family, I'm the only one who knows where she is."

"Are you still in danger?" Ollie asks, her dark brow pinched.

"Nah." Fiona dismisses her concern with a flick of the wrist. "I'm not worried about Tyler anymore. I'm sure he's moved on. He's torturing some other unsuspecting girl."

Cecily smiles over at Fiona. "I'm relieved to hear I'm not the only one whose love was blind. Earlier tonight, Parker described Lyle as a 'punk.'" She uses air quotes. "'An adolescent lax bro.' Lyle's boyish charm is one of the things I love most about him. But he's spoiled and irresponsible. It took me months to see the immature side of him. But it's the thing that ultimately drove us apart."

"Not to mention he's a cheater," Fiona says.

"What a jerk," Ollie says, smacking the water with her palm.

Peaches rolls her eyes. "Once a cheater, always a cheater."

"Right," Cecily says. "He claims his *fling* with the girl is over. He thought I would just forgive and forget."

"Love is blind for everyone, Cecily. At least to some extent," Ollie says.

"So true," Fiona says. "My mom can't see how irritating it is when Dad chews with his mouth open. And Dad looks past her clutter that litters every surface of the house."

Cecily thinks about how her father always forgives her

mother's crass statements. "I call that tolerance that comes with years of marriage. But I get your point." She notices Ollie's face has grown dark. "Have you experienced blind love, Ollie?"

"In the worst way." Ollie shivers, even though her body is submerged in warm water. "You're lucky, Cecily. You realized your mistake before you married."

"Wait, what?" Fiona's warm brown eyes are like thin mint cookies. "You mean, you're married? Where's your husband?"

"I'm divorced." Ollie hoists herself out of the tub, leaving her legs dangling over the side and wrapping herself in a towel. "For several years after college, I roamed around California teaching exercise classes and guiding hiking trips. When I was twenty-eight, my parents summoned me home. It was time for me to get serious about managing the family's winery. I fell in love with our foreman, a man ten years my senior. My parents would never have approved if it had been anyone other than Sergio. But he had worked for them for years. He was like a second son to my dad. They trusted him. And they were thrilled to see me settle down with someone who could handle me." A smile creeps across her lips. "I was a bit of a wild child."

Peaches rubs her hands together. "This is getting juicy."

Ollie drops her smile. "But I wasn't finished sowing those wild oats. Sergio tried to control me. He was ready for children. I wasn't. He disapproved of my friends, which only made me want to hang out with them more. Our fights were vicious. My father had to come to our house many times to break them up. Our marriage lasted two years."

Three sets of mesmerized eyes are glued on Ollie. "Go on," Cecily prompts.

"Sergio turned on my family. He sued my family for a fourth of the winery, half of my half, compensation he felt entitled to for the pain and suffering I'd caused him. The lawsuit was bogus. Of course, he didn't win. But he made our lives hell for more than a year."

Silence falls over the foursome, each lost in her own thought. Finally, Cecily asks, "How was your love for Sergio blind? What did you see in him that made you fall for him?"

"Great question. It took a lot of therapy to figure that out. There was much to love about Sergio before I ruined him. Before I made him bitter and resentful. He was handsome and gentle, the salt of the earth kind of man. I was blind to reality. I imagined myself being his wife, having his children, running the winery. But when it came down to it, I wasn't ready or willing to stop the partying." Ollie swings her legs over the side and stands up. "So now you know my sad story."

Cecily gets out of the pool and gives her a hug. "Thanks for sharing. I know it wasn't easy. You've been through a lot."

Ollie's smile is sad. "It's life. We're all on our journeys. Some roads are smoother than others."

Cecily thinks about this during her walk home. She's not afraid of taking the road less traveled. She's more afraid of arriving at the wrong destination.

15

OLLIE

On Thursday afternoon, Ollie fills in for a spa attendant who needs to leave early to prepare for her husband's fiftieth birthday dinner party. Ollie's last client of the day shows up a few minutes early for her six o'clock soaking tub appointment. Maureen Graves, a woman in her early forties, wearing a pink scarf over her bald head, tells Ollie she's battling pancreatic cancer.

"I refuse to let this disease beat me." She touches her fingers to her scarf. "My doctors insist on a grueling course of chemo and radiation, but I'm trying homeopathic remedies as well. I'm eating healthy and exercising regularly. Who knows, the healing waters might offer the miraculous cure."

While Ollie doubts such a miracle is possible, she can't bring herself to squash this woman's optimism. "You never know. Having a positive attitude is key." She shows Maureen to the nearly vacant dressing room. "Are you from around here?"

"Richmond." Maureen tugs off her scarf, revealing a shiny pale scalp. "I drove up for the treatment. I'm headed back afterward."

"You couldn't find anyone to ride with you?" Ollie doesn't

think a woman undergoing chemotherapy should be driving alone on the mountain roads of Virginia at night. Even in the summertime.

"I'm all alone these days. Divorce, thank goodness. My ex and I hardly speak. And my daughters live out west. They're coming home for Christmas. I hope I'm still alive by then."

Ollie is caught off guard. "Oh ... I ..."

Maureen grabs her arm. "I'm teasing. I fully intend to be here for Christmas."

"Of course, you will," Ollie says with more conviction than she feels. She knows firsthand, from a friend whose father died from pancreatic cancer, the average life span after the disease spreads is three to six months.

"Do you have any other family? Any siblings?" Ollie empathizes with this woman who is battling the biggest challenge of her life alone.

"Nope. It's just me and the cancer."

At a loss for words, Ollie says, "I'm sorry."

Ollie shows Maureen her locker. Inside the locker hangs a terry cloth robe and a drawstring bag with a pair of one-size-fits-all slippers. Ollie studies Maureen as she places her belongings in the locker. A faint tan line runs along her previous hairline. Her eyebrows are sparse, but her eyelashes have yet to fall out. Her green eyes are bright and, surprisingly, her complexion has a rosy glow.

Maureen takes the robe out of the locker and disappears inside a dressing room. Ollie tidies up the sink counter while she waits. She doesn't want to leave the woman alone in case she needs help.

When Maureen emerges from the dressing room, Ollie shows her down the quiet hall to the treatment room where a steaming tub awaits.

After the fifty-minute time allotment, Ollie waits, once again, for Maureen to change in the locker room before walking her out to the parking lot.

For the rest of the evening, Maureen Graves weighs heavily on Ollie, and she discusses it with the girls later that night in the hot springs.

"I can see where the mineral water might cure certain skin conditions. Since the skin comes into contact with the water. But curing cancer is a stretch."

"I agree," Presley says. "Has there been any documented proof of anyone having a miraculous cure for cancer or diabetes?"

Ollie shakes her head. "Not that I'm aware of."

Fiona rubs her elbow. "My tendonitis is much better."

"Well, my anxiety isn't," Peaches snaps. "I'm not sure I can go through with this wedding."

Fiona crosses her eyes. "Ignore her. She's in a mood."

Ollie hasn't had a panic attack in days. But she attributes the stress reduction to her newfound friendships with these women, not the mineral water. "Maybe talking about what's causing your anxiety will help," she suggests. "Confessing about my failed marriage helped me."

"My problem isn't with Nathan," Peaches says, as though nothing could possibly be wrong with her fiancé. "He's made a whole new friends group without me, a group of wealthy Brits who invite Nathan to go to their country homes on the weekend."

"Sounds like my kinda friends." Cecily says what Ollie's thinking.

"Except that now those friends are going on our honeymoon with us," Peaches says sticking her lower lip out in a pout.

Presley cuts her gray eyes at Peaches. "How's that?"

"Daddy has chartered a superyacht for Nathan and me out of Montenegro. Some of Nathan's new friends will be down there at the same time. It's a coincidence. Apparently, they go the last week in July every year. But still. Some honeymoon. I haven't seen Nathan since Christmas. Instead of relaxing, I'll be spending my time trying to impress his friends." Peaches falls back against the side of the pool. "They'll probably all hate me."

"Or they'll find you intriguing," Presley says with a smile. "A Southern girl whose father is the governor of Georgia."

Cecily looks at Presley, as though she's lost her mind. "Yeah, but you might want to tone it down a little."

Peaches glares at Cecily. "Tone what down?"

"The pampered Southern belle act," Cecily says. "Others may find it offensive."

Tears well in Peaches's eyes. She blinks several times as she looks down at her Apple Watch. "Would you look at the time? I have a trial run with my hair stylist first thing in the morning. I want to look my best." She sucks in her gut, bringing herself to her full height, and gracefully exits the pool. "You ladies have a good evening."

Ollie hates to see Peaches's feelings hurt, but Cecily's criticism, while harshly stated, was well intentioned. Isn't that what true friendship is about? Telling secrets and being honest with one another, even if the truth hurts?

Presley reaches into the water and splashes Cecily. "Good job! You probably just got us all fired."

Cecily gives her a playful shove in return. "What're you talking about? You're not officially working here."

"Trust me, I am. Stella has pulled me in on nearly every wedding planned for the next few months."

Cecily pats Presley on the head. "Calm down. It's not good for the baby. I'm joking. I know you work hard. Stella won't fire us. We run this place."

Fiona reaches for a towel, blotting the perspiration from her face. "Peaches isn't going to tell on you anyway. She knows what you said is true. I've told her the same thing a thousand times. She needed to hear it from someone other than me."

"I agree," Ollie says. "For her own good, she needs to toughen up. Once she's married and living in London, she won't be able to run to her daddy when something doesn't go her way."

Ollie's father never pampered her. When she got into trouble, he let her figure her own way out. But he was good at giving advice. If only she'd listened to him more often. She'd do anything to learn just one more lesson from him. Ollie has only herself to blame.

Maureen Graves occupies Ollie's thoughts over the coming days. Her heart breaks for the woman, having to endure cancer alone. Shame on her daughters. Ollie fears they'll one day regret not spending more time with their mom. Ollie knows all too well that turning back the clock is impossible.

A nagging feeling warns Ollie she hasn't seen the last of Maureen. She wonders if their two worlds have brought them together for a reason. On Wednesday of the following week, when Ollie turns on the local morning news while getting ready for work, she's stunned to see Maureen holding a press conference in front of a two-story brick row house in Richmond.

Ollie drops her coffee mug, the porcelain shattering on the tile floor. Reaching for the remote, she turns up the volume.

A reporter—identified by the banner at the bottom of the screen as Nicole Lambert—asks Maureen, "Is there any other explanation for your sudden cure? Are you involved in any clinical trials?"

"No. I'm telling you. The mineral water in the natural hot springs at Hope Springs Farm has magical healing powers. I visited their soaking tubs last Thursday. I went for a CT scan on Monday. Late yesterday afternoon, my doctor"—she gestures at the woman standing next to her—"informed me my cancer is in remission."

Ollie moves closer to the television to get a better look at Maureen's doctor. Something about the woman is oddly familiar.

The reporter turns to the doctor. "We're joined today by Dr. Wilma Matthews, a well-known local oncologist. Dr. Matthews, how do you explain this sudden development?"

"There is no explanation, aside from divine intervention." The doctor casts her gaze heavenward. "Only a few days ago, Maureen Graves was deathly ill. And now she's made what appears to be a miraculous recovery."

Ollie smells a rat. If Maureen Graves was deathly ill last week, how do you explain her rosy glow?

Ollie's phone vibrates her kitchen counter with a call from Stella. "Turn on the news!"

"I'm watching. I'll be there in a few minutes." Powering off the TV, Ollie grabs her purse and racewalks down Main Street to the inn. She's entering the main building when Mark and Marcia Porter, the town's power couple responsible for the inn's marketing, pull up in their Tesla.

The threesome walk together to the general manager's office where they find Stella pacing the floor and raking her fingers through her unruly hair. "Ollie, do you know this woman? This Maureen Graves?" Her arm shoots out, finger pointed at the television.

Ollie quickly fills them in on her encounter with Maureen Graves. "I have an uneasy feeling about this. I'm not certain she's telling the truth. At the risk of being unsympathetic toward this woman's situation, she appeared too healthy to be critically ill." Ollie describes Maureen's rosy glow and the tan line.

"Are you suggesting she's an opportunist?" Stella asks.

Marcia's hands fly up with palms out. "Hang on a sec. The quickest way to lose the success we've achieved these last few months is to accuse a dying woman of lying."

"No one's accusing anyone of anything. Let's all calm down and think this situation through." Stella lifts the receiver on her desk phone. "Have a seat. I'll order coffee."

Ollie and the marketing experts sit down across from one another at the conference table, and Stella takes her seat at the head a minute later when she gets off the phone. For the next thirty minutes, they discuss the potential ramifications of Maureen's press conference. The promise of miracle cures will bring new guests to the inn. But can they handle more business? And is it the type of clientele they want?

There's a knock on the door, and Stella calls, "Come in."

Rita enters the office. "Phones are ringing off the hook, and the reservation system keeps crashing. As of now, we're booked through next February. What on earth is going on?"

"I'll hold a meeting and explain later," Stella says. "For now, don't take any more reservations. Get the guests' names and tell them we'll call them back."

Rita is on her way out of the office when Ollie receives a call from Lucinda, the manager of the spa. After listening briefly, Ollie says, "Stop answering the phone. I'll be down in a minute."

"They're overwhelmed at the spa, Stella," Ollie says. "Phones are ringing off the hook with some guests desperate to soak in the tubs and others claiming they've been miraculously cured of a number of diseases."

"This is out of hand." Stella looks from Mark to Marcia. "What do we do?"

Mark massages the bridge of his nose. "I suggest scheduling a press conference for this afternoon. We need to play the situation down before it gets out of hand."

The color drains from Stella's face. "What will I say?"

"The truth. There's no evidence the mineral water has magical healing powers. I'll help you. We'll devise the statement together."

Stella's gaze lands on Ollie. "As manager of the wellness center, you'll need to be there to answer questions."

"Stella, no! I can't." Ollie's mind races for an explanation and comes up with a weak one. "I'm camera shy."

"Get over it. I need you," Stella says in a demanding tone Ollie has never heard her use.

Feeling the walls closing in on her, Ollie stands to go. "Okay. Just text me the time, and I'll be here."

Ollie feels a panic attack coming on as she hurries out of the building and down the hill toward the wellness center. Taking deep breaths, she reminds herself this is local news. No one outside the Commonwealth of Virginia cares about a woman who claims spring water cured her cancer. No way her brother will see the press conference all the way out in California.

16

STELLA

At one o'clock in the afternoon, with Ollie at my side, I exit the main building through the front doors to face an army of reporters who shove microphones and video cameras at me. My knees go weak, and my hands shake as I approach the podium.

"Good afternoon. My staff and I would like to express our sincere best wishes to Maureen Graves for her continued recovery." I pause to take a breath. "We're all about health and wellness at Hope Springs Farm. Our restaurant provides diners farm-to-table produce as well as the highest quality meats and seafood. Our spa offers beauty treatments and relaxation therapies. And we encourage guests to take advantage of the unspoiled countryside by hiking and biking, fishing and kayaking. Dreams come true here every day. Guests fall in love. Babies are conceived. Couples begin their lives together as man and wife. If ever there was a place for a miracle to happen, Hope Springs is it. With that being said, I believe Maureen's team of skilled doctors is more responsible for her cancer's sudden remission than the mineral water in the springs here. Thank you for your time."

I hadn't planned to answer questions, but as I'm turning away from the podium, a reporter calls out, "Have there been any other miracle cures relating to the hot springs?"

Turning back to the podium, I recognize the reporter as Nicole Lambert from the local NBC news affiliate in Richmond. A number of responses come to mind, but I've learned from past experiences that lies almost always come back to haunt me.

I readjust the microphone. "A couple of guests claim they've seen improvement in skin and muscular problems."

"How many guests?" another reporter asks.

I gesture at Ollie whose face goes pale. "I'll let Ollie, the manager of our wellness center, answer that question."

Ollie takes a tentative step forward. "A few guests. A handful at the most."

More questions follow, but I take Ollie by the arm and guide her back inside. Martin, my large and solidly built head of security, is waiting for us in the front hallway.

"We have a situation at the wellness center," he says in a low voice. "Thirty minutes ago, a mob of sick people swarmed the building. We evacuated the pool and have locked down the building. But they refuse to leave. They're demanding time in the hot springs."

"How do you know they're ill?" I ask.

"Some are in wheelchairs and others are pushing walkers. A few have lost their hair and a couple are emaciated."

"All right. I'll deal with it." With Martin and Ollie on my heels, I storm past reception, out the back door, and down the hill to the wellness center.

The sufferers wait patiently in a long line that wraps from the main door around the building and out onto the pier. My heart breaks when I see these people of various ages in different stages of illness and disease. What if the mineral water really does heal? Who am I to deny these people the chance to be cured?

Cupping my hands around my mouth, I yell, "Can I have your attention, please?"

When they continue talking amongst themselves, I nod at Martin who finger whistles them into silence.

I wait for them to settle down. "Thank you for coming today. I appreciate your interest in our wellness center. Unfortunately, all treatments are booked solid for months."

The crowd responds with a chorus of boos.

"Please be patient with us. We were blindsided by today's events. *If* it turns out the waters have magic healing powers, and that's a very big if, I'll make certain every one of you has your share of time in the hot springs. I'll have someone collect your names and contact information. Once you've provided these details, please leave the property without disturbing our guests." I turn to Ollie. "Will you please get some staff members out here with clipboards?"

"I'm on it," Ollie says and disappears inside.

I look up at Martin. "I'm afraid this is only the beginning. We'll need to beef up our security patrol. Can you handle that?"

Martin snaps his heels together. "Yes, ma'am. I belong to a network of local and state police officers. I'll send out a request for anyone looking to earn extra money."

"Thank you. I'm calling a meeting for three o'clock in my office. You can report your findings then."

I spend a few minutes speaking with the sick folks. They tell me about their ailments and dismal prognoses. In many cases, a miracle seems to be their only hope.

Upon my return to the main building, I instruct my administrative assistant to email key members of my staff about the meeting, and I lock myself in my office.

I'm exhausted, and even though it's after two o'clock, I

haven't eaten lunch. I call Jameson's and ask for a server to bring me the salad special of the day. I'm surprised when Cecily delivers the order herself.

She hands me the silver-domed plate and sits down opposite my desk. "I thought you might need to talk."

I need a few minutes alone to gather my thoughts for the meeting more than I need to talk to Cecily, but she genuinely wants to help, and I don't want to hurt her feelings. I remove the silver dome and dig into the salad—a delicious mixture of greens, melon scoops, prosciutto, and grilled chicken with a citrusy dressing.

Cecily babbles on while I stuff my face. "Something smells fishy about this woman's story. Miracle or not, cancer doesn't go away overnight. Although, Jazz's ankle healed pretty quickly. And Fiona swears her tendonitis is almost gone."

"I honestly don't know what to think, Cecily. I'm just trying to get through the day." I look up from the salad. "Have you heard any more from Lyle?"

"Not since last week. Rumor has it, he's seeing Whitney. And I'm fine with it. Makes it easier to move on. We're crazy busy in Jameson's." Cecily gets to her feet. "Speaking of which, I need to check on some things before the meeting. I'll be back in a few."

I smile, watching her go. Cecily is one of the strongest people I know. She'll be fine ... better than fine, without Lyle.

While I finish my salad, I jot notes on a legal pad.

My staff arrives promptly at three o'clock for the meeting. There are more people than chairs, and some staff members are forced to stand.

I come from behind my desk with my legal pad. "It's crowded in here, so I'll be brief. As of this minute, we're operating in partial lockdown mode. The safety and wellbeing of our paying guests is our primary concern. Martin, let's start with you. Were you able to pick up some additional security?"

"Yes, ma'am. I'm working out a plan. You and I can discuss it in detail later. But we're in good shape."

Some of the tension drains from my body. "That's excellent news." I consult the notepad. "So, for the foreseeable future, Parker and Cecily, we will serve by reservation only in Jameson's as well as in Billy's Bar." I gesture at Elton, our bell captain. "Advise your bellmen to be on alert for anyone who isn't a paying guest. With the exception of the regular locals. You know most of them by name. They are always welcome."

Elton nods. "Yes ma'am."

"Ollie and Rita, have your staff hold off on taking any new spa and room reservations. At least for a couple of days. Hopefully, this whole thing will blow over," I say without much conviction. "Everyone else, please be on constant alert for anything out of the ordinary. If you have any concerns at all, call Martin or me immediately."

My staff members stand at once and file out of the office. I drop the legal pad on my desk and grab my bag. I need a break from the drama, some fresh air to clear my head. Jack is picking Jazz up from Bible camp this afternoon, which gives me a couple of hours to spare. I run across the street to the manor house and jump in my Jeep Wrangler. While I never met my father, driving his Wrangler makes me feel close to him. As I head up into the mountains, I wonder how Billy and his father would've handled the situation. *If* they ever had to handle a similar situation.

I park at the overlook, get out of the Wrangler, and sit on a large rock, looking down at Hope Springs Farm below. Opal brought me here when I first came to town. I didn't know she was my grandmother at the time. And I had no idea how much the farm and my family would come to mean to me.

My mind drifts back over the crises I've weathered during the past thirteen months. I'm so lost in thought, I'm unaware I'm not alone until someone taps me on my shoulder.

Startled, I look up to see Opal looming over me. "I thought I might find you here."

"Our special place." I move over to make room for her, holding onto her arm as she lowers herself to the rock beside me.

"You handled the press conference with grace and dignity," Opal says. "Your father and grandfather would've been proud."

"Thank you for saying that, but I'm not sure it's true."

Opal tilts my chin toward her. "This is your birthright, Stella. For someone who wasn't raised to take over the inn, you have certainly risen to the occasion this past year."

My throat thickens. "That really means a lot." I pause, composing myself. "Do you think there's any truth to Maureen's claim? Is it possible the mineral water has healing powers?"

"That's for you to find out." Her index finger shoots up. "I will say this, though. I've soaked in the hot springs at least twice a week for most of my adult life. And while I find the water relaxing, it didn't prevent me from getting leukemia. Or cure me after my diagnosis. Although, admittedly, I wasn't soaking much while undergoing chemo."

My heart skips a beat. "You're so right, Opal. I didn't think of that." I rest my head on her shoulder. "How did I survive three decades without you in my life?"

Opal strokes my hair. "Your mamas did a fine job of raising you."

"What do you think I should do about the situation?"

Without hesitation, Opal says, "Ride out the storm. The inn has weathered much worse. Somehow it always manages to persevere."

"There's not much else I can do short of shutting the place down, which is out of the question." I slide off the rock to my feet. "I should get going. I have to stop by the market for a couple of things on the way home." I hold out my hand to my grandmother. "Are you coming?"

"Nah. I'm gonna sit a while. This is my favorite time of day."

I lean in to kiss her cheek. "Drive carefully on your way home. And come for dinner soon. Jazz will show you her gymnastic moves. She's getting quite good."

Opal snickers. "I have no doubt. She's good at everything she puts her mind to."

"Love you," I call over my shoulder as I head back to my car.

I drive slowly back to town, taking the long way in order to stop by the grocery. After grabbing a carton of milk and a package of chicken breasts from the market, I drive toward the center of town. As I near Main Street, traffic is at a standstill with cars bearing license plates from states up and down the East Coast.

I call Martin for an update. "I've never seen so much traffic in town. Please tell me all these people aren't headed to the inn."

Martin chuckles. "They're trying. But I have plenty of guards stationed about. No one is allowed on the property without a reservation."

"How are the guests reacting to the additional security?" I ask.

"They appear unfazed. Don't worry, Stella. We've got things under control."

"Okay. Call me during the night if you need me," I say and end the call.

After another ten minutes, I finally make a left-hand turn onto Main Street. The inn is in sight. I'm almost home.

I notice a woman standing at a table on the corner up ahead to my right. As I drive nearer, I see plastic cups of water stacked in a pyramid on her table with a chalkboard sign that reads: HOPE SPRINGS MIRACLE WATER, 8 OUNCES FOR $20.

What the heck? I maneuver the Wrangler to the curb and get

out. I march up to the woman, who is wearing one of the blue uniform shirts with the inn's logo that we issue to our maintenance staff.

"What do you think you're doing?" I demand.

"I . . . um . . ."

My blood boils. "What's your name?"

The woman stares down at her feet. "Sandra Welch."

"You're exploiting my business. And you're fired." One by one, I rip the lids off, dump the water onto the sidewalk, and drop the empty cups into a nearby trash can.

Fuming, I get in my Wrangler and drive home. I'm entering the back door when I hear Jack calling me. "Stella! Come quick! You've gotta see this."

I pass through the mudroom to the kitchen doorway. Across the room, my face fills the screen on the wall-mounted television.

"You're breaking news. All the major networks are covering the story." Jack flips through the channels. "Poor Ollie. She looks terrified."

"She's camera shy. Or so she says." I suspect Ollie's reason for not wanting to be televised has to do with whatever it is she's hiding. And there's no doubt in my mind she's hiding something. My gut tells me she's not a bad person. I don't think she's done anything illegal. I sense her sincerity. As much as I sense her turmoil. Her problem is eating her up inside. And I need to reach out to her.

Ollie wakes from a restless sleep feeling hungover, even though she had nothing to drink on Wednesday night. She slips out of bed and goes to the window. Heavy gray clouds cover the sky. Gloomy weather to match her mood. She can't go to work today, can't face the reality of her life. She'll call in sick and hide out in her apartment.

She crawls back in bed, pulling the covers over her head. When she closes her eyes, sounds and images from that tragic night flood her mind and ring out in her ears. Her past is catching up with her, and there's nothing she can do to stop it.

Feeling the onset of a panic attack, she throws the covers back and swings her legs over the side of the bed. She showers and dresses in pale gray trousers and a white blouse. She clicks on the television while her coffee brews. The story of Maureen's miraculous cure is still headline news. Stella and Ollie are featured on every morning show. Her brother is a news junky. There's no way Alexander will miss this.

Ollie takes her time walking to the inn, stopping to speak with Rita at the check-in desk upon her arrival. "Our security team has everything under control," Rita assures her. "Fortunately, there was no drama overnight. "

Ollie continues to the wellness center where everything appears to be operating as normal with the exception of the reservation staff who is overwhelmed with the constant ringing of the phone. Ollie assigns another attendant to field the calls, answering questions and taking names for waitlists. When one of the fitness instructors calls in sick with a head cold, Ollie jumps at the opportunity to teach her classes. She meets Presley for a quick lunch at Roots before going back to the exercise studio to lead a yoga class.

After the class, Ollie is making her rounds at the pool when she receives a call from Elton.

"Miss Ollie, there's a young man here to see you. He claims he's your brother."

Ollie's hand begins to tremble, and she nearly drops her phone.

"Hello? Are you still there, Miss Ollie? Would you like me to send him down to the wellness center?"

Ollie checks her watch. Four o'clock. She has an hour to get rid of Alexander before her private yoga session at five. "That's okay, Elton. Tell him to wait for me there. I'll be up in a few minutes."

Retrieving her purse from her office, Ollie hurries to the main entrance where she finds her brother leaning against the brick wall, thumbing his phone's screen. Six years her junior, Alexander celebrated his thirtieth birthday a month ago. He's aged since the last time she saw him on that dreadful night. He's thinner, his facial features more defined and more handsome, if that's even possible.

"Alexander."

He looks up from his phone. "Ollie." He eyes her exercise

clothes. "You're still teaching yoga? I thought you were managing the wellness center."

"One of my instructors is sick. Why are you here?"

He pushes off the wall. "You know why. Is there somewhere we can talk in private?"

"My apartment's a block away on Main Street. You can leave your car here." She takes off ahead of him. He catches up with her, and they walk the short distance in silence.

When they arrive at her apartment, Alexander circles the room while she pours two glasses of sweet tea.

"Nice digs." He plops down on the sofa. "You don't have to worry about getting lost."

"Ha ha. The small space suits me. I don't need anything bigger." She hands him a glass of tea and sits down beside him.

"Why did you leave California?" he asks.

"I needed a fresh start," she says, and thinks, *To get away from you.*

"I figured as much." He shifts on the sofa to face her. "Do you think you'll ever come back to California?" His tone is soft. He almost sounds like he cares.

"Who knows? I'm taking one day at a time."

Alexander sips his tea and sets his glass on the coffee table. "The attorneys want to settle the estate, Ollie. Dad's and Mom's wills were identical. If one of them were to pass first, the other would've inherited everything. Since they both died at the same time, you and I split everything fifty-fifty. Which includes the winery and vineyards and a sizable stock portfolio." He speaks as though discussing a business deal and not their parents' estates.

"Let's be realistic, sis. There's no love lost between us. We've never gotten along. Perhaps our age difference has something to do with it."

"Perhaps it's because you're an ass."

He lets out a humph. "Perhaps it's because you're a self-absorbed immature brat."

"At least we're on the same page about our feelings for each other." She nods at him. "Go on."

"Our forefathers poured their hearts into making Hendrix Vineyards a success. The property is priceless, some of the best grape growing soil in the Russian River Valley. And I refuse to let it go to waste. I'm ready to re-establish the vineyard and rebuild the winery. If we liquidate the portfolio, I'll have the equity to buy your half of the land."

He's pushing her out like she knew he would. But she doesn't have to make it easy for her brother. "I'm entitled to half of the brand as well."

He sets his smoldering eyes on her. "So, you're going to be difficult. Fine, I'll pay you for the brand."

They glare at each other for a long minute, a lifetime of animosity passing between them. When did things go so wrong in their relationship? It couldn't have been easy for him, the perfect child who never did anything wrong, to have a sister like Ollie who was always causing trouble.

He gets up and moves to the window. With his back to her, Alexander says, "Truth be told, you should do the honorable thing and disclaim your inheritance. After what happened, no one would blame you. In fact, everyone expects it."

Anger sends Ollie to her feet. "You'd love that, wouldn't you? Even before the fire, you felt entitled to the business. Tell me, Alexander, why is that?" She knows why. She needs to hear him admit it.

Her brother's eyes are dark. "Because you don't deserve it. You never caused Mom and Dad anything but heartache." He produces a sheaf of papers. "I had the attorney draw up a disclaimer. This agreement allots you the sum of one hundred thousand dollars."

Ollie's jaw drops. "You're outta your mind. That's a fraction of what the estate is worth." She tears the agreement in half and throws it at him. "Get out of my apartment."

"Not until we figure this out. I flew all the way to Virginia to see you. You owe me that much."

"I owe you nothing. Tell the attorney to settle the estate. I'll move back to California. We'll rebuild together." Ollie has no intention of doing either. She wants to make her brother stew for a while.

"Look, Ollie, my flight home isn't until tomorrow. I'll get a room at your inn, and we'll have dinner together. If we put our differences aside, we can come up with some sort of agreement."

"The inn is booked." Ollie crosses the room to the door. "Now, run along home to California. I'll be in touch with Dad's attorney about my half of the estate."

"I'll take you to court. When the judge hears how you killed our parents, he'll give everything to me."

"Don't bet on it." She points at the doorway. "Out. Now."

Alexander strides across the apartment, pausing in front of her. "This isn't over."

He exits the apartment, and she slams the door behind him. Bending at the waist, with hands planted on knees, she sucks in big gulps of air to ward off the rising panic. She can't fall apart now. Not until after her private yoga session.

She rushes back to the wellness center, arriving with only minutes to spare before her five o'clock shows up.

Ollie manages to keep it together during the session, despite Alexander's voice replaying over and over in her mind like a broken record. *How you killed our parents.*

Gathering her belongings from her office, she retraces her steps toward the inn. She's staring at the sidewalk, concentrating on holding back the tears, when she hears Stella calling her name.

"Wait up, Ollie!"

Lifting her head, Ollie slowly turns around to face her boss.

"I was just looking for you at the wellness center."

Despite her best efforts, Ollie bursts into tears.

"Oh, honey. Come here." Stella draws Ollie into her arms. "What's wrong?"

"Everything!" Ollie sobs.

"The porch is empty. I don't know about you. But I could use a drink."

Ollie pulls away, sniffling and nodding.

Wrapping an arm around Ollie's waist, Stella walks her across the lawn to the dining porch. She seats her in a chair at a table for two beside the railing. "I'll get us some drinks from Billy's. Is wine okay?"

Afraid to speak, Ollie bobs her head.

While she's gone, Ollie stares out over the mountains, inhaling and exhaling to steady her breath.

Stella returns with a wine cooler, a bottle of Pinot Grigio, and two glasses. "According to Parker, this is your favorite vintage. He amazes me the way he always remembers what everyone likes to drink." She fills the glasses with wine and hands one to Ollie. "We made it through the day with no more drama from Maureen."

Ollie smiles, despite herself. "That's a miracle in and of itself."

Stella sips her wine. "Crisp and clean. I see why you like it." She sets down her glass. "Wanna talk about it?"

Ollie looks down at her wine. "I don't. But I need to, if you don't mind listening."

"I'm all ears. In my experience, putting voice to the demons that plague us is therapeutic."

Ollie sits back in her chair, wine glass in hand. "I was a party girl in my previous life. A headstrong wild ass who let the good times ruin my marriage." She pauses to take a sip. "My family's homestead was a hacienda-style house with stucco walls and red clay roof tiles. It was shaped like a horseshoe with bedroom wings stretching deep off the main living areas, one wing for family and the other for guests. The house burned to the ground last summer when the fires raged through Napa Valley. My parents died in the fire."

"Oh, Ollie. I'm so sorry. I wished you'd told me sooner."

Ollie bites down on her quivering lip. "I was living at home at the time. I'd moved back in with my parents after the divorce. I'd been out with friends that night. I passed out on the sofa, too drunk to make it to my bed. I could've saved them."

"Or you could've died."

"Sometimes I wish I had. Death would've been easier than the hell I'm going through."

"I can't imagine how devastating this has been for you. Do you have any siblings?"

"A brother. Alexander blames me for our parents' deaths. When I left California, I didn't tell him I was coming to Virginia."

Understanding crosses Stella's face. "But he saw the press conference."

"Exactly. He didn't waste any time. He flew out here today to talk about our parents' estate. Alexander thinks I should disclaim my inheritance."

Stella frowns. "I hope you told him no."

"I did better. I kicked him out of my apartment." Ollie hangs her head. "I don't deserve half of the estate. Mom and Dad would still be alive if not for me."

"You're being too hard on yourself, Ollie. What if you'd stayed home that night? What makes you think you could've saved them when they couldn't save themselves?"

Ollie pauses, considering this. "I haven't thought about that. The fire was raging. It desecrated everything in its path."

"You're lucky you survived. Your parents are resting easier in heaven, knowing you got out alive."

Ollie hasn't thought of this either. But Stella is right. Her parents would be grateful she didn't perish in the fire. They also wouldn't want her to bear the burden of guilt. They would want her to lead a productive and happy life.

Ollie explains, "My father and I were close. Dad excused my rambunctious behavior, because he understood me. He, too, had a wild streak in his younger years. Dad treated me differently than my brother. It's not unusual for dads to feel more protective of their daughters. But my brother viewed it as favoritism. And he's always resented me for it."

Ollie finishes her wine and pours more. "The vineyard was in my blood. From the time I was a small child, I helped harvest the grapes. I had my first taste of wine at age six. After the divorce, my father began grooming me to take over. I was working hard and doing a good job. I was finally growing up. Before the fire, I hadn't been out with my friends in weeks. But that night, one of my friends was in from out of town. I hadn't seen Jess in years. We got carried away."

"It happens, Ollie. That's what people do when they have reunions."

When the hostess sits a large boisterous crowd at a table near them, Stella says, "Let's go somewhere quieter." She grabs her glass and the bottle, and they move to the rockers at the opposite end of the porch.

They sit in silence for a minute, enjoying their wine while watching the sun sinking toward the mountain range. "How does your brother fit into the picture? Were you going to run the business together?"

"That was the plan. He was to handle the winery and me the vineyard."

"Don't give away your inheritance, Ollie. It's your birthright. Regardless of what happened, half that property belongs to you. I inherited all of this from a man I never met." Stella spreads her arms wide at the landscape. "But I've come to know Billy Jameson through photographs and stories told by friends and acquaintances. I am his daughter, as much as Jazz is his daughter. Not only am I preserving the resort my forefathers built, I'm making it bigger and better. I'm doing it as much for me as for Jazz. When she's old enough, I hope she'll take her rightful place beside me as co-owner. Because that's what siblings do for each other."

"That's what loving siblings do for each other. Greedy siblings try to force their sisters out. I'm not ready to go back to California. I'm not sure I'll ever go back. The memories are too close."

"Or maybe you need to face the memories so you can put them to rest."

"Maybe." Is it possible? Could she rid herself of the nightmares by returning to Hendrix Estate and reliving that night?

"I don't blame you for wanting to stay in Hope Springs." Stella chuckles. "I grew up in New York. I never thought I'd last a day in the mountains of Virginia. But I love it here."

Ollie closes her eyes and rests her head against the back of her chair. "I do too. And I love my job and all my new friends. Thanks for listening. Talking about the fire really helped. I feel more relaxed than I have in a long time."

"We're your family now," Stella says in a sincere tone. "You can count on us—Cecily and Presley and me. We've got your back. You can talk to us about anything."

Ollie rolls her head against the back of the chair as she looks over at Stella. "I've been afraid to confide in anyone, for fear they'd blame me for the fire."

Stella places her hand on Ollie's. "No one blames you, Ollie. Except your brother. But he doesn't count because his heart is not in the right place. You've got to stop blaming yourself."

Ollie wants this more than anything. If only she knew how.

18

PRESLEY

Presley is pinning images to Pinterest boards late on Thursday evening when Chris bangs on her cottage door. He's still wearing his uniform with the shirt untucked and a backpack slung over his shoulder. He wears an anguished expression, and his eyes are red rimmed as though he's been crying.

Presley is almost afraid to ask. "What's wrong?"

"My mom caught Amy and me . . . um . . . you know, doing it. Having sex. Amy's car was parked out front. Mom knew she was there. My bedroom door was closed, and Mom barged in without knocking. I still can't believe she did that. She said some awful things." Chris's eyes glisten with fresh tears. "She called Amy a whore to her face."

Presley flinches. "Where's Amy now?"

"She went home, I guess. I'm not sure. She won't answer her phone. She'll probably break up with me. Can I crash on your sofa tonight? I can't live with Mom anymore. I'll try to reach my dad. Maybe I can stay at his house until I leave for school."

"I have a spare bedroom, Chris. You're welcome to stay here as long as you'd like."

Chris swipes at his eyes. "Really? Do you mean it? That'd be great."

"Of course. And Amy is welcome here any time. To the cottage. Not in your bed." She slaps him playfully on the arm.

"I understand."

"Come. I'll show you the room." Taking him by the hand, she leads him through the kitchen and down the short hallway to the second bedroom. She walks past the queen beds and opens another door. "You even have your own bathroom."

"Sweet. Can I live with you for the rest of the summer?"

Presley hesitates. What does she know about taking care of a teenage boy? Then again, Chris is her brother. This will give them a chance to really get to know each other. "We'll see how it goes." A smirk appears on her lips. "As long as you keep your room clean and don't eat my yogurt."

"Deal." He tosses his backpack on the bed and heads for the door. "I need to find Amy. To apologize."

Presley walks with him back to the living room. "I have a spare key to the cottage. Let me get it for you." She retrieves the key from her top desk drawer and gives it to him. "If you decide to sleep over at Amy's house, text me so I won't worry."

"Yes ma'am," he says, and she backhands him. "Call me ma'am again, and I'm kicking you out."

Chris laughs. "I was kidding, sis. Take a joke."

Presley musses his hair. "Good luck with your girl. And try not to worry about your mom."

After Chris leaves, Presley remains on the porch a few minutes breathing in the crisp night air and listening to the cicadas. The peacefulness of the mountains is growing on her. Small town living isn't so awful after all.

She's no sooner returned to her computer when there's another knock on her door, and she's not surprised to see Lucy staring in at her. When Presley opens the door, Lucy blurts, "Is Chris here?"

Presley steps out of the way to let Lucy in. "Not at the moment. He went to smooth things over with Amy."

Lucy grimaces at the mention of her son's girlfriend. The expression is ugly and twisted, hinting at the anger eating this woman alive. "With any luck, she'll break up with him."

Presley glares at her. "What do you have against Amy? Have you even tried to get to know her? She has an adorable personality, and she seems to really care about Chris."

Lucy pins Presley against the wall with a death glare. "She'll break his heart."

"Most first loves end with broken hearts. It's a rite of passage. Suffering builds character."

"I don't need a lecture from you." Lucy eyes Presley's baby bump. "When you've been parenting for eighteen years like me, *then* you can give parenting advice."

"It's not parenting advice. It's life advice." Presley softens her tone. "What're you so afraid of? You were young once. You survived teenage drama." The words leave Presley's lips before she realizes what she's said. "That's it, isn't it? You're afraid he'll get her pregnant, that a baby will ruin his life like it ruined yours."

"That's ridiculous. This isn't about you, Presley. This is about Chris." Lucy spins on her heels and storms out of the cottage.

Presley follows her out to the porch. "You're ruining your relationship with your son."

Lucy stops in her tracks. "My relationship with my son is none of your business." She turns to face Presley. "I resent you intruding in our lives. There's a reason I gave you up for adoption."

"And I'm glad you did. Renee was a wonderful mother." Presley studies Lucy's face more closely, noticing the deepening lines around her eyes. Her addiction has been hard on her. "You once told me you were obsessed with finding the baby you'd given up. That was before you realized that baby was me. Why do you detest me so?"

Lucy gestures at Presley's face. "Every time I look at you, I'm reminded of the boy who raped me."

"How can that be when I'm the spitting image of your mother?"

"You're nothing like my mother," Lucy snaps.

Presley's shoulders slump. She's fighting a losing battle with this woman. "You seem so unhappy, Lucy. What is the true source of all this hostility? I don't think it's me. I think I'm an easy target for your anger and sorrow."

Tears well in Lucy's eyes, and her chin trembles. "It's everything. But mostly it's Brian. I thought we had something special. I don't understand what's changed."

Presley knows what's changed. Rita and Brian fell in love. "Have you tried talking to him?"

"Yes, he keeps blowing me off. Whatever, it's not your problem." Lucy spins on her heel and disappears into the dark night.

Presley goes inside and locks the door. She calls Rita, who answers on the fourth ring in a raspy voice. Was she sleeping? Or having sex with Brian? "Lucy was just here. She's a mess, Rita. She ran Chris out of the house."

"Oh no! What did she do to poor Chris?"

Presley explains about Lucy walking in on Chris and Amy. "He needs a break from his mom. He's staying with me for a while. Maybe until he goes to school in August."

"Good! I'll text him. But please tell him I'm here for him if he needs anything."

Presley grips the phone. "Lucy is really hung up on Brian. For her sake, you should tell her the truth. She'll be hurt at first, but she can begin the process of moving on with her life."

Rita exhales loudly. "Brian and I were discussing that earlier tonight. We're going to tell her soon."

"Be sure and let me know when you do it, so Chris and I can prepare for the fallout."

Rita chuckles. "Will do."

Presley ends the call, but she's too distracted to return to work. She plops down on the sofa and flips on the television, surfing the channels. The Country Music Station is broadcasting Everett's concert live from Madison Square Garden. A stunningly beautiful young woman is on stage with him, singing a duet. A love song. And they're making goo-goo eyes at each other as though they're in love. She watches them more closely. Is that an act? Or are they lovers? Is her husband having an affair? The woman has crazy mad vocals. They make a dynamic duo. Who is this person?

The banner crawling across the bottom of the screen tells Presley the young woman's name is Audrey Manning. With a quick Google search, she discovers Audrey Manning is last season's *American Idol* winner. She clicks on Everett's website and checks his schedule. It appears Audrey Manning has joined his tour. The bottom falls out of Presley's stomach. What other secrets is Presley's husband keeping from her?

The team from *Virginia Living Magazine* arrive around ten on Friday morning and stay until dinnertime. The young journalist, Liz Baker, is a striking brunette with an infectious personality. She's genuinely interested in Hope Springs Farm and insists on a tour of all the facilities. Liz samples lunch in the kitchen. Tastes wine with Lucy in the cellar. And experiences a reflexology foot massage at the wellness center.

When it's time for Liz to leave, Cecily and Stella walk her to the parking lot. As her photographer is storing his equipment in the trunk, Liz says, "We originally planned to publish the Jameson article in the August edition. But I think my editor will agree your charming resort deserves a bigger feature. I'm thinking a multipage spread in the October issue with Cecily on the cover."

Cecily's heart skips a beat. "I'm honored. Thank you so much."

Stella extends her hand to Liz. "We look forward to seeing the article. I hope you'll come back soon for the weekend. Our treat. And bring your significant other."

Liz beams. "I'd love that. And so would my boyfriend."

Cecily walks on a cloud throughout the evening. Even an unusually grumpy patron complaining of an overdone steak doesn't drag her down.

The dinner rush is coming to an end when Stella shows up in the kitchen with several bottles of champagne for the staff. She pulls Cecily to the side for a private toast. Touching her glass to Cecily's, she says, "We've come a long way in a short amount of time. A year ago, you and I were girls, searching for our life's purpose. And now we've come into our own. We're building something special here, Cecily. You have an amazing talent. You could go anywhere you want. Selfishly, I hope you stay in Hope Springs."

Cecily kisses Stella's cheek. "I'm not going anywhere. This town is my home. I want to raise my children here, if I ever find a man who understands how important my career is to me."

"You will. I'm absolutely certain of it," Stella says and wanders off to mingle with the rest of the staff.

Parker enters the kitchen. "Awesome job, Cecily!" He throws his arms around her, liftingher off her feet. "Let's celebrate."

"What do you have in mind?" Cecily asks when he sets her back down.

"We'll go somewhere for drinks. I'm winding things up in Billy's Bar. Go home and change. By the time you get back, I'll be ready to go." When she hesitates, he says, "Come on, Cess. It's Friday night. When's the last time you went out on the town?"

Cecily shakes off her uncertainty. "You're right. This occasion is worthy of a celebration. I'll be back in a few."

Grabbing her purse from her office, she hurries across the street to her apartment. She rinses off in the shower, touches up her makeup, and gathers her hair into a messy bun at the crown of her head. She slips on the new black sundress with the sexy back she bought in May but hasn't yet worn. Stepping into a pair of black wedges, she twirls in front of the full-length mirror, admiring the way the dress dances around her thighs.

When she returns to the inn, Parker has changed into jeans and a striped polo and is waiting for her at the front entrance. "Where are we going?" she asks.

He offers her an arm. "How about Town Tavern?"

She loops her arm through his. "Perfect."

They talk about the *Virginia Living* feature as they stroll down Main Street to Town Tavern. The bar is crowded and noisy. Cecily spots Fiona and Peaches at a large table of young women, and while Parker goes to the bar for drinks, she makes her way over to speak to them.

Fiona stands to greet her. "Peaches's bachelorette party is this weekend," she yells over the din of the crowd.

Cecily nods. "Right. You mentioned that. What're the plans?"

"The other bridesmaids flew in this afternoon. We've chartered a party bus for a tour of the local wineries tomorrow."

"That sounds like fun. Are the bridesmaids staying in Hope Springs until the wedding next weekend?"

"No. They're taking the whole week off, but they're going on a shopping trip to DC for a few days. They tried to get Peaches and me to go, but neither of us is comfortable leaving with the wedding so close."

"I don't blame you," Cecily says. "Is Peaches feeling any better about moving to London?"

"She's getting there," Fiona says. "She's really taken what you said to heart. She's toned down the Southern belle spoiled brat act. She didn't even get upset when the florist failed to come through with the peonies."

"Wow! I'd definitely call that a miracle."

Fiona says, "Right? Truthfully, I think peach roses will be a better choice this time of year."

"I agree." Across the room, Cecily notices Parker has secured two seats at the bar and is waving for her to join him. "You've done an amazing job, Fiona. Sometime this week, we should talk about what's next for you. You may aspire to bigger and better things, but if you're interested, I'd love for you to stay on at Jameson's."

Fiona nods enthusiastically. "I'd be interested to hear what you have in mind for me. I've been networking with a few other places. But I haven't received any official offers yet."

Cecily smiles. "We'll chat on Monday."

She fights her way through the crowd to the bar and sits down beside Parker. Pete, the bartender, yells, "I hear congratulations are in order. Way to go, Cess!" After finishing up with his customer, he moves toward them and lines up three tequila shots on the bar, and they each down one.

The mood at the Tavern is upbeat with funk music blasting from the speakers. For the first time in a very long time, Cecily allows herself to relax.

Her back is to the door, and she doesn't see Lyle enter the bar until he taps her bare shoulder. She cranes her neck to see behind her. "Oh. Hey."

Lyle's eyes are red rimmed, and his words slurred when he says, "I can't believe it! You're taking a night off from work. Your new boyfriend obviously rates higher than your fiancé."

She spins on her stool to face Lyle. "Parker isn't my boyfriend."

"Yeah, right. I can't believe you ditched me for this manwhore." When Lyle sweeps an arm at Parker, he loses his balance and stumbles into the guy standing next to him.

The guy shoves Lyle off. "Get off me, dude. You've had too much to drink."

"Ha. I haven't had enough to drink." Cupping his hands around his mouth, Lyle calls out, "Hey, Pete, give me a beer, will ya?"

Pete shakes his head. "Sorry, bro. Looks to me like you've been overserved already. Do you need me to order you an Uber?"

"Nah. Whitney's in the bathroom." Lyle stumbles again, this time in the opposite direction. Whitney arrives in time to catch him before he falls into a table.

"Let's get outta here," Cecily says under her breath to Parker.

"Good call," Parker says. "If we stay, I might punch him."

When she slaps her credit card on the bar, Parker snatches it up. "No way! I invited you out to celebrate. Drinks are on me."

Cecily flags Pete down. "Can we get the check please, Pete? And split it down the middle," she says, sticking her tongue out at Parker.

Parker gives her card back. "Have it your way."

They exit the bar and walk back toward the inn. "That was embarrassing," Cecily says. "What he said about you being a manwhore was uncalled for."

Parker laughs. "I'm aware of what people say about me. Do you know how many women I've slept with since I started working at the inn?"

"Um . . . no! It's none of my business."

"None! Contrary to what everyone thinks, I don't sleep around."

Cecily jerks her head back. "Seriously? You could have your pick. All the girls lust after you."

"I prefer committed relationships to one-night stands. I was involved with someone a few years ago. It ended badly, and I'm still nursing those wounds." Parker stops suddenly on a street corner. "Wanna come over for a drink? I live just down the road," he says, throwing a thumb over his shoulder.

Cecily checks her phone for the time. "It's almost midnight. I should probably get home."

Parker holds up a finger. "Just one drink. I want to show you something."

Cecily shrugs. "In that case, why not? Since I don't have to worry about you hitting on me."

Parker places a hand on the small of her back and walks her across Main Street. "I would hit on you in a heartbeat, Cess. But you just broke off your engagement. You need time to recover before I make a move on you," he says with a mischievous twinkle in his blue eyes.

Cecily doesn't know how to respond. She can't deny her attraction to him. But she's not ready for romance. "The houses on this street are charming. Are you renting?" she responds, opting for a safe topic.

"Nope. I'm a first-time homeowner," he says proudly.

They come to a small house with taupe-colored siding, a blue front door, and dormer windows. He stands out of the way, gesturing at the sidewalk. "After you."

He unlocks the door, and they enter a small foyer. Off the foyer is a living room, handsomely decorated with caramel-colored leather furniture and a navy handwoven rug. On the far wall between two windows, a serene painting of a sailboat hangs over the mantel of a stone fireplace. A built-in bar with blue cabinetry and brass pulls stretches the length of the wall to her left. Liquor bottles in unique shapes bearing fancy labels line the glass shelves.

"What do you think of my project?" Parker asks.

"It's amazing." Cecily runs her hand across the smooth mahogany top. "Did you have this installed or did it come with the house?"

"Designed by me and custom-built by a local kitchen contractor."

Cecily's jaw drops. "Remind me to ask Stella for a raise."

His handsome face grows serious. "I couldn't afford this on

my salary. My father passed away a few years ago. He was a successful software developer. As his only child, I inherited his entire small fortune."

Her fingers brush his arm. "Oh, Parker. I'm so sorry about your father. I can't imagine how hard that must have been for you."

"Yeah. He was a good dude. I really miss him. But I'm grateful to him. He set me up for life. I can do what I love doing. Which is serving cool drinks to fun people."

She smiles at him. "Sounds like you and I are kindred spirits."

"Being a chef takes a lot more talent."

"I don't know about that. The goal is the same. We're both artists. We just work with different mediums." Cecily pulls down a bottle of Rhum Clement from Martinique. "What is this?"

"Rum. Here, have a taste." He pours a finger into a glass and hands it to her.

She takes a sip. The deep golden liquor is both spicy and fruity. "Yum." She drinks the rest. "I've never tasted anything like it."

"Collecting liquors from all over the world has become a hobby." He gestures her to the sofa. "Have a seat while I make our drinks." He turns on soft jazz music and positions himself at the bar.

She can't see what he's mixing with his back to her. When he's finished, he hands her a glass with a single cube of ice and clear bubbly liquid. He clinks his glass to hers. "Cheers."

"What is it?" she asks, bringing the glass to her lips.

He raises an eyebrow. "You tell me."

She sips and licks her lips. "Tequila."

"Correct. Tequila, club soda, and a splash of freshly squeezed lime juice."

"So simple. But so good," she drinks more of the liquid.

"The quality of the tequila makes a difference," he says.

"I'm impressed, Parker. I didn't know you were so into your career."

He sits down beside her on the sofa. "I'm hoping to take my mixology skills to the next level. I'm collaborating with a photographer to create a coffee table book. And Stella's agreed to sponsor another book, *Cordials at Hope Springs Farm.*"

"That's so cool! We should consider doing a cookbook."

His blue eyes get big. "Yes! And coordinate them so the branding is the same."

Cecily kicks her shoes off and tucks her feet under her, settling back on the sofa. "Tell me more about your exotic liquor collection."

While she finishes her drink, he holds her spellbound with expert talk about the liquors he has flown in from all over the world.

This guy is not who she thought he was. He's an enigma. They have much in common except the most important thing. He's looking for a relationship, and she's looking for a good time.

20

PRESLEY

P resley is moseying her way back from lounging by the pool late Saturday afternoon when Rita catches up with her. "I did it! I told Lucy about Brian and me. As expected, she didn't handle it well."

Presley casts a sideways glance at her aunt. "What happened?"

"She sped out of the parking lot like a maniac. She'll probably wreck and kill someone."

Presley stops walking. "Why on earth would you break the news to her in a parking lot?"

Rita, with a huff of exasperation, tosses her hands in the air. "I had no choice. Lucy was in her car, pulling out of the parking lot when I flagged her down. I invited her to go for coffee or to take a walk. I told her I had something important to talk to her about, but she demanded I tell her right then. I called Brian, warning him to be on the lookout for her. You and Chris should do the same."

"Poor Chris. All of this is so hard on him." Presley starts walking again, and Rita steps in line beside her on the sidewalk.

They arrive at Presley's cottage, and Rita collapses in a

rocking chair. "I've thought about my sister so much these past few days my brain hurts. I know her so well. This is not who she is deep down. Lucy has battled depression on and off for as long as I can remember. She was doing so well when the inn first reopened. She was seeing a therapist and getting her act together. Then she slipped off the deep end."

"When I came along," Presley says, lowering herself to the rocker next to Rita.

Rita gives Presley a scolding look. "No, honey! This is not your fault. Things may have headed south about that time, but it wasn't because of you."

"You're wrong about that, Rita. Lucy was desperate to find her biological daughter. Until she found out said daughter was me. She claims I remind her of my father, the boy who raped her."

Rita slaps the arm of the chair. "That's ridiculous! You remind everyone of our mother."

Presley grunts. "According to Lucy, I'm nothing like your mother." She removes her phone from her pool bag, checking for messages from Everett. She hasn't heard from him since she left a voice message accusing him of sleeping with Audrey Manning. Her stomach churns at the memory of what she said. She sounded like a whiny, insecure housewife. She's sunk to a new all-time low. She's teetering close to the edge of the cliff. If she falls, she may lose herself. Her pride might never recover. And she can't let that happen because of a man.

"Earth to Presley," Rita says, jerking her back to the present.

"Sorry." Placing her phone on the arm of the chair, Presley smiles over at Rita. "Chris should be home soon. Can I get you some tea or lemonade while you wait? Sorry I can't offer you any wine."

When Presley moves to get up, Rita grabs her by the arm,

holding her down. "I can tell something's on your mind. Is it Everett?"

Presley relaxes in the chair. "Yes. The newest American Idol, the drop-dead gorgeous Audrey Manning, has joined his tour. I saw his Madison Square Garden concert on television the other night. Audrey and Everett were all lovey-dovey, like they were really into each other."

Rita furrows her brow. "Are you sure it wasn't just the one performance?"

"According to the schedule on his website, Audrey is here to stay. *And,* he promised me the tour would be over by the end of September, so he could be home when the baby comes. But his manager keeps adding dates. As of now, he's on tour through November. He mentioned coming to Hope Springs the weekend of Peaches's wedding, but I have no clue if that's still a possibility." Presley lowers her head. "What am I gonna do, Rita? If I go back to Nashville, I'll be alone for the birth."

"No way you're going back to Nashville. You'll have the baby here. Do you like the obstetrician you've been seeing here?"

"Yes, but I have plans to start my own event planning firm in Nashville."

Rita shakes her head. "Those plans can wait. You need to be with your family right now. Besides, I'm dying to give you a shower. I even volunteer to be your birth partner. My mom will be thrilled. She loves babies!"

"Where will I live? Cottage row is booked for at least one wedding this fall."

"Multiple weddings, actually." Rita taps her chin. "You're welcome to stay with me. But I know you need your space." Her face lights up. "You could rent the caretaker's cottage. Have you seen it since the renovations?"

Presley thinks about the charming cottage near the main

building where Stella lived when she first came to Hope Springs. "From the outside, but I haven't been in."

"They updated the kitchen, turned the original master into a study, and raised the roof, adding two bedrooms upstairs. It'd be perfect for you. No one is living there now. Stella plans to hire a caretaker when she has a baby, but that won't be anytime soon."

The thought of staying in Hope Springs another few months appeals to Presley. The idea of not being alone when the baby comes appeals to her even more. Presley's lips turn downward. "I honestly don't think Everett is cheating on me. I'll have to get used to his lifestyle if I want our marriage to survive. I refuse to be the jealous, nagging wife."

"You're doing the right thing by building a career you can count on. You'll always have that to fall back on."

Presley is eager to get started on that career. "But our home will be in Nashville. I need to be establishing myself there instead of wasting my time here in the mountains."

"There'll be plenty of time for that *after* the baby comes, Presley. Why not stay here with your family and friends while you adjust to motherhood? You can go back to Nashville next spring or whenever you're ready."

Presley is secretly terrified of giving birth and taking care of a newborn. Being around people who care about her lessens that fear. "I'll think about it."

Presley sees the top of her brother's head and hears the sound of him whistling. "Here comes Chris. Sounds like he's in a good mood. Too bad we have to spoil it."

If Chris is surprised to see his aunt, he doesn't show it. He gives Rita a kiss on the cheek and sits down in the rocker beside Presley. "I'm starving." He whips out his phone. "I'm gonna order a pizza. Anybody want some?"

Presley slaps his arm. "Bro! I bought sushi from the Sooshie Bar. Remember, we talked about it last night?"

"I'd rather have pizza." Chris curls his upper lip. "The thought of eating raw seafood makes me want to hurl." He looks around Presley at his aunt. "Presley keeps making me try the weird food she eats."

Presley laughs. "I'm broadening your horizons before you go to college. You'll thank me for it."

"Be real. Come September, I'll be existing on a diet of pizza and beer." His thumbs fly across the phone screen. "I'm ordering you a vegetarian pizza. A large, considering your appetite of late."

"Ha ha. You're hilarious." Presley waits until he sets the phone down. "Rita has something she needs to tell you."

Chris's chest deflates as he exhales. "What now?"

Rita explains about her relationship with Brian, about how they grew close after his mom went into rehab and how they became attracted to each other. Chris keeps a straight face as though this neither surprises or alarms him.

"I broke the news about our relationship to your mom a little while ago," Rita says. "She didn't take it well."

"Of course, she didn't," Chris says in a tone of indifference. "I'm glad I'm not at home to experience the fallout."

Presley narrows her eyes. "I thought you'd be more upset."

"I'm trying not to let Mom get to me so much." He offers Presley a genuine smile. "I realize I've been living with you only a few days, but you've given me back my sanity."

Rita's phone rings with a call from Brian. Presley can hear most of what he says. Lucy showed up at his house. She's hysterical. He thinks she's having a mental breakdown.

"Has she been drinking or taking pills?" Rita asks.

"I don't think so," Brian answers.

"We're on the way." Rita ends the call and leaps out of the rocking chair. "Let's go."

Presley is on her feet, digging her keys out of her pool bag. "I'll drive. My car's out back."

Chris is on their heels as they hurry around to the back of the cottage. "Hey! What about my pizza?"

Over her shoulder, Presley says, "Call Ruby's. Tell them to leave it at the front desk."

Rita shouts out directions to Presley who speeds down Main Street to Brian's House on the opposite side of town. She parks behind Lucy's car in the driveway so Lucy can't escape. Brian, as though he was watching for them, dashes out the front door. "She was furious when she got here, screaming and throwing fists. She clocked me good in the eye." He places his hand on the left side of this face.

Presley looks closer. She can already see the beginning of a black eye.

"She started crying and she won't stop. I've tried everything. She needs psychiatric help." Brian waves his phone. "With your permission, I'll call a psychiatrist friend of mine, Dr. Randall Scott."

"But they'll put her in the psych ward," Chris says, his expression serious, his pizza now forgotten.

Rita places an arm around him, pulling him close. "We don't have much choice. Maybe this time, the doctors will finally be able to help her."

Chris sags against his aunt. "I guess you're right."

Rita nods at Brian. "Make the call, please."

Brian presses his phone to his ear and steps away while he talks to the doctor. Five minutes later, Brian returns with a grim face. "Scott says to bring her in now. He'll meet us at the hospital. He'll observe her overnight before deciding how to proceed. If he can't effectively treat her here, he'll transfer her to the psychiatric hospital in Roanoke."

"I want to go with her." Chris's face is tormented and tears glisten in his eyes.

Rita looks past Chris to Brian who shakes his head.

Presley hooks an arm around her brother. "Know what, buddy? I think you and I should let the grown-ups handle this. We'll go back to the cottage and gorge ourselves on pizza while we wait for Rita to give us an update."

"Okay." He stares down at the ground, kicking at a rock. "I should call my grandparents anyway, to give them the news."

Rita tilts Chris's chin up. "I'll take good care of your mama. She's gonna be okay. This time, I'm going to make certain she gets the help she needs."

21

STELLA

Presley is waiting for me in my office when I arrive on Monday morning. She stands to greet me. "We need to talk," she says in a troubled tone.

"Okay." I drop my bag behind my desk. "I need coffee. Let's go out to the porch."

We pass through the lobby, pausing to speak to guests and stopping at the self-serve coffee carafes before exiting the french doors. We move to the rockers at the far end of the porch for privacy.

I suck in a deep breath of clean mountain air. There's not a cloud in the bright blue sky and rays of sunshine sparkle on the lake like diamonds.

A moment of silence passes, and I sense Presley is stalling for time. I prompt her by asking, "What's up?"

Staring out at the mountains, Presley says, "Lucy was admitted to the hospital on Saturday night. She had a mental breakdown when she found out Rita and Brian are together."

My jaw drops open. "Together, together? As in a relationship?"

"Together," Presley repeats sipping her decaf coffee. "Their friendship developed into something more serious after Lucy went to rehab."

I imagine Brian and Rita enjoying dinner at a romantic restaurant with a bottle of red wine on the table between them. "Good for them! They make a cute couple. The Lucy situation has weighed heavily on both of them. I'm glad they've found some happiness."

Presley flicks her auburn mane over her shoulder. "I agree. In my opinion, they're better suited than Brian and Lucy."

I drum my fingers on the chair's arm as I consider what Lucy's absence will mean for the wine shop. "I have to admit I'm growing irritated with Lucy's constant stream of problems."

Presley shifts her weight toward me. "I don't blame you, Stella. You've been more patient than most employers would have been. The doctor is optimistic about Lucy's prognosis, though. He thinks adjusting her medications will make a huge difference. They are transferring her this morning to a psych ward at a hospital in Roanoke where they are better equipped to treat her. The doctor thinks she'll be there for a week. Maybe ten days."

I scroll down my mental list of employees. "We'll have to juggle some staff around. This will be a busy week with everyone focused on Peaches's wedding. We can count on Holly to help, since she's already been working some with Lucy."

"We can pull Fiona if necessary. She knows a ton about wine, and she's incredibly organized. Her food and beverage plans for the wedding are buttoned up tight."

I smile, thinking about our enthusiastic intern. "Cecily needs to hire Fiona full time."

"She's considering it." Presley looks away, staring out across the grounds. "I know you're frustrated with Lucy. But can you give her one more chance? Rita is determined to get the old Lucy back. I only got a glimpse of that Lucy when I first came to Hope Springs. I'd like the chance to get to know her better."

"And I want that for you," I say, patting Presley's hand. "Of course, I'll give Lucy another chance. We'll survive this week. We always do."

Presley smiles. "All hands on deck."

Exhaustion overwhelms me, and I rest my head against the back of the chair. "I don't know why I'm so tired. Jack, Jazz, and I had a relaxing weekend."

"You're probably worn out from the Maureen Graves drama last week."

I snicker. "True. Fortunately, things have settled down. I'm going to scale back the security patrol this week for the wedding. I don't want Peaches's guests thinking they're entering a third world country."

Presley's gaze shifts to the caretaker's cottage down the hill. "On a different subject, what're your plans for the cottage?"

"I don't have any at the moment. I'll eventually hire a caretaker, but not in the foreseeable future. Why do you ask?"

"I'm considering staying in Hope Springs until after the baby comes. Maybe even until next spring. Would you consider renting the cottage to me?"

"Heck, yes! It would be perfect for you. It's fully furnished. Would you like to see it?"

Presley looks over at her. "You mean now?"

"Sure." I dig in my pocket for the keys and dangle them in front of her.

Presley gets to her feet. "In that case, what're we waiting for?"

We cross the stone terrace and walk down the steps to the cottage. When I open the door, Presley gasps at the creamy walls and random-width oak floors. "Wow! You did an amazing job with the renovations."

"Thanks. I'll give you the tour." We pass through the living room to a small office big enough to house a desk, sofa, and two comfortable chairs. I gesture at the stairs leading to the second floor. "We carved out a sliver of the original master for the staircase."

I follow Presley up the stairs where two generous-sized bedrooms share a Jack and Jill bath. "This is impressive, Stella. And plenty of room for the baby and me."

We return to the kitchen on the first floor which boasts new stainless-steel appliances, white cabinets, and quartz countertops.

Presley roams the kitchen, opening and closing cabinet doors. I lean against the doorjamb while she explores. "What does Everett think of you staying in Hope Springs?"

"I haven't talked to him about it yet. His managers have extended his tour. I have no reason to return to Nashville." She holds her hands out by her sides. "Might as well stay here." Despite her wide smile, Presley's voice is tight. There's something she's not telling me.

"Your services are certainly needed. Lia's learning, but she's not up to your standards yet. When you leave, *if* you leave, I'll have to hire another event planner."

"You know me. I'm a big-city girl. I can't stay here forever." Something in her chuckle makes me think she's considering just that.

"Sometimes our aspirations change with our needs."

We walk back through the living room and out the front door to the wraparound porch. Presley stands at the railing, watching people come and go.

"Did all this foot traffic bother you when you were living here?" she asks.

"Not at all. Although it's definitely not as private as Cottage Row." I lock the door behind us. "Think about it. The cottage is yours if you want it."

"Thanks, Stella," Presley says when we part on the sidewalk.

I watch her amble down the hill toward Cottage Row. Her posture is stooped. Something is definitely troubling her. Presley is a private person. I trust she'll tell me when she's ready.

I head back toward the main building, stopping in the lobby for a second cup of coffee. Instead of boosting my energy, the caffeine gives me the jitters.

For the rest of the morning and into the afternoon, I trudge through my daily routine as though walking through quicksand. Around four o'clock, when I catch myself nodding off while trying to review a budget report, I give up and call it a day.

I stroll across the street to the manor house where I find the back door unlocked but no one home. I've cautioned Jazz's teenage babysitter about locking doors when they leave on outings. They've probably taken Angel on a hike. They're not expecting me home until six. Which gives me plenty of time to take a long nap.

In my bedroom, I take off my white jeans and beige linen blouse and slip beneath the covers in my bra and panties. I'm asleep before my head hits the pillow. When I wake an hour later, my missed period is the first thought that crosses my mind. Grabbing my phone off the bedside table, I access the calendar app. I'm three days late. Swinging my feet over the side of the bed, I cross the room to the en suite marble bathroom. Opening the medicine cabinet, I remove the pregnancy test leftover from the previous time I thought I was pregnant.

I pee on the stick and set it on the counter to bake. While I wait the requisite five minutes, I dress and splash cold water on my face. When I look at the test window again, there's a faint line next to the control line.

My stomach does a somersault as I stare up at the ceiling. I'm pregnant.

I hear noises downstairs, the pitter-patter of Angel's paws on hardwood floors and Jazz's voice calling out to Jack. "Can I feed Angel?"

Jack calls back, "Yes. Then take her outside to potty."

I pause a minute to compose myself. I consider waiting to tell him the news. But I can't. I'm too excited. By the time I get down the stairs, Angel has already gobbled up her food and Jazz is throwing the tennis ball for her in the backyard.

I find Jack in the kitchen watching the news and sipping a beer. I kiss his cheek. "Close your eyes and hold out your hand."

He does as I ask, and I place the pregnancy test in his palm. Opening his eyes, he looks at the test and then at me. "I assume the line means we're pregnant."

I bob my head. "Very early. I'm only three days late."

Jack picks me up and spins me around. "Sweetheart, this is the best news ever."

I bury my face in his neck, breathing in his woodsy scent. "This is the happiest moment of my life."

"Uh-oh." He sets me down. "I'm afraid the happiest moment of your life may be short-lived."

My gaze follows his to the television where the reporter from Richmond, Nicole Lambert, is standing in front of the inn.

I reach across the counter for the remote. "Quick! Turn up the volume."

"This is Nicole Lambert, reporting tonight from Hope Springs Farm with breaking news regarding the magic healing powers of the property's hot springs."

To my horror, Nicole tells the story of the beautiful debutante from Charleston whose fiancée drowned her and her lover in the hot springs in 1958.

"How'd she find out about the debutante? Besides me, only Ollie, Presley, and Cecily know the story. Did she . . ." I leave Jack standing in the kitchen and dart up the stairs to my bedroom.

My great-grandmother's journal has disappeared from my bedside table. I yell for my husband. "Jack!"

He comes running. "What is it?"

"My great-grandmother's journals are missing. Lacey forgot to lock the door again today when she and Jazz went out. Do you think Nicole Lambert could have snuck in while they were gone? Should we call the police?"

"That's a stretch, Stella. She's a journalist, bound by a code of ethics. She could lose her job for breaking into someone's home."

"That's true. I didn't think of that."

When we hear Angel barking outside, Jack moves to the window and looks out. "The press is in our front yard."

I bolt back down the stairs, throwing open the front door and hollering for Jazz and Angel to come inside. The dog bounds up the sidewalk with Jazz chasing after her. I step aside and the dog and child enter the house. I'm closing the door when I notice the mob migrating toward me. Hovering near the back are Nicole Lambert and Maureen Graves.

"Stella! Can we have a statement?" a reporter on the front line calls out.

An older woman waves her hand. "Did you know about the 1958 double homicide?"

A male reporter runs toward me, holding up his phone as he videotapes me. "What else are you hiding? Are your guests in danger?"

A surge of anger propels me forward, and I step out onto the brick stoop. "My guests are most certainly not in danger. I only recently learned the tragic story of the young debutante from my great-grandmother's journal. I have researched the story, and there is no mention of the circumstances surrounding the debutante's death, or her lover's death, in any Virginia or South Carolina newspaper. Unfortunately, my great-grandmother's journal, which I last saw this morning on my bedside table, is now missing." I move to the edge of the stoop. "There is no point in stirring up a nest of hornets over a story we're not even sure is true. For all we know my great-grandmother made it up. Now, I ask you all to kindly leave my property."

I go inside and close the door, leaning against it as my breath steadies. Nicole wouldn't risk her career by breaking into my home. Maybe she got Maureen to do her dirty work. How did she find out about the debutante's tragic story in the first place? Only a few people know about it, all of whom I trust. Maybe she overheard us talking. Has she been spying on us, eavesdropping on our conversations?

I push off the door and head down the hall. I'm jumping to conclusions. There must be another, more reasonable, explanation for the missing journals.

22

OLLIE

Ollie watches the press conference in disbelief. She yearns to smack the smug smile off that reporter's face. She clicks off the television and tosses the remote on her desk.

Her inbox dings with an incoming email from her father's attorney. Karl Keller has reached out to her several times in the past few days. She needs to respond to him. Problem is, she doesn't know what to say. She has three choices. Rebuilding and running the family business with her brother as a partner is her least favorite option. Selling her share of the vineyard and winery to Alexander is the most reasonable solution. But she can't eliminate the possibility of disclaiming her inheritance. While that might unburden Ollie of some of her guilt, the idea of surrendering to her brother, of giving him what he wants, makes her blood run cold. Stella's words ring out in her head. *Don't give away your inheritance, Ollie. It's your birthright. Regardless of what happened, half that property belongs to you.*

Ollie can't leave the attorney hanging forever. She sends a curt response to his email, letting him know she'll have a decision within the week.

Ollie makes a point of speaking to the spa and pool

managers on her way out, alerting them to the potential for more intruders. As she walks down Main Street toward her apartment, her thoughts drift to Maureen Graves, and she replays in her mind the day the woman came to the spa for her treatment.

At her apartment, she pours a glass of wine and makes a salad of mixed greens, fruit, and sliced grilled chicken. While she eats, she opens her laptop on the breakfast bar and searches for information about Maureen Graves. She's still sitting at the counter two hours later when she hits the jackpot.

She slides off the barstool and makes a victory lap around the apartment. *I knew it! Wait until Stella sees this!*

It's too late to call her boss tonight. She'll have to wait until in the morning. But when she arrives for the meeting about Peaches's wedding, the other staff members are already gathered around the conference table in Stella's office.

Stella claps her hands to get everyone's attention. "Before we discuss the wedding, in case you missed last night's media circus, I need to tell you about the crisis du jour." Stella recounts the details of Nicole's press conference and her response to it. "I expected hordes of crazies to be lined up and down the front drive this morning. Perhaps rumors of a decades-old double homicide will deter these unwanted visitors instead of encouraging them." She flips open her laptop. "Now, we have a wedding to put on. Who wants to start?"

Presley raises her hand. "All systems are a go. There's a chance of rain in the forecast for Saturday. We may have to use the inn's tents for the ceremony on the terrace."

"Rain?" Peaches removes her phone from her clutch and taps on the screen, accessing her weather app. "No one said anything to me about bad weather."

Presley takes the phone from her. "Let us worry about the weather. Your job this week is to enjoy yourself."

"I can do that!" Peaches sits up straight in her chair. "My parents and fiancé are arriving tomorrow, which makes tonight my last night to cut loose." She looks over at Ollie. "Can we have a girls' night bash at the hot springs after work? I want everyone here to come. You've all been so good to me these past few weeks."

"Fine by me. Stella?" Ollie looks down the table at Stella who nods her approval.

"Yay!" Fiona comes out of her chair a little. "I'll bring the wine."

"I'll check the schedule and email everyone the time," Ollie says.

They talk about the wedding a few more minutes before Stella announces the meeting is adjourned. The other staff collect their belongings and file out of the office. Ollie brings up the rear, but instead of following them into the hall, she closes the door.

She turns to face Stella who has moved from the conference table to her desk. "You won't believe what I found out about Maureen Graves."

"What?" Stella says, appearing alarmed.

Crossing the room, Ollie gestures at Stella's computer. "May I?"

Stella steps out of her way. "Of course."

When Ollie sits down at the computer, Stella stands behind her, peering over her shoulder as she types. Ollie pulls up the website she discovered last night—Maureen's personal blog with the most recent post, dated seven years ago. The post features a photograph of Maureen and her sister on vacation in Europe. The sister is none other than Maureen's supposed oncologist, Dr Wilma Matthews.

Stella lets out a gasp. "Why that lying bitch."

Ollie bites her lip to keep from smiling. She's never heard Stella swear before.

Grabbing her phone, Stella taps a few keys and presses the phone to her ear.

"Who are you calling?" Ollie asks.

"Nicole Lambert." Stella says.

Ollie moves in closer to Stella to hear what Nicole is saying. When Stella explains why she's calling, Nicole eagerly agrees to look into the situation.

"If you make this right, Nicole, we will forget the little matter of my great-grandmother's missing novels."

Ollie's eyes go wide, and Stella holds the phone away from her ear for Ollie to hear Nicole's stuttered response, "I . . . I . . . I'll call you back as soon as I know something."

When Stella ends the call, Ollie offers her a high five. "You handled that brilliantly."

Stella tosses her phone on the desk. "Nicole's reaction just now is proof she took the journals. Or had Maureen take them for her. Since I have no way of proving it, there's no point in going to the police. But I learned my lesson, and I won't make that mistake again. Jack is having security cameras installed. Going forward, we will be more vigilant about keeping our doors locked."

"You can't be too careful these days."

Stella lets out a deep breath. "Excellent detective work, Ollie. You may have salvaged the inn's reputation."

"I knew from the beginning something was fishy about that woman's story." Ollie moves toward the door. "Let me know if you hear from Nicole."

"Will do. Hopefully we won't have to wait too long," Stella says. But when she shows up for the girls' night bash at nine, Stella still hasn't heard from Nicole.

"Wonder why she hasn't called," Ollie says.

Stella shrugs. "Let's hope she's doing her job."

Because the governor is spending a small fortune on his daughter's wedding, Stella insists on providing the food and booze for the party. Champagne bottles are uncorked, and several rounds of toasts are made.

Peaches, who is more than a little tipsy, jumps to her feet. "Let's play a game. We'll go around in a circle, and everyone will talk about how the hot springs has changed them over the past two months. I'll go first. And when I'm finished, I'll tag the next person." She loses her balance and wine sloshes onto the stone paving. "Oopsy."

"Give me that," Fiona says, taking the wine glass from her.

Peaches throws her arms over her head. "I'm magically cured of my anxiety." She scrunches her face, as though trying to figure something out. "Although truth be told, Cecily deserves more credit than the hot springs." She points at Cecily. "You set me straight on my pampered Southern belle act. I feel more like myself than I have in years. I'm a product of my mama's making. But I don't wanna be that person anymore. I'm really trying to change."

"And it shows." Fiona gives her a hug. "The old Peaches, the Peaches from our childhood, is back. I really like that girl."

Peaches crosses her hands over her heart. "I like that girl too. I'm excited about moving to London now. I have the opportunity to reinvent myself. I'm actually planning to get a job. For the first time in my life, I'm gonna work." She slips into the pool, going all the way under and coming up with hair wet. "That's it for me. I tag Fiona."

"I'm not in the market for a miracle," Fiona says. "But I believe this place is magical, the friendship and the environment. I've enjoyed working here this summer. Thank you for the opportunity." She looks first at Cecily and then Stella.

"You're a breath of fresh air," Stella says. "I hope you'll consider staying on permanently."

Fiona casts a mischievous glance at Cecily. "I'm waiting for Cecily to make me an offer."

"We'll talk. Ten o'clock tomorrow. In my office." Cecily's hand shoots up, offering Fiona a high five.

"Awesome!" Fiona grabs Cecily's hand and pulls her to her feet. "You're it."

Cecily groans. "I hate this game." She shifts her weight. "I can't say the hot springs have worked wonders for me. But I'm feeling better every day about my breakup with Lyle. I miss him sometimes. But I love having my own apartment and my freedom back. And having a crush helps." She drops back down to the edge of the pool as the others bombard her with questions about her crush.

Cecily drags her fingers across her lips. "I'm not looking for a serious relationship. Right now, I just wanna have some fun. Oh, and I tag Amelia."

Amelia sets down her champagne flute and gets up. "I'm still waiting for my miracle. Every day I pray for God to grant me Presley's magic. If only I had a tenth of her talent as an event planner."

"You have plenty of talent," Presley says. "You're just learning to use it."

Amelia's cheeks pinken. "Thank you for saying that." She looks across the pool at Ollie. "You're it."

Ollie remains in the pool. "The springs haven't taken away my heartache over losing my parents, but being surrounded by people who care about me is giving me the strength to make some difficult decisions. I tag Presley."

Presley slowly rises, with a hand against her lower back. "I ditto Ollie. I, too, am figuring some things out." Her gaze travels the group. "Your love and support help me get through the day. Stella, you're up next."

Ollie has been curiously keeping an eye on Stella since she arrived wearing a sundress instead of her bathing suit. She accepted a glass of champagne and pretended to take sips during the toasts. But the still-full glass sits beside her on the pool surface. Ollie smiles to herself at the thought of Stella having a baby. She'll be a great mom. For the first time ever, Ollie wanders what it would be like to carry her own child, to produce another living being that is part of her, that she's responsible for raising from infancy to adulthood.

Stella says, "My first miracle happened when I came to Hope Springs Farm. I've been blessed with miracles nearly every day since. I discovered the family I never knew I had. I've made life-long friendships with all of you wonderful ladies. And I found the man of my dreams."

Stella's phone vibrates the pavement, and when she looks down at it, the color drains from her face. She snatches up the phone. "Nicole Lambert texted me. She's reporting live about Maureen Graves on the eleven o'clock news."

"The nearest television is in the Poolside Cafe," Ollie says, hoisting herself out of the pool.

The others grab towels and follow Ollie out of the hot springs area to the cafe. Locating the remote, she clicks on the television and Nicole appears in all her stunning beauty.

"I'm Nicole Lambert reporting to you live from the home of Maureen Graves, the woman who claims her pancreatic cancer was miraculously cured by the mineral water at Hope Springs Farm in Hope Springs, Virginia. Channel eleven news has discovered Maureen's head oncologist, Dr. Wilma Matthews, is Maureen's sister. According to a whistleblower who works in the oncologist's office, Maureen Graves never had cancer. Of any form. Her conspiracy was a ploy for fame and fortune. She's in the process of negotiating with a publisher for a book deal for the story of her miraculous cure."

Stella snatches the remote from Ollie. "No more book deal for her," she says, clicking off the television.

Presley shakes her head in disbelief. "I can't believe anyone would do something so underhanded to achieve fame."

Peaches fingers a lock of her blonde hair. "I mean, seriously. She shaved her head and everything."

Fiona runs her hands through her pixie cut. "Can you imagine?"

"What a psychopath," Cecily mumbles in a disgusted tone. "Can we sue her or something?"

"I don't think we have grounds for a lawsuit, although I'll check with my attorneys to make certain," Stella says.

"Thank goodness Nicole outed her," Amelia says.

Stella draws Ollie in for a half hug. "Nicole didn't out her. Ollie did. She discovered Maureen and Wilma are sisters."

A flush creeps up Ollie's cheeks. "The whistleblower, whoever he or she is, gets the real credit."

"You all deserve some of the credit," Stella says. "I just hope things will go back to normal around here now."

Ollie wonders what Stella's definition of normal is. Everything she's experienced since coming to Hope Springs Farm is anything but normal. Some of it good. Some of it not so much.

23

CECILY

The days leading to Peaches's wedding are thrilling for the kitchen staff with exotic foods arriving from all parts of the world. One minor crisis after another prevents Cecily from talking to Fiona about her future until mid-morning on Friday.

When Cecily finds Fiona standing alone at the window counter, studying the wedding menu, she drags her outside to the herb garden and pulls her down to the teak bench, the newest addition to her garden. "We need to talk fast before another catastrophe happens. I'd like to offer you a permanent position at the inn. Although it might not be exactly what you're hoping for."

Fiona's lips turn downward. "Go on."

"I'm fully staffed in the kitchen. However, I'm in desperate need of a catering assistant. You've worked wonders with Peaches's wedding events, both the reception and the rehearsal dinner. And you're the ideal candidate for the job. I'm not sure how this fits with your long-term goals. Going forward, you'll have first dibs on any culinary positions that open up."

"I'm intrigued." Fiona gets up and wanders around the

garden, inspecting the herbs and edible flowers, as she considers the offer.

"You'll be well compensated, Fiona. You'll start at a much higher salary than you would as a line cook. The catering menu needs updating. You'll have full creative control."

Fiona's head jerks up as she looks at Cecily. "Are you serious?"

"Absolutely! You've earned it."

Fiona bends down and pinches off a sprig of basil. Sniffing the herb, she returns to the bench. "I accept the position. I can't promise I'll stay forever, but working with you is the most valuable experience I can get at this point in my career. You're amazing, Cecily. I've learned more from you these past weeks than I did in culinary school."

"I think you're pretty amazing too, Fiona. You have a bright future ahead of you. Be warned, I'm going to hang on to you as long as I can." Cecily settles back on the bench. "Now, let's talk logistics. You'll need to find an apartment."

"I already have one. Holly is looking for a roommate. My parents are coming for the wedding. If it's okay with you, I'll follow them home to Atlanta on Sunday, pack up my stuff, and come back midweek."

"That works for me. As long as you're back by Friday. We have another big wedding next weekend."

Fiona runs her hand over the bench's weathered teak. "When did this bench get here?"

"I had the grounds crew bring it over from the barn," Cecily says. "Coincidentally, if you need props for weddings, in the attic of the barn you'll find a large inventory of benches and planters and garden statues."

"Good to know." Fiona closes her eyes and tilts her face to the sky. "Ahh, the sun feels so good. What a shame Peaches couldn't have a day like today to get married."

"The forecast is dismal. Do you have a backup plan? We can easily clear out the tables in Jameson's and the furniture in the lounge if Peaches wants to move the wedding inside."

"Presley already offered that as an option. But Peaches is adamant. Her wedding will be outside, torrential downpours be damned." Fiona sighs contentedly. "It's quiet out here."

Cecily snickers. "Isn't it? I've been spending a lot of time out here lately, away from the hubbub in the kitchen. Hence the reason I had the bench brought over. Stella wants to open the garden to guests. I'm sure people would love to see our chef's garden. But I refuse to give up my sanctuary." She rises slowly off the bench. "Sadly, we've gotta get back to work. We have a rehearsal dinner to put on."

The groom's mother, Grace Malone, is equally persnickety but way more reserved than the bride's mother. The rehearsal dinner goes off without a hitch. Every table in Jameson's is filled. The guests have a choice of surf or turf—Trout Almondine or roasted beef tenderloin. Champagne is served with fruit tarts for dessert. Wedding guests toast the bride and groom for hours. When the gathering finally disperses, the older folks head to bed leaving the younger ones to party at Billy's Bar into the wee hours of the morning.

Despite the gloomy weather forecast, the storm system stays well to the south of the Virginia mountains. Saturday dawns with bright blue cloudless skies and mild temperatures in the lower seventies.

Peaches is beside herself as she oversees the removal of the terrace tent. At six o'clock in the evening, she floats down the aisle in a strapless satin gown, with her hair styled in an elegant chignon, to meet her handsome groom under an arbor of peach roses. After they exchange vows, when the minister gives Ethan permission to kiss his bride, a thousand peach balloons are released into the air.

The guests migrate down to the lawn where food stations are set up under one tent, and the band, dance floor, and an enormous circular bar are set up under the other tent. Cecily is overseeing the shucking of raw oysters when Fiona appears in her peach-colored bridesmaid's gown. "There's a long line at the seafood taco bar, and the California roll platter is empty at the sushi station."

"I'll take care of it," Cecily says. "You're officially off the clock tonight. You're the maid of honor. This is your best friend's wedding."

Fiona hesitates, and Cecily shoos her away. "Go! Enjoy the band. When else will you get to hear Earth, Wind, and Desire?"

As the words leave Cecily's mouth, a horn blasts and the band's lead vocalist, Booker Lee Boss, announces the bride and groom will now dance. Fiona purses her lips, blowing Cecily a kiss, and heads for the band tent.

The next few hours pass in a blur of activity as Cecily bustles about making certain everything runs smoothly at the food stations. When she notices Presley standing alone at the edge of the band tent, watching the activity on the dance floor, she takes a break from work to speak to her. "You and Amelia outdid yourselves. This is a wedding for the Pinterest boards."

"Thanks! We had a lot of help from the food geniuses."

Cecily follows Presley's gaze to the dance floor where a tall guy with ginger coloring is swinging Ollie around. "Who's she dancing with?"

"One of Nathan's British friends. They're both really good dancers."

Peaches and Nathan work their way through the crowd toward them. "Outstanding job, ladies," Nathan says with a slight bow.

"Your bride had the vision," Presley says. "We simply executed it."

Cecily gestures at the band. "I'm sorry to say, the band has stolen your thunder."

Peaches laughs. "I'm grateful for the reprieve."

"Are you escaping to a secret spot after the reception for your wedding night?" Cecily asks.

Peaches shakes her head. "We're staying in the cottage."

Nathan places an arm around Peaches's waist, pulling her close. "We want to party with our friends and family. We'll have brunch with our parents in the morning, and then we've hired a car to drive us to Dulles Airport for our flight to France tomorrow afternoon."

"Would you like me to arrange a private room for your brunch?" Cecily offers. "The morning sun is glorious in the solarium."

Peaches and Nathan exchange a look. "Thanks," Peaches says. "But all these people came here for us. We want to spend as much time as possible with them. Who knows when we'll see them again?"

"I get it," Cecily says. "Best of luck to you in London. I'll be following you on The Gram."

Nathan smiles lovingly at his bride. "Peaches will light London up like a firework. My new friends will never know what hit them."

"Stop!" Peaches leans in closer to him. Her rosy cheeks give her away. She considers his compliment high praise, the endorsement Peaches needs as she becomes a part of the life he's built for himself in a foreign country.

The bride surveys the crowd. "I see several people we need to speak to." She entwines her fingers with her new husband's. "How long before we cut the cake?"

Presley consults her watch. "About thirty more minutes. I'll send someone to find you when it's time."

Cecily and Presley watch the happy couple being swallowed

up by the crowd. "I'm actually going to miss her," Cecily says. "I was beginning to like her."

"Nathan is not at all what I expected."

Cecily's gaze shifts to Presley. "How so?"

"I thought maybe he'd be an opportunist. Because of her father's wealth and power. But he's really into her."

Cecily detects a sad note in Presley's tone. "What's wrong, Presley? Is it Everett?"

Tears well in Presley's eyes. "He was supposed to be here this weekend. But I haven't heard from him in days." She bites down on her quivering lower lip. "Make that weeks."

Cecily furrows her brow. "That doesn't sound like Everett."

"I know. I keep telling myself there's a logical explanation. I don't doubt his love for me. Being the wife of a country music star is way harder than I thought it would be."

Cecily's green eyes pop when Everett appears behind Presley. He's wearing gray slacks, a crisp white shirt, black tie, and a black baseball cap pulled low to hide his face. "Hey, baby," he says, wrapping his arms around his pregnant wife.

A broad smile spreads across Presley's face as she turns toward him, throwing her arms around his neck. The music's tempo changes as the band launches into one of their most popular slow songs.

"Dance with me," Presley says, walking him onto the dance floor with her arms still around his neck.

A wave of melancholy washes over Cecily as she watches the couple dance. Presley and Everett will work through whatever growing pains they're experiencing. Their devotion to each will bind them together through difficult times. That devotion was the key ingredient missing in her relationship with Lyle.

The song is almost over when Peaches's loud squeal comes from deep within the crowded dance floor. "Everett Baldwin's in the house!" She throws her hands over her head. "Everett! Everett! Everett!"

The wedding guests begin chanting along with her.

Cupping her hands around her mouth, Peaches yells, "I'm a huge fan, Everett! It would mean so much if you'd sing 'Show Me the Way' on my wedding day."

Everett looks from Peaches to Booker. "With the band's approval."

Booker waves him on. "Come on up, bud!"

The guests go wild for Everett's deep sexy voice and heart wrenching song lyrics. He could easily steal the show from Earth, Wind, and Desire, but to his credit, he only sings the one song despite the crowd pleading for more.

The bride and groom cut the cake, and shortly thereafter, fireworks explode off in the distance. When Peaches and Nathan leave the reception to change, Cecily instructs her staff to slowly begin the cleanup process.

She's overseeing the dismantling of the raw oyster bar when Parker approaches with a martini glass filled with a light green liquid. "Here. Try this."

Cecily eyes it suspiciously. "What is it?"

"Cucumber vodka, mint syrup, and soda."

Cecily takes a small sip. "Yum."

He leans against the banquet table. "After the bride and groom make their fake exit, the party is moving to Billy's Bar. Rumor has it, the band has promised to join in for drinks and more entertainment. I'm going to need all the extra hands I can get. Any chance I can convince you to help?"

Her lips part in a mischievous smile. "Only if I get to sling drinks behind the bar."

He offers her a high five. "You're on."

Cecily helps pass out tiny bottles of bubbles and sachets of peach rose petals. The newlyweds return to the reception, posing a striking couple with Peaches wearing a lacy white sundress and Nathan in khaki linen pants and crisp white shirt with sleeves rolled up. The exodus is over in minutes. When the crowd migrates up the hill, Cecily gives her staff final instructions before following them to the main building.

When she arrives at Billy's Bar thirty minutes later, the after-party is already raging with Everett and Booker taking turns at the microphone. Cecily jumps behind the bar, and even though she's never bartended before, at that time of night, the drink orders are simple—beer, wine and champagne, and tequila shots.

Cecily pours herself a glass of champagne, sipping as she works. She's more than a little tipsy when the last partiers leave around two thirty. While the barbacks clean up behind the bar, Cecily helps Parker gather dirty glasses from tables. "I can't remember when I've had so much fun," she says.

"Tell me about it! I know it's late, but I'm too wired to sleep. Wanna hang out with me?" Parker's words are slurred. He's had his share to drink as well.

Cecily taps her chin. "What do you have in mind?"

Glasses in hand, Parker shortens the gap between them. "I have you in mind, Cecily. I've thought of little else since the night at Town Tavern."

She places a hand on his cheek. "I'm looking for fun, Parker, not commitment. Are you okay with being my rebound guy?"

He brings his face in close, his lips a whisper away from hers. "For now. When I'm finished seducing you, you won't remember Lyle's name."

She hooks an arm around his neck. "Bring it on." As she presses her lips to his, her legs go weak, and jolts of electricity travel her body.

24

PRESLEY

Presley sits bolt upright in bed at dawn on Sunday morning. She'd been dreaming about Chris. He was drowning in the lake, and she was standing on the pier, holding a round orange life ring in her hand. The life ring's long rope was wrapped around her body, binding her arms and preventing her from tossing the life ring to her brother.

Presley shakes her head to clear the dream from her mind. Whose life was she trying to save anyway? Her brother's? Or her own? Chris is safe. He's visiting friends at Virginia Beach with Amy. Her husband is the only threat of danger in Presley's life.

She glances over at Everett, snoring softly beside her. She was the only sober one at Billy's Bar last night. But Presley didn't mind. The music gave her a natural high. She sat on the barstool nearest the dance floor, sipping club soda and watching her husband perform. Watching how the crowd responded to him. Everett has a gift. And he must share that gift with the world.

Later, when they finally fell into bed at almost three in the morning, he'd made love to her with exquisite tenderness. But now, in the dim light of morning, lingering doubts cast shadows of the memories of that lovemaking. She needs answers. She needs to know where she fits into his life. She needs to know what Audrey Manning means to him.

Presley slips out of bed, pulls on her robe, and goes to the kitchen. She brews a cup of Earl Grey tea and takes it out to the porch. The morning is cool, the sky clear. The cottage next door is quiet, the bride and groom sleeping off their hangovers.

She's still sitting in the rocker, contemplating her life, when Everett emerges from inside two hours later. He kisses the top of her head. "Good morning."

She cranes her neck to look up at him. "Morning. Are you hungry?"

"I'm starving."

She rocks out of the chair to her feet. "I'll make you some breakfast."

Following her into the kitchen, he pops a pod into the Keurig while she removes eggs, bacon, butter, and milk from the refrigerator. "How long can you stay?" she asks as she places strips of bacon in a skillet.

His eyes remain on the coffee streaming into his cup. "My flight leaves at five this afternoon from Roanoke. Which means I need to leave the inn around three."

Irritation creeps up her neck. Why can't he stay longer? His next concert isn't until Wednesday. She cautions herself not to complain. "I could make us some sandwiches, and we could hike up to the overlook. Or we could lounge by the pool."

"How about if we take a long walk on the trails around the farm and then grab some lunch by the pool?"

"Sounds like a plan," Presley says, cracking an egg into a bowl.

"Do you have any Advil," he asks, opening and closing cabinets.

"No. But I have some Tylenol. Do you have a hangover?" She studies her husband closely as she retrieves the Tylenol from the cabinet next to the refrigerator. Everett's electric blue eyes are red rimmed, and he winces as though in pain when she slams the cabinet door. If he'd been drunk last night, he'd hidden it well. Everett is a recovered alcoholic. After watching her adopted mother die from cirrhosis of the liver, Presley had been hesitant to get involved with him when they first met. But he'd promised her his addiction was under control.

"Don't look at me like that, Presley. Partying is part of the culture. But it's not a problem."

Presley's mother went to rehab several times. She knows all too well how these things go. It's not a problem now. But it soon will be. She should call him out on it, but they have so little time together, she doesn't want to start an argument. Handing him the bottle of Tylenol, she returns her attention to frying bacon.

He shakes three tablets into his hand, pops them into his mouth, and chews them up.

Their unresolved issues hang in the air between them, and an awkward silence settles over the kitchen as she finishes preparing breakfast. She sets two places at the breakfast counter, and they sit down to eat.

Presley doesn't criticize him for not calling more often, but her tone is accusatory when she says, "Why didn't you tell me you were coming? Back in June, you mentioned the possibility of visiting this weekend, but you never said anything else about it."

"I wasn't sure I could get away until the last minute. I have a long weekend over Labor Day and a week in October when the baby comes."

If the baby comes on her due date. She knows his tour schedule by heart. If the baby is seven days early or seven days late, he'll miss the birth.

He sighs. "I'm sorry, babe. I know this is difficult. But this is what life will be like when I'm on tour."

"I understand," Presley says, and doesn't speak again until they've finished eating.

Everett stands and stretches. "How about that walk? I could use some fresh air."

"Sure! Why don't you change while I clean up?" Presley prefers to be alone in the bedroom when she dresses her swollen body in exercise clothes.

Ten minutes later, they set out on the trails surrounding the farm. Everett takes hold of her hand. "We should clear the air."

"We should," Presley says without hesitation. "You go first."

"You surprised me by coming to Hope Springs. I thought small town living suffocated you. You couldn't get out of here soon enough after our wedding in December. But you seem happy now. Has that changed?"

Presley stares down at the ground as she walks. "My circumstances have changed. Being near my family and friends is more important now that I'm pregnant. Now that I'm alone."

"Welcome to our new life, Presley. You're going to have longs stretches of time alone. Being on tour isn't easy either. You saw that for yourself. It's certainly no place for a baby. I rarely have a free minute for myself."

"No time to call your wife." She nudges him with her elbow, a gesture intended to be playful, but she's not joking around.

"I haven't called on purpose. After our argument back in June, I thought you needed time to figure out what's best for you and the baby. Everything happened so fast for us. We met, married, and conceived within a few months. Not to mention the launch of my career." He stops walking and turns to face her. "You're the love of my life, Presley. I'm committed to you a hundred percent. And I will support you in whatever you decide about the future."

Presley longs to talk to him about her plans for the future, but her tears are close to the surface, and she doesn't want him to see her cry. She nods and starts walking again.

They leave the trail and cut across the lawn to the caretaker's cottage. "Stella renovated the cottage and added a second floor. What do you think?"

He ignores her question. "I didn't see Stella last night. Was she at the wedding?"

"At the beginning. But only for a short time. I have a sneaking suspicion she might be pregnant."

"Good for her." Everett steps onto the porch and peers through the window.

Presley joins him at the window. "Stella offered for me to lease the cottage if I decide to stay in Hope Springs until the baby is born. There are two bedrooms upstairs, and she converted the downstairs bedroom into a home office."

He sits down in a rocking chair, pulling her onto his lap. "Are you thinking of having the baby here?"

Presley shrugs. "Maybe. I might stay through the winter, until I adjust to motherhood. Would you be okay with that?"

He smiles at her. "I told you, I'll support whatever you decide. I'm making plenty of money. If you want to buy a house in Hope Springs, I'm all for it. This is a wonderful place to raise a family. And I'd feel better knowing you have family and friends looking out for you. When I'm not on tour, I'll have to spend a fair amount of time in Nashville. But I'll come up to see you every chance I get."

If Presley didn't know better, she'd think her husband was trying to get rid of her. "We don't have to decide today or next month or even this year. Right now, I'm focused on bringing this baby safely into the world."

He runs a finger down her cheek. "I must say, all this fresh mountain air agrees with you."

"I feel safe here. And that's the most important thing right now, with the baby on the way." Presley jumps up and pulls Everett to his feet. "Let's put on our swimsuits and go to the pool. I have a hankering for a juicy hamburger. And the Poolside Cafe has the best burgers in town."

Everett trips along beside her. "But we just finished breakfast."

She laughs. "In case you haven't noticed, I'm pregnant. Which means I'm hungry all the time. But I'm exceptionally hungry these days. I wouldn't be surprised if this baby is a boy."

"Really? That'd be cool! Although I'm hoping for a girl, since I already have a son. You wouldn't believe how much Lee has grown these past few months."

Presley stops walking. "You've seen him?"

A flush creeps up his neck. "Um . . . yeah. Didn't I mention it? We had a pop-up concert in Atlanta a few weeks ago. I stopped in to see Carla and the baby while I was there." Carla is Everett's previous girlfriend, the young pediatric nurse who tried to trick him into marrying her by getting pregnant.

Presley stares at her husband. He's lying. The pop-up concert wouldn't have been on his schedule, but there would've been social media pics galore. Why does he feel he has to lie about making a special trip to see his son?

Not knowing what else to say, she takes off jogging across the lawn, calling over her shoulder, "Race you back to the cottage."

They spend the afternoon together at the pool, swimming and soaking up the sun, eating hamburgers and ice cream. But their alone time is minimal with all the fans hanging around, asking for autographs.

At three o'clock, she walks him to the cottage's driveway where he parked his rental car.

Everett tosses his overnight bag into the back seat. "Tell Chris I'm sorry I missed him. I left some swag on his bed."

"That's thoughtful of you. Thank you." She kisses him on the lips.

She's been delaying the inevitable for fear of starting an argument. But she can't let him go until she has an answer. "Where does Audrey Manning fit into your life?" She sounds like a jealous wife, but she can't help herself. She needs an answer.

"Audrey Manning is this year's American Idol. The audience loves her, and she draws a huge crowd. Her presence on my tour benefits both of us. She's a good kid, and we've become friends, but we are not romantically involved." He opens his car door and gets behind the wheel. "Our marriage is complicated, Presley. It won't survive without trust."

He closes the door and drives off without so much as a wave.

Tears stream down Presley's cheeks as she watches his taillights disappear around the bend. How dare he accuse her of not trusting him? She trusted the Everett she married. But this Everett has changed in only a few short months. This Everett has done the one thing he promised he wouldn't do. He let his success go to his head. He lied to her about the pop-up concert in Atlanta. And she suspects he's lying to her about the drinking. Who knows what else he's lying to her about?

O n Sunday afternoon, I'm lying on the sofa with a cold washcloth covering my eyes when someone bangs on the terrace doors. "Come in!" I yell without removing the cloth.

There are footfalls on the hardwood floors followed by Cecily's voice. "What's wrong, Stella? Do you have a hangover?" she says with a little snicker.

"I wish I had a hangover. At least then, the agony would soon be ending." Snatching the cloth off my eyes, I ease into a sitting position. "As it stands, I'm destined to feel like hell for the next six weeks."

Cecily's jaw drops open. "You're pregnant. That's awesome, Stella. Congratulations." She plops down beside me, sending a jolt of pain to my brain.

"I'm not very far along, and you're the first person I've told, so please keep it to yourself."

Cecily drags her fingers across her lips. "Mum's the word. Are you throwing up and stuff?"

"I haven't actually vomited yet. But I feel nauseous all the time."

"You should talk to Katherine. Didn't she feel bad in the beginning?"

"Katherine felt bad all the way through her pregnancy. Don't you remember? She called in sick more than she came to work. Which worries me. I can't afford to feel bad like that."

Cecily falls back against the sofa cushions. "Isn't morning sickness a sign that all is well with the baby?"

"Yes! And that's the good news." Tucking one leg beneath me, I angle my body toward hers. "I shouldn't complain. I'm thrilled about the baby. What're you up to today?"

Cecily examines her fingernails. "I have the Sunday scaries."

"Based on what I saw during the short time I was there, everyone who attended the wedding last night, with the exception of Presley and me, should have the Sunday scaries. Did you disgrace yourself?"

Cecily laughs out loud. "I never disgrace myself, Stella. But I hooked up with Parker. I don't regret it, though. He's easy to be around, and we have a lot in common."

"Did he spend the night?"

A naughty smile spreads across her lips. "There wasn't much night left. He was gone when I woke up this morning. Even though he has the day off, he went to the inn to make certain everything was in order when Billy's Bar opened." She grabs onto my arm. "It's okay for me to have a rebound person, right?"

I thumb my chest. "Why are you asking me? Sounds like you've got everything figured out."

She lets go of my arm. "What if he ends up being more than my rebound person? I just broke off my engagement. I need time for myself."

I tuck a stray strand of honey hair behind her ear. "Then take it slow. Don't dive headfirst into the deep end."

"Parker is looking for a serious relationship. He's been texting me all day. He asked me to go on a hike. And then fishing. And then to the Dairy Deli for ice cream." Her phone buzzes, and she tugs it out of her pocket. "Now he wants to know if I can come over for dinner. I should tell him no." Her thumbs fly across the screen as she responds to his text. "There." She drops the phone in her lap.

I stand and stretch. "I'm thirsty. Do you want something to drink?"

"I'm parched," Cecily says, licking her lips. "I'd love some water."

Cecily follows me into the kitchen. I fill two glasses with ice and water and slide one across the counter to her.

"It's so quiet around here," Cecily says in a hushed voice. "Where is everyone?"

"Opal needed Jack to help her with a leaky faucet. He took Jazz and Angel with him to give me some time to rest."

Cecily's phone buzzes again, and she looks down at the screen.

"Parker again?" I ask.

Cecily looks up with a dreamy expression. "Yes. He's begging me to come to dinner." She guzzles the water and goes to the sink for a refill. "You don't think I should have a fling with Parker, do you?"

I stare at her, mouth agape. "I didn't say that."

"No. But you're thinking it."

"I'm thinking you should be careful." I drain the water from my glass. "I'd hate to see you get hurt. And I don't want you to make the same mistake twice. You rushed into a relationship with Lyle before you really knew him."

"The only way to get to know Parker is to hang out with him. And we only have one day off a week. Why shouldn't I have dinner with him?"

"There's something to be said for playing hard to get, Cecily."

Cecily lifts a shoulder. "That's true." Her eyes narrow as she looks closer at me. "Something's wrong. Other than morning sickness."

"That reporter, Nicole Lambert, contacted me again. She wants to go through the inn's history books. She's determined to find out more about the Charleston debutante."

Cecily's body goes rigid. "I hope you told her no."

"Of course, I told her no. Nicole Lambert is trouble. But what if she's right? What if there's more we don't know about the hot springs? My great-grandmother's last journal ended abruptly. What if there are more journals?"

"Hmm." Cecily strokes her chin. "Where'd you find the first ones?"

"In the mini warehouse where Billy stored the contents of this house when he sold it."

"Is there more stuff in the warehouse?"

I nod. "You can hardly open the door it's so packed."

"What're we waiting for?" Cecily snatches my keys off the counter. "I'll drive, since you're not feeling well."

Grabbing my purse, I traipse behind her through the mudroom and out the back door to the driveway. I lack the energy to tackle the warehouse today, but my curiosity won't let me rest until I know if there are more journals.

I spout off directions as Cecily drives my Wrangler like a bat out of hell through the winding mountain roads to the mini warehouse on the outskirts of town.

She risks a glance over at me. "What happens if you find out some dark secret about your family's history?"

"Please, keep your eyes on the road," I say, pointing at the windshield. "I doubt we find anything, but if we do, I'll deal with it. Why are you suddenly so interested in my family's history anyway?"

"I'm not. I need a distraction. I'm trying not to think about Parker. Should I have dinner with him?"

"Sure! What else will you do on your night off? Although you're welcome to have dinner with us. Jack is barbecuing chicken on the grill."

Cecily bites down on her lower lip. "Parker is cooking steaks."

I roll my eyes. "Seriously, Cecily. You work harder than anyone I know. You might as well enjoy your one day off. If you want to spend time with Parker, do it. You've been through a lot these past six months. You deserve to have some fun."

Cecily screeches to a halt in front of the mini warehouse and kills the engine. "What if fun turns into feelings?"

"Proceed with caution. Let the situation play itself out and see where you land." I hold my hand out for the keys. "I'm driving home. Riding with you is a risk to my unborn child's life."

She sticks her tongue out at me. "Ha ha."

I open the passenger door. When Cecily makes no move to get out, I say, "Are you coming?"

"After I text Parker to tell him I'm coming for dinner."

When I start off toward my unit, Cecily falls in line beside me. With her eyes glued to her phone, she says, "Parker wants me to come over in an hour. What time do you think we'll be done here?"

"Shouldn't take more than a half hour." I stick the key in the padlock and roll up the warehouse door.

"Ugh!" Cecily says about the three rows of boxes and furniture piled from floor to ceiling.

"It's not as bad as it looks," I say, stepping inside the air-conditioned warehouse. "You take one aisle, and I'll search the other."

Cecily ventures down her aisle. "At least it's cool in here. What're you gonna do with all this stuff?"

"I plan to slowly work my way through everything. There's plenty of junk in here. But there are priceless antiques, works of art, and my ancestor's personal belongings as well."

I go silent as I shine my phone's flashlight up and down the rows of stacked boxes. From the next aisle over, Cecily argues out loud with herself about whether or not she'll have sex with Parker tonight. A few minutes later, I'm nearing the end of my aisle, ready to give up, when I hear groans followed by a loud thud. Cecily lets out a loud *Ouch!*

"What happened?" I ask, rushing to her aid.

"This box fell on my foot," she says, hobbling around in pain in the tight space.

I kneel down to inspect the box. Someone has scrawled photo albums across one side. The old packing tape crackles when I peel it back. I pick up the top album and thumb through, glimpsing photographs of my father at various stages of his life. Removing the albums one at a time, I stack them on the concrete floor beside the box. At the bottom, I find two leather journals identical to the others with my great-grandmother's meticulous cursive handwriting. The date of the first entry in one journal is June 15, 1960. The second journal begins two years later in 1964.

I look up at Cecily who is staring down at me. "Bingo!" I say, giving her a high five.

Setting the journals aside, I pack the albums neatly back in the box. When I move to pick up the box, Cecily brushes me out of the way. "Here, let me get that. In your condition, you should be careful about what you lift."

She hoists up the box and carries it out to the car while I lock up the warehouse behind us.

During the drive home, my mind is on the journals while

Cecily babbles on about what she should wear on her date. When I pull into the driveway, I say, "Wear white jeans and a cute top, not too casual or overdressed."

"Of course," Cecily says, smacking the side of her head as if to say why didn't I think of that.

"Thanks for your help today, Cecily. And have fun tonight. But take it slow."

We get out of the Wrangler, and Cecily heads off toward the garage apartment. I'm struggling with the box of albums when Jack's pickup truck pulls into the driveway.

"Cecily and I went to the mini warehouse," I explain when Jack and Jazz come to greet me. "We found a box of old family photo albums and two more of my great-grandmother's journals."

"Ooh! Photos! I wanna see," Jazz says, dancing on her toes.

"Me too, kiddo! I can hardly wait." I hand the box to Jack and follow him inside.

Jack prepares the chicken for the grill while Jazz and I peruse the photo albums at the kitchen counter. The albums chronicle our father's life from the time he was a baby. Birthdays, Christmases, and his first day of school every year. Summers at the inn, swimming and fishing in the lake. Him playing guitar at different ages.

Jazz finger-stabs a photograph of Billy. "Check it out! That looks like me! He's about my age. Even his skin is the same color."

I study the photograph. Billy's dark curls are unruly, and his amber eyes are like gold coins. He's wearing cutoff shorts and no shirt, his tanned skin the same caramel color as Jazz's. "Wow! It's eerie how much you look like him."

I've always been a little envious of my half sister's relationship with our father. Jazz and Billy shared a close friendship when he was alive. She didn't find out he was her father until after his death.

"Can I have this picture for my room?" Jazz asks.

"Of course." I gingerly remove the aged photograph from the album and hand it to her. "It's old and fragile, so be careful with it."

Jazz presses it against her chest. "I'll put it on my nightstand. Can we keep the albums here, or do we have to take them to the inn with the rest of the family books?"

"I say we keep them on the bookshelves in the family room, so we can look at them any time we want. Do you want to help me do that now?"

"Yes! Let's!" Jazz slides off the barstool to her feet. We each gather several albums in our arms and walk them to the family room. We clear a spot on the bookshelves, and while I work on dinner, Jazz meticulously arranges the albums to her liking.

The topic of Billy occupies the conversation during dinner at the kitchen table. Jazz is suddenly obsessed by his life as a child growing up at the inn. "Can I work at the inn when I grow up?" she asks.

"After you finish college and win six gold medals at the Olympics."

Jazz gives me a sassy head bob. "Seriously, Stella."

I set down my fork and wipe my lips. "My hope is for you and me to one day run the inn together. I'm expanding our facilities to accommodate our growing business. By the time you're ready to come to work, we'll be operating a mini Disney World."

"Can I live here, in the manor house?" she asks with a mischievous grin.

"We'll toss a coin. We have plenty of land. Whoever loses can hire Jack to build another house somewhere on the property." I wink at my husband, and he smiles back at me.

After dinner, the three of us snuggle on the sofa for an hour of television. Jack and Jazz are partial to animal shows, which is fine by me. I can hardly wait to start reading the journals. When the show ends at nine o'clock, Jack surfs the channels for an old war movie while Jazz and I take Angel outside to do her business.

On the way back inside, Jazz asks, "Can I give Angel her bedtime snack and put her in the kennel?"

"Of course." I wag my finger at her. "But remember, only half a stick of jerky. When you're finished, brush your teeth and put on your pajamas. I'll be in to read you a story in a few minutes."

"Okay. Come on Angel," Jazz says and slaps her thigh for the puppy to follow her into the kitchen.

I retrieve the journals from the bookshelves and climb the stairs to my room. Changing into my pajamas, I wash my face and brush my teeth. Jazz is nearly asleep when I enter her room, and we agree to skip story time tonight. I tuck the comforter around her, kiss her forehead, and turn out the light.

I slip beneath the covers, settling in to read a few pages of my great-grandmother's journal. I'm soon engrossed in the tale of the tumultuous relationship between my great-grandmother and her daughter-in-law, Janis, my grandmother and Billy's mother. Two hours later, I read the last word. What I've learned has soured my stomach, and I suddenly crave ginger ale.

When I stand up, dizziness overcomes me, and I grab on to the bedpost until it passes. I plod in bare feet down the semi-dark hallway to the stairs. I don't notice Angel sleeping at the top of the stairs until I trip over her and tumble down to the marble floor in the front hall.

26

CECILY

Parker greets Cecily at the door, carrying a yummy raspberry basil mojito and wearing a delicious smile. She wants to lick his lips. She sips the drink instead.

"Are you hungry?" he asks. "I have some nibbles in the kitchen."

"I'm a chef. I eat, even when I'm not hungry." She follows him into a part of the house she didn't tour during her previous visit. A thin pine farm table separates a small sitting area from the kitchen, which has been recently renovated with stainless appliances, marble countertops with heavy gray veining, and sage-green cabinets.

He gestures at the tray of hummus and vegetables on the table. "Help yourself. It's nothing fancy, but I grew most of the veggies in my garden."

She inspects the appetizer presentation. "Wow. These veggies are magazine worthy. Peppers and tomatoes and cucumbers." She drags a cherry tomato through the hummus. "And homemade hummus. You've been holding out on me, Parker. I didn't know you could cook."

He shrugs. "I find cooking relaxing. I wouldn't want to do it for a living. The steaks are marinating. What time do you want to eat?"

"Whenever. I'm not in a hurry." She moves over to the french doors and steps out onto his bluestone terrace. A wood pellet grill occupies one corner. Opposite the grill are four lounge chairs surrounding a fire pit. His yard is small but well tended with a vegetable garden taking up one side of the fenced-in area. She plops down in one of the chairs and he sits down beside her.

"We should talk about last night," he says with a sexy smirk on his lips.

Cecily would rather repeat what happened last night than talk about it. But she says, "You go first."

"Being with you was lovely. You're a special woman, Cecily."

She peers at him over the top of her glass. "But?"

He cuts his eyes at her. "But I can't be your rebound guy. I won't like it, but I'll totally understand if you need to find some other guy to help you get over Lyle."

Is he blowing her off? She can't tell. "I don't understand. You've been texting me all day."

"Because I enjoy hanging out with you." He sets his drink down on the arm of the chair and reaches for her hand. "Despite being more than a little drunk last night, I felt a strong connection with you. We have a chance at something special, but you need to clear your head of Lyle first."

Cecily gets up and walks to the edge of the terrace. "This feels heavy to me."

He waits a beat before joining her. "I'm offering you friendship with no benefits. How is that heavy? I want to get to know you. I wanna hang out. Do fun stuff together. Maybe things will naturally progress between us in the next few months."

Cecily's jaw slackens. *Months*? She has to wait *months* to have sex with him again? She cringes at the thought. What is she, a slut now? On the other hand, maybe sex with no strings attached is what she needs. Maybe she should look for someone she doesn't like to be her rebound person. Someone she won't fall in love with.

"And if things don't progress."

"Then neither of us gets hurt. Then *I* don't get hurt. This is mostly about self-preservation. I stand to lose the most, since you're still hung up on your fiancé." Parker's expression is genuine, and she suspects he's given this a lot of thought.

"What makes you think I'm still hung up on Lyle?"

"Because you were going to marry him. You don't strike me as the kind of person who takes marriage vows lightly."

"Or maybe I am. Lyle and I hadn't been dating very long when I began pressuring him to propose. I'm impulsive by nature, one of my many character flaws."

"Something else we have in common." Parker squeezes the back of her neck. "We don't have to talk about this anymore tonight. But I wanted you to know where I'm coming from. And when you figure it out, I'd like to know what you're thinking as well."

"Okay. Can we eat soon? I'm starving."

"Yep," he says with a laugh. His laughter carries a melodic note that makes her feel happy and carefree.

He walks over to the grill and lifts the lid. She follows, peering over his shoulder. "What're we having? Can I help cook?"

"No, you may not. Today is your day off."

Twenty minutes later, they sit down at a beautifully set table on the terrace. Parker lights fat pillar candles in hurricane globes and fills two stemmed red wine glasses with semichilled pinot noir. "You're so domesticated," Cecily says. "Are you sure you're not gay?"

Leaning across the table, with mischief playing on his lips, he says, "You tell me."

She glares at him. "You can't flirt with me like that if we're going to be friends without benefits."

He straightens. "Fair enough," he says, placing his linen napkin in his lap.

She stares down at her scrumptious plate of filet mignon, tender fingerling potatoes, and a green salad with unique lettuces grown in his garden. She carves off a bite of steak, groaning as she savors the flavor. "Cooked to perfection. Seriously, Parker. Your home decor is magazine worthy. You're an amazing cook. You're an enigma. If you're not gay, then what gives?"

Parker swirls the wine around in his glass before taking a sip. "I was ten when my mom left. She chose career over her family. She just up and moved out to the West Coast with no discussion about me going with her. My dad took care of me the best he could, but his career demanded much of his time. And he traveled a lot, two or three days a week. I had sitters at first, until I was old enough to stay home alone."

"That must have been hard for you at such a young age."

He sets his glass down and picks up his utensils. "I learned to take care of myself. I spent a lot of time at my best friend's house. Judd's mom practically raised me. She had three sons and always wanted a daughter. She was thrilled when I asked her to teach me to cook."

Parker stabs a forkful of salad. "The Cole's house always smelled like cinnamon, and Judd's mom had a snack waiting for us every day after practice. For a kid like me, with no parents at home to care for him, those things mean a lot."

Listening to Parker makes Cecily feel guilty for her traditional upbringing. "Did you major in home economics in college?" she asks in a teasing tone.

"Ha ha. Aren't you funny? Actually, I majored in creative writing, which is a hobby of mine. I have a secret ambition to be the next Tom Clancy."

Cecily pauses in mid chew to stare at him. "Every time you open your mouth, you say something that surprises me."

"Good. I like to keep you on your toes."

She points her fork at him. "There you go with that flirting tone again."

"Sorry." He pops a potato into his mouth. "You're making me out to be a freak. But I'm just a normal guy. In high school, I was the star quarterback of the football team and starting attackman on the lacrosse team. In college, I was president of the most popular fraternity. I'm comfortable in my own skin, Cecily. So what? I like to cook and play house. I'm not embarrassed about that."

"And you shouldn't be. I dare say, most people our age haven't figured out who they are yet."

"That doesn't include you."

"No, but Lyle's name is on the top of that list."

Cecily can't help but compare Parker to Lyle. While they both came from money, their backgrounds are very different. Lyle's mom pampered him while Parker's mom left him to fend for himself. Lyle wants a woman like his mother to provide a nurturing home for their children. Is that what Parker wants as well? A wife to replace the mother who abandoned him? If so, he's barking up the wrong tree.

Later, after the dishes are put away, Parker mixes creamy, salty caramel martinis, which they take outside to the lounge chairs. Cecily says, "I would think a guy like you would be looking for a girl like Judd's mom. The Susie Homemaker type. Just so you know, *if* a relationship between you and me were to develop, I am definitely not that type."

Parker laughs. "I view marriage as a partnership, an equal

fifty-fifty split. Your drive to succeed is one of the things I admire most about you. I told you I aspire to be the next Tom Clancy. In a perfect world, I will stay home with the kids, writing my life away, while my wife brings home the bacon. When the kids are young, we'll have to hire a nanny, so I can get my daily word count in."

Cecily stares at him over the top of her martini glass. "You're serious. You've given this a lot of thought."

"Yep. Like I said, I'm comfortable in my own skin."

Cecily's infatuation with Parker is growing by the minute. And that scares the heck out of her considering only a few weeks have passed since she broke off her engagement. She drains the rest of her martini. "I should go. I have an early day tomorrow."

"I'll walk you home."

"You don't need to do that. I'm a big girl. I can walk myself home."

"But I want to." Taking her glass from her, Parker deposits them in the kitchen while she retrieves her purse from the sofa in the adjacent sitting room.

As they start off toward Main Street, Parker says, "We've been talking about me all night. Tell me about your family."

"They are boisterous and often rude. And my mom never does anything without her sister, Amelia's mom. They were all here at Christmas for the wedding. When Lyle and I decided not to get married, we had a family reunion instead."

Nearing the manor house, they increase their pace when they see red flashing lights in the driveway. "What in the world?" Stella's pregnancy comes to mind. "I hope no one is sick."

When they arrive, two EMTs are wheeling a stretcher out the front door. Stella's body is strapped to the stretcher, her head immobilized in an orange brace and a large white bandage covering her right temple.

Jack emerges from the house, carrying a crying Jazz. "What happened?" Cecily asks.

"Stella fell down the stairs," Jack says. "She hit her head on the marble floor. She's unconscious."

Cecily can see the worry in Jack's face. He, too, is thinking about their unborn baby.

"It's all my fault!" Jazz cries. "She tripped over Angel. I didn't lock the kennel all the way and Angel got out."

"It's not your fault. It was an accident." Cecily holds her arms out to Jazz. "Why don't you stay here with me while Jack goes to the hospital with Stella?"

Jazz leaps into Cecily's arms.

Jack appears relieved. "Thank you, Cecily. Opal's on her way. She should be here soon." He jogs over to the ambulance and climbs in the back with Stella. Seconds later, the ambulance speeds off toward the hospital.

Parker takes Jazz from Cecily. "Come here, you. Let's go check on Angel. I imagine she needs some loving right about now."

Cecily's heart melts. How does this guy always know the right thing to say?

27

OLLIE

Ollie has twenty-four hours to report her decision to her father's attorneys. She's leaning toward disclaiming her inheritance. But Stella's words play like a broken record in her head. *Don't give away your inheritance, Ollie. It's your birthright. Half that property belongs to you.*

Her anxiety level reaches an all-time high on Tuesday morning. She breaks the rule about employees using the facilities during working hours and swims two miles in the spa pool. The exercise doesn't touch the apprehension brewing inside of her.

To make matters worse, she's having hallucinations about her ex-husband. She sees Sergio checking in at the front desk, and lunching on the porch at Jameson's, and strolling down the sidewalk toward the spa. After close scrutiny, she decides the man is not a figment of her imagination but a guest who looks enough like Sergio to be his twin. Only this man has a beard and Sergio detests facial hair.

Around three o'clock that afternoon, no closer to making a decision about her parents' estate, with the clock ticking rapidly, she goes in search of Stella. She needs her boss's voice of reason. But Stella isn't in her office.

She stops by the front desk to speak to Rita. "Where's Stella? Will she be back soon?"

Rita gives her a curious look. "Haven't you heard? Stella fell down the stairs at the manor house on Sunday night. She has a concussion and a broken arm. She'll be out for a few days."

She steps back from the desk. "Oh, no! Poor Stella." The walls begin to close in on her, and she escapes through the front door. *Breathe.* She tells herself. But sucking in deep gulps of air does little to stifle the panic gripping her chest. She needs to focus on something or someone other than herself. She'll go to the farmer's market and buy a bouquet of zinnias for Stella.

She hurries up Main Street to her apartment building and retrieves her beat-up sedan from the parking lot. But she drives past the farmer's market and enters the highway heading east. She rolls down all the windows and blasts classic rock music from the radio. The open road helps clear her mind, and she's able to contemplate her options. An hour later, as she's approaching the outskirts of Charlottesville, she comes to a conclusion. A business relationship with Alexander will never work. Rebuilding the family business with her brother is no longer an option. She'll either disclaim the inheritance or Alexander buys her out of her share of the property and branding rights.

Ollie drives the long way back to Hope Springs, through winding mountain roads. She passes many charming vineyards along the way. Maybe she could buy a vineyard in Virginia. Or even start her own. If she keeps her half of the inheritance, she'll have money to invest.

The idea takes root, and her excitement about the prospect grows. By the time she stops at the farmer's market in Hope Springs, she's practically floating on a cloud. She needs more time to think through the prospect. She'll call her father's attorneys tomorrow and ask for an extension.

She purchases a ginormous bouquet of wildflowers in a large mason jar and drops the arrangement at Stella's front door on the way back to the inn. She's surprised to find Sergio's looka-like sitting on a bench at the spa's front entrance.

He stands to face her. "Hello, Ollie."

She freezes with her hand on the door handle. "Sergio? I thought you were someone else. What's with the beard? You detest facial hair."

Sergio chuckles. "Not anymore. I met someone. We're to be married in October. She convinced me to grow a beard." He strokes his bushy chin. "I kinda like it."

Ollie drops her hand from the door handle. "You must like her too, if you let her convince you to grow hair on your face. What're you doing here? We're already divorced. You don't need my permission to get married."

"I need to talk to you about the fire. It's important."

Her heart rate quickens. "I guess so, if you flew all the way across the country."

He holds a gift bag out to her. "For you."

Inside are two stemless glasses and a bottle of wine. She pulls the wine out and studies the label of the 1995 Cabernet Sauvignon. "This was our best year."

"Indeed, it was," he says. "I thought we could share it. What I have to tell you won't be easy for me to say or you to hear. Is there somewhere we can talk?"

She looks past him at the deserted pier.

Sergio follows her gaze. "I have a corkscrew," he says, tugging a wine opener out of his pocket.

They walk to the end of the pier, kick off their shoes, and sit down with their legs hanging over the side. He opens the wine and fills their glasses.

Sergio swirls, sniffs, and sips his wine. "First of all, I owe you an apology. I should've never married you." He holds his hand up. "Don't misunderstand me. I loved you. Like a sister. And I loved your father. I was misguided in thinking that fathering your children would make me a legitimate member of your family. But I couldn't tame you."

"Because I wasn't ready to grow up."

He touches her chin. "But you've grown up now. I see it in your face. In your eyes."

She stares down into the inky lake. "Losing one's parents in a fire will do that to you."

Sergio pauses a beat. "I was there the night of the fire."

Ollie jerks her head up. "You were where?"

"At the Rolling Rock. And then later at the estate. I saw you leave in the Uber. The driver looked sketchy, and I followed you home, to make sure you got there safely. I parked on the street, and when you went inside, I walked over to the winery. When I moved out of my office, I left something important, and I wanted it back."

She eyes him suspiciously. "Like two cases of the 1995 vintage."

"Ouch." He hangs his head. "I guess I deserved that."

"After what you did to my family, hell yes you deserved it. You made the last two years of my parents' lives miserable."

"I can't undo what I did, Ollie. But I can make amends for my actions."

Nothing he can do will bring back her parents. "So, what did you take from your office that was so important?"

"A framed photograph of your father and me at the awards ceremony when we won vintage of the year for this." He clinks his glass to the bottle.

A stab of guilt pierces Ollie's heart. Sergio worked for Hendrix Estate for twenty-five years. He was like a son to her father. And Ollie ruined that relationship by divorcing Sergio.

Sergio continues, "I was coming out of the winery when

flames engulfed the house. I saw a figure in dark clothing, carrying a red plastic gas can, dart off toward the vineyard. I spent untold hours helping your brother improve his times when he was on the track team in high school. I would know Alex's gait anywhere."

Ollie's body goes still, her wineglass stalled on the way to her mouth. "Wait. Are you saying Alexander started the fire?"

Sergio gives her a solemn nod.

"But the fire chief ruled burning debris from the fire at the Santos farm the cause."

Sergio shrugs. "A plausible explanation. But that's not what actually happened. Your brother had an evil streak. Remember that cat you had when you were young, the black one with the yellow eyes you thought ran away?"

Ollie's chest tightens at the mention of her beloved pet. "Her name was Tinkerbell. I cried for days when she disappeared."

"I caught your brother mutilating it with your mother's butcher knife behind the cellars."

A wave of nausea overcoming her, Ollie scrambles across the boardwalk and vomits over the side of the pier. A minute later, she feels a hand on her back. "I'm sorry, Ollie. You need to know this stuff to understand what a monster he is."

She pushes Sergio away and leans back against a piling, collecting herself. "This doesn't make sense. Alexander was the perfect child. I was the one with all the problems."

"He put on a good act. But he's a demon."

Several long minutes pass as Ollie reflects on her past. Things suddenly make more sense. Even when she wasn't at fault, Alexander was always quick to blame her when something got broken or when chores were left undone. Because he was the one responsible.

"What happened after you saw Alex fleeing the scene of the fire?" Ollie asks.

"I ran to the front of the house. I got you out, but I couldn't save your parents. Alex intended for you to die in the fire that night, Ollie. He wants the business all to himself."

"He's been trying to guilt me into disclaiming my inheritance."

Sergio's jaw tightens. "I figured as much, the little bastard."

Ollie fits the remaining pieces into the puzzle. "So, you're the one who called nine-one-one. Why did you leave? Why didn't you tell the police any of this?"

A pained expression crosses his face. "The police would've blamed me for starting the fire. After losing the lawsuit, I had motive."

Ollie considers this. "You're probably right. How do I know you're not lying now?"

"You don't. You have to trust me. It's my word against Alex's." Sergio pours more wine into her glass and hands it to Ollie. "Remember that girl who accused Alex of raping her in high school?"

Ollie takes a gulp of wine, washing down the taste of bile. "How could I forget her? She put us through hell and then recanted her story."

"She recanted the story because Alex ran a smear campaign against her. Not only that, but he also threatened her."

Ollie furrows her brow. "How do you know that?"

"I overheard him talking to his friends."

Ollie jumps to her feet. "Seriously, Sergio? We're talking rape here." She glares down at him. "Why didn't you tell my father?"

Sergio averts his eyes. "I did."

The implication hits Ollie like a wrecking ball. "And Dad protected him," she says in a disgusted tone. "This is too much for me to process."

Ollie starts off down the pier, and Sergio comes after her. "I promise that's the worst of it. But you need to know these things."

"I don't understand. Why are you coming forth with all this now?"

Sergio runs his hands over his face. "This past year has been hell. This secret is eating me up inside. May, my fiancé, knows how hard this has been for me, and refuses to marry me until I go to the police."

"And have you? Gone to the police?"

"I'm flying out at the crack of dawn tomorrow morning in order to make a midafternoon meeting with a homicide detective. I fully expect Alex to try and weasel his way out of this. But I'm prepared. I've already hired an attorney." Sergio glances at the half-full bottle of wine. "What say we finish the bottle over dinner? We have a lot to talk about."

Ollie doesn't know whom to trust. She certainly doesn't trust her brother. There's always been something off about Alex. But she never thought him to be a psychopathic murderer. Is she in any danger? Alex visited her a week ago. She was alone with him in her apartment. He tried to kill her the night of the fire. What's stopping him from trying again?

"Okay. Dinner sounds good."

Sergio grabs the bottle, and they stroll together up the hill toward the inn. "You have a good gig here, Ollie. Running a wellness center suits you. Do you like it?"

"I do," she says with an enthusiastic nod. "I've made a lot of new friends here. But I miss the vineyard. I was toying with the idea of returning to California."

"You were born to be a vintner. It's in your blood. Alex cared more about entertaining the wealthy clients. You, on the other hand, understand and appreciate the process of making wine. I took the scenic route over from Charlottesville today. I saw many small wineries along the way. Perhaps you could buy one, establish your own winery."

"I took a drive in the country today too. And I was thinking the same thing. Regardless, now that I know Alexander's responsible for our parents' deaths, I will not be disclaiming my inheritance."

"I'm glad to hear it," Sergio says in a satisfied tone.

When they arrive at Jameson's, Sergio asks the hostess to seat them on the porch. At a private table at the far end of the railing, Ollie and Sergio talk shop as they finish the wine and order dinner. They slip into their old comfortable relationship, before they were married, when they were still friends.

They both order the crab cake special, and Sergio selects a pinot noir from a local winery. "What happened, Sergio? Why did you sue my family when I asked for a divorce? That's not who you are."

"I was hurt and angry when your father fired me. But I realize now, he had no choice. Tension in the family had gotten so high. That was a troubled period in my life. I'd like to put it behind me. If the police press charges and the case goes to trial, these coming months could be difficult for both you and me. Let me help you, Oll. I watched you grow up. You're like a baby sister to me. I let you down once. I won't let you down again."

"Thank you for saying that." She falls back in her chair. "Wow. This is all so hard for me to wrap my mind around. Not only is my brother a murderer, he killed his own parents. And I can't believe Dad protected him against the rape allegations. If Alexander had been made to pay, Mom and Dad might still be alive today."

Sergio considers this. "Maybe."

"Still, I'm partially responsible for their deaths. If I hadn't been in an alcohol coma, I could've saved them."

Sergio shakes his head vehemently. "There's absolutely no

way. The fire ravaged that house. I was there, and I hadn't been drinking. I barely got you out. I couldn't have gotten to your parents. You're lucky you passed out on the sofa. Otherwise, you wouldn't be alive."

She thinks about what Sergio said earlier. *Alex intended for you to die in the fire that night, Ollie.* But she didn't die. She now knows the truth. And she will make certain he pays.

28

STELLA

A light tapping on my door wakes me from a deep sleep early on Wednesday morning.

"Come in," I say, groggily.

Cecily tiptoes into the room, carrying a covered basket with a blue checkered cloth peeking from beneath the lid. The aroma of warm blueberry scones makes my mouth water.

I look from the basket to her. "You didn't?"

Cecily holds up the basket. "I did. I personally baked them just for you." She eases herself to the edge of the bed. "How're you feeling?"

I touch the bandage on my right temple. "Like I fell down the stairs and cracked my head open on the marble floor."

Cecily looks at the bandage from different angles. "How many stitches did you get?"

"Eleven." I hold my broken arm close as I struggle to sit up in bed.

Cecily eyes my cast. "Good thing you broke your left arm and not your right."

"No kidding. The left presents enough challenges as it is." I open the basket and remove a scone. "This smells divine."

Cecily hands me a linen napkin. "I understand you have a nasty concussion."

"Unfortunately. The doctor prefers I not take pain medicine because of the baby. But the throbbing in my head is unbearable. My eyes are incredibly sensitive to light. I have to keep the drapes pulled tight. No way can I read anything." I pinch off a bite of scone and pop it into my mouth. "Yum. Let's hope I can keep it down."

"Is the nausea from the concussion or morning sickness?"

"A little of both, I think." Under my breath, I add, "I hope."

"So, everything's okay with the baby?" Cecily asks in a hopeful tone.

"As far as we know. It's too early to hear a heartbeat. But I haven't had any bleeding. I have an appointment with my obstetrician on Friday. I'm praying she hears the heartbeat then."

"I'm sure everything is fine," Cecily says, holding up her hands to reveal crossed fingers.

I take another bite of the scone. "How is everything at the inn? Can I rely on you and the other team leaders to hold down the fort until I come back?"

Cecily pats my blanketed knee. "Don't worry about a thing. We have everything covered. If we need you, we know where to find you." She stands to go. "Get some rest. And let me know if there's anything I can do for you."

"Thank you for the scones," I say, blowing her an air kiss.

I wait for her to leave before putting the half-eaten scone on the nightstand. As with most food these days, my mouth savored the scone, but it made me nauseous. Sliding deeper beneath the covers, I sleep for most of the morning. When I wake again, Opal is entering the room with a bamboo tray.

"I made you a grilled cheese sandwich. I had horrible morning sickness when I was pregnant with your mother. Grilled cheeses were one of the few things I could keep down."

I ease up the headboard to a sitting position. Taking the tray from her with my right hand, I say, "This looks delicious. Did you have morning sickness with Uncle Brian too?"

"Nope. Only with your mama." Opal pulls a chair closer to the bed. "If you're up to talking about it, I'd like to hear what you learned from Imogen's journals."

I gesture at my great-grandmother's journals on the night table. "You're welcome to read them if you'd like."

Opal crosses her legs and folds her hands in her lap. "I'd rather hear about them from you instead."

"Okay." I take a bite of my sandwich, savoring the rich blend of cheeses as I arrange my thoughts. "You've told me about my grandmother, how Janis cussed like a sailor and drank whiskey like water, and everyone loved her because she didn't put on airs. Did you ever meet my great-grandmother?"

"A time or two. To say Imogen and Janis did not get along is an understatement. Imogen, who was a royal priss pot, disapproved of Janis's devil-may-care attitude. Truth be told, I think Imogen was jealous of the way the guests fawned over Janis."

"That reinforces what I've read." I finish the sandwich half and set the tray aside. "In the early sixties, my grandmother and grandfather decided to start a family. After a few years of trying without success, Imogen arranged for Janis to see a specialist at UVA University Hospital. Imogen doesn't go into detail in the journal, only to say the doctors ultimately concluded Janis would never be able to conceive."

"But she did have children," Opal says, confused.

"Let me finish. So, Janis came to see Imogen one day, asking for the key to the hot springs. Remember, my great-grandfather had closed the hot springs years earlier after the debutante's tragic drowning."

"Right." Opal uncrosses her legs and moves to the edge of her seat. "Did Imogen give her the key?"

"Nope. But Janis snuck into the house the next day and took it. She soaked every day for a month. And guess what happened?"

"She got pregnant," Opal whispers.

I grin, which makes my head hurt. "Exactly."

Opal's olive eyes get wide. "How did Imogen react?"

"She should've been thrilled for her son and daughter-in-law. But she was furious. Reading between her lines, I got the impression she felt like a fool for refusing to give Janis the key." I pick up the other half of the sandwich and gobble it down. "The grilled cheese was incredible, Opal. Does this mean my appetite's back? What if the morning sickness is gone? Do you think I'm having a miscarriage?"

Opal points a gnarled finger at my midsection. "That baby is fine as a fiddle, loving grilled cheeses just like your mama did. I think this is a sign you're having a baby girl."

"I hope you're right."

Opal slaps her thigh. "On with the story. What happened next?"

"Nine months later, Ethan junior was born. With a rare blood disorder."

Opal gasps. "I didn't know."

My throat thickens. "I actually cried when I read this part. The doctors diagnosed his condition as terminal. They warned he wouldn't see his first birthday."

Opal sits straight up in her chair. "But he saw well past his first birthday. Let me guess. The healing waters of the hot springs cured him."

"Correct." I grab one of the journals and thumb through it. "Once again, Imogen refused access to the hot springs. Can you believe that? What kind of monster grandmother was she? This time, Janis busted down the hot springs' door. The doctors were dumbfounded. They warned Janis not to get her hopes up, that Ethan's improvement was only temporary."

"But Ethan lived to be twenty-six—"

I finish her sentence. "When he died in a plane crash."

"Your father is only two years younger than Ethan. Did Janis have trouble getting pregnant with Billy?"

I run my hand over the journal's worn cover. "There's no mention of that pregnancy. But Imogen became greedy with the hot springs after Ethan's miraculous recovery. She was convinced the mineral water not only healed but prevented aging."

"Hmm." Opal looks away as she considers this. "Now that I think about it, Imogen was a striking woman with flawless skin and toned muscles. If she had any health issues, I'm not aware of them. She died in her sleep at the ripe old age of ninety."

I pick up the second journal and flip through the pages. "I can't find the entry. But sometime in the mid-seventies her sister was diagnosed with breast cancer. Imogen refused to let her soak in the mineral water. Her very own sister, who eventually died from that cancer." I toss the journal on the bed. "I'm glad I never met her. I don't think I would've liked her very much."

"Sadly, not many did."

I swing my legs over the side of the bed and slowly get to my feet. I walk to the window and peek through the drapes, but the bright sunlight hurts my eyes, and I turn back toward the room. "I'm curious, Opal. What did Billy think of the hot springs? With all his health problems, did he ever try to soak his way to a cure?"

"Your father didn't believe in miracle cures. He called it hocus pocus. I encouraged him to at least try, but he refused. He never admitted it, but I got the impression he disapproved of his grandmother's obsession with the hot springs." Opal stands to face me. "We could use you as an experiment. Why don't you go dunk your head in the hot springs? Maybe the waters will heal your wound and make your concussion go away." The smirk on her lips tells me she's joking.

"No thanks. I'm enjoying being pampered." I return to the bed and crawl back beneath the covers.

"I've been thinking a lot lately about my leukemia." Opal lowers herself to the edge of the bed. "The doctors attributed my quick recovery to my strength and determination. Even though I wasn't soaking in the mineral water during my treatment, I'd been soaking regularly before the diagnosis. Therefore, I believe the mineral water was at least partially responsible for my rapid recovery."

I smile at her. "So, you do believe in the hocus pocus?"

"Look at me, my darling girl." She sweeps her hands down her body. "I'm a flamboyant artist. Of course, I believe in hocus pocus."

My mood turns serious. "I'm not like my great-grandmother. If the mineral water truly heals, who am I to deny the terminally ill the opportunity to be cured?"

Opal stares into my eyes. "I see the wheels spinning in your head. What're you planning?"

I bark out a laugh, despite the pain in my head. "I haven't figured that out yet. But I'm working on it."

Opal pats my leg. "I have no doubt about it."

29

PRESLEY

Late Wednesday morning, Presley is meeting with Cecily and Lia about the upcoming wedding on Saturday when Rita knocks on the door of Stella's office. "Sorry to interrupt. Presley, Can I have a word with you in private?"

The bottom falls out of Presley's stomach. Something bad has happened. Is it Lucy? Or Chris? Please don't let it be Everett. She's mad as heck at her husband, but she still loves him.

Presley leaves the conference table and joins Rita in the hall. "What is it? Is someone hurt?"

"It's nothing bad. I got a call from Lucy's doctor a few minutes ago. She's releasing her from the hospital today. Lucy wants you and me to attend a family session and drive her home."

Presley pats her chest. "*Me*? She wants *me* to come?"

"According to Dr. Norman. I talked to the doctor for a few minutes. She's very encouraged by Lucy's progress. She thinks we'll be pleasantly surprised."

Presley narrows her eyes. "So, you're going to give her another chance after all she's done to you?"

Rita's lips part in a soft smile. "That's what sisters do, Presley.

I'll keep giving her chances until there are no chances left to give."

Presley inhales, pulling herself to her full height. "Okay then. What time do we leave?"

"Our appointment is at four. We should leave here around three."

"I'll meet you at the check-in desk at three," Presley says. "What should we tell Chris?"

"Nothing for now. Let's see how the session goes, and then we'll decide."

Presley kisses Rita's cheek. "You're an amazing woman, Rita. You have the biggest heart of anyone I've ever met."

Rita gives her a hug. "You have a beautiful heart yourself, my sweet niece."

The next hours pass in a blur. Presley avoids Chris for fear she'll spill the beans about his mother's homecoming. After tying up a few loose ends for the wedding, she changes into exercise clothes and hikes up to the lookout.

Presley hasn't heard from Everett since he left on Sunday afternoon. And she doesn't expect to hear from him anytime soon. He seemed different while he was here. Uncharacteristically self-absorbed. Never once did he ask about her professional life. And he seemed a little too eager to keep her hidden away in the mountains. Is his pregnant wife suddenly cramping his style? If her husband can do whatever he wants without any consideration of her feelings, Presley can do the same. As for Audrey Manning. *If* Everett is having an affair with his current co-star, the media will break that news soon enough.

Presley showers and chooses a knit maternity dress with a cheerful geometric pattern of grays, pinks, and blues.

"Any idea what we should expect?" she asks Rita during the forty-five-minute drive to Roanoke.

Rita glances over at her from the driver's seat. "Not really.

When Lucy was in rehab, I attended the family sessions out of a sense of obligation. Someone in the family needed to be there. And I worried it would be too stressful for our parents. Lucy never said much during these sessions. But this is different. She asked us to come today. Maybe she's going to apologize."

"If that's the case, why didn't she ask Chris to come?"

"Your guess is as good as mine. Maybe she thought it'd be easier to talk about her problems without him being present."

When they arrive at the hospital, the receptionist shows Rita and Presley to a lounging room with a variety of options of comfortable seating and a large picture window overlooking a colorful perennial garden. Presley chooses the love seat and is comforted when Rita sits close beside her.

The psychiatrist enters the room first. Raquel Norman is an attractive middle-aged woman with a thin figure and a silver bob grazing her shoulders.

She sits in an overstuffed chair opposite the coffee table. "Thank you for coming on such short notice. Lucy insisted I be present when she speaks to you. She admits to having treated both of you unfairly, and she very much wants to make amends. She's worked hard these past few days, and she's making headway, although she still has a long way to go. If she angers you or says anything inappropriate, please refrain from lashing out. It's best to let me handle it."

Presley gulps and Rita says, "Understood."

The door opens again, and Lucy enters the room wearing jeans and a pink blouse. Her skin has a healthy glow, her mahogany hair shines, and when she smiles at Rita and Presley, her brown eyes are warm. Based on her appearance, the old Lucy has returned.

She parks her small rolling suitcase beside the door and settles into the matching chair next to her doctor. "Thank you both so much for coming. I have a lot to tell you. But first, I want to apologize. The last months are a blur, but I remember being unkind to both of you. And to my son and his girlfriend. How is Chris by the way?" she asks Presley.

"He's working hard and saving lots of money," Presley says. "We've been shopping for his dorm room. He's very excited about college."

Lucy has work to do where her son his concerned. Chris hasn't mentioned his mother in days. Presley's tried talking to him about her, but he's made it clear the subject is off limits.

"Good." Lucy sits back in the chair. "I'll start with you, Rita. Although I don't really know where to start. You've been an amazing sister to me. You've supported me through thick and thin during these difficult years. And I've repaid you by being a bitch. I wish you and Brian the best. And I mean that from the bottom of my heart. Of course, I'm jealous. Who wouldn't be? He's a great guy. You've had your share of life's disappointments, and you deserve happiness."

Presley senses the tension draining from Rita's body. "Thanks, Luce. We both do."

"Do you think you can find it in your heart to give me another chance?"

Rita, as though remembering their conversation from earlier, looks over at Presley. *I'll keep giving her chances until there are no chances left to give.* "We're sisters, Lucy. Whether you like it or not, I will always be here for you."

"You are too good to me. This time, I won't let you down." Lucy twists her body toward Presley. "I've felt an emptiness inside of me since I put you up for adoption. Even marrying the love of my life and giving birth to my precious son couldn't make up for what I'd lost. For years, I desperately wanted to find you, to be reunited with my precious baby girl. Then you appeared out of nowhere, and I fell off a cliff."

Lucy looks uncertainly at her shrink who nods for her to

continue. "I told you once that I saw a therapist when I was pregnant with you, but she wasn't very helpful. Dr. Norman thinks I never properly addressed the rape. Seeing you brought it all back. I had nightmares and panic attacks. I was flattered when Brian expressed an interest in me, and I had to pretend I wasn't coming unglued at the seams. Hiding my distress became increasingly more difficult, and I began self-medicating. I dealt with the physical aspects of my addiction at rehab, but not the mental issues. At least not the *real* mental issues."

Lucy pauses to take a sip of water. "You're a lovely girl, Presley. You're talented and you have a special way with people. Any mother would be thrilled to have a daughter like you. My problems were never about you. Coincidentally, I'm thrilled you and Chris have forged a bond."

Presley's eyes well with tears, and she doesn't trust herself to speak.

"Now for the difficult part." Lucy gets up and goes to the window. "In order to properly work through what happened to me, I have to face my rapist. Levi doesn't know about you, Presley. I never told him I was pregnant."

An awkward silence overcomes the room. Presley glances at Dr. Norman, waiting for her to speak, but she's preoccupied with the iPad in her lap. Presley ventures, "You once told me my biological father wasn't such a bad guy. That he was handsome and smart."

Rita says, "Good people make bad decisions. Especially when they're in college."

"I know," Lucy says to the window. "I need to confront him. I need for him to tell me why he did it. Then, with Dr. Norman's help, I can put this whole thing to rest."

The psychiatrist looks up from her iPad. "I truly believe that once she faces the past, she'll be able to move on with her life."

"Do you know anything about his current life?" Presley asks.

Lucy turns away from the window. "Dr. Norman and I looked him up. We can't find any mention of him on social media."

"How will you find him?" Rita asks.

"I have a few college friends I can contact," Lucy says.

"So, there's a chance I have more half siblings," Presley says.

"A very good chance." Lucy stares down at the floor. "Dr. Norman thinks it's a good idea for you to come with me when I confront him. I know it's asking a lot. I just thought . . ."

Presley moves to the edge of her seat. "Of course, I'll go with you."

Relief crosses Lucy's face. "Thank you."

Rita says, "It's none of my business, but since I'm your closest relative, I should be aware of any medications you're taking."

"The doctor has me on an antidepressant that controls anxiety. It's making a huge difference already. And it's totally your business." Lucy pulls Rita to her feet. "You're my sister, Rita. And I love you. I haven't been very kind to you these past few years, but I plan on making it up to you."

Rita flashes a bright smile, revealing her dimples. "I look forward to it."

Lucy loops an arm through Rita's. "In that case, let's go home."

Lucy thanks her doctor and retrieves her suitcase from beside the door. On the way out to the car, she stops to say goodbye to a number of nurses. Seeing this genuine interaction gives Presley hope of having a meaningful relationship with her biological mother after all.

They make small talk as they leave the Roanoke city limits. Once they're on the highway, Lucy says, "I have to figure out how to approach my son. He's terribly upset with me and rightly so. I was horrible to him and his girlfriend."

Presley, who is sitting alone in the back, says, "Would you like for me to talk to him first?"

Lucy shifts in her seat to look at Presley. Instead of being offended as Presley expected, Lucy appears grateful. "Would you? He'll listen to you. I understand if he wants to continue living with you. But I'm hoping to spend some time with him before he leaves for college. If he'd let me, I'd like to take him and Amy to dinner."

"I'm not making any promises, but I'll do my best. He's hurt, Lucy. It may take some time, but he loves you, and he'll eventually come around."

"Stella must be furious with me," Lucy says. "Do you know if I still have a job?"

"You still have a job," Presley says. "And I hope you're ready to come back to work, because we desperately need you."

"Stella is one of the most forgiving people I know," Rita says. "I'm saying this for your own good, Luce. Don't screw it up. I don't think there'll be a next time."

Tears well in Lucy's eyes. "Don't worry. I have no intention of blowing it again."

Presley wants so much to believer her, for her sake as well as her brother's.

When Rita suggests stopping for an early dinner on the way home to Hope Springs, Presley and Lucy eagerly agree.

"I'm always hungry these days," Presley says.

"The hospital food was the worst," Lucy adds.

Rita locates a quaint roadside diner, and all three women order the cheeseburger platter. Presley is quiet while she eats, listening to Rita and Lucy talk about old times. The sisters laugh at pranks they pulled on their parents as children and become weepy when they speak of the summers they spent at their grandparents' beach cottage at Figure Eight Island.

"I miss that cottage," Rita says with a faraway expression. "I wonder who owns it now."

"We should try to rent it next summer. I would love to get Mom and Dad and all the kids together." Lucy looks over at Presley. "Your baby will be crawling by then."

Presley's heart swells. She takes this to mean she's included in the family vacation plans for next summer. "And into everything, I'm sure."

The women linger over warmed slices of blueberry cobbler and decaf coffee. It's almost nine o'clock when Rita drops Presley at the inn. She takes her time strolling back to the cottage. Despite the problems in her marriage, she feels more hopeful about the future than she has all summer.

Presley arrives at the cottage to find Chris and Amy, snuggled on the sofa watching a rom-com.

"Where have you been?" Chris asks.

"Rita and I drove to Roanoke to bring your mom home."

Chris sits up straight, gently pushing his girlfriend away. "Why didn't you tell me?"

"It was arranged at the last minute. I didn't know myself until late this morning." Dropping her bag on the floor, Presley plops down in a comfortable armchair. "Your mom seems in a good place. Her doctor believes Lucy's problems are a result of what happened to her in college. Because she never properly addressed the rape."

Presley watches for Amy's reaction. She's curious how much Chris has told her about his half sister. Amy doesn't flinch, as though she knows about the rape.

Chris clicks off the television. "And how does this doctor think she should address it now, thirty years after the fact?"

"By confronting the man. Apparently, she never told him she was pregnant. He doesn't know about me."

Chris tosses his hands in the air. "Great! More drama! Just what we need. Is she gonna make me move back home?"

Statements like these remind Presley of how young and immature her brother is. He's eighteen. Lucy can't make him do anything. "No. She's fine with you living here. But she would like to spend some time with you before you leave for college. She feels terrible about the way she treated you and Amy. She'd like to take the two of you out to dinner."

"No thanks," Chris snaps.

"Chris," Amy says in a warning tone. "She's your mother."

"And she's put me through hell these past few months." Chris stands to face Presley. "How can you forgive her so easily after what she's done to you?"

"Because she wasn't in her right mind. She's now under the care of a compassionate and capable doctor. She's taking the right medications. Once she faces her past, she'll be able to put all this behind her."

Chris steps closer to Presley, staring deep into her eyes. "You actually believe that, don't you? Well, I know Mom a lot better than you. There's always another crisis where she's concerned. I've put up with her theatrics long enough. As far as I'm concerned, I no longer have a mom."

Amy leaps off the sofa. "Chris! You don't mean that."

"Yes, I do." Chris takes Amy by the hand. "Come on. I'll drive you home." On the way out the door, he tosses over his shoulder, "Don't wait up for me, Presley."

He's more upset than Presley realized. And he's right. He does know Lucy better. Maybe that's part of the problem. He's too close to the situation. *I'll keep giving her chances until there are none left.* Presley considers it her duty as an older sister to help him change his mind.

30

OLLIE

Ollie is on pins and needles, waiting for further word from Sergio. Last night he had called to report that his meeting with the homicide detective went well. The detective planned to look into Sergio's allegations against Alexander and promised to let Sergio know something soon. Ollie pressed him, but Sergio was unable to give her more of a definite time.

Ollie's meeting with the bride du jour on Thursday morning does little to alleviate her anxiety. While the wedding will be an elaborate affair with several hundred guests soon descending upon the inn, the bride is much easier to work with than Peaches. Katie Robinson is a stunning brunette in her mid-thirties with realistic expectations. Together, Ollie and Katie map out a plan for the spa party for her bridesmaids on Saturday morning. After facials and massages, the group will move downstairs to the indoor pool where the staff will serve a lunch of cold chicken and fruit salads and champagne. Ollie has reserved the larger, more comfortable, of the two spa locker rooms for the early afternoon hours when hair stylists and makeup artists will work their magic on the bride and bridesmaids for the four o'clock wedding.

Ollie sees Katie to the elevator before returning to her office to send the appropriate emails to her staff with the notes from their meeting. Despite being focused on the task at hand, she's still on edge, and her cell phone vibrating her desk startles her.

She snatches up the phone, expecting Sergio. But the call is from her boss. "Stella! How're you feeling?"

"A little better. Thanks for asking. I'd like to meet with my key staff members before the weekend. After work tonight is the only time that fits everyone's schedule. I thought we'd make a party of it and gather at the hot springs. Does that work for you? Say around nine o'clock?"

Ollie has no other plans, and she's grateful for the distraction. "Sure! I'll make certain the hot springs are cleared out by then."

She hangs up with Stella and goes downstairs to Roots for a quinoa bowl. As she eats, she replays the conversation with her father's attorney in her mind. She spoke with him at length yesterday when she called to tell him she would not be disclaiming her inheritance.

"Good! I'm glad to hear it," Karl Keller had said in a genuine tone. "This is what your father wanted. If I were you, I wouldn't trust your brother. He doesn't have your best interests at heart."

"Don't worry. I'm aware of Alexander's agenda," Ollie had said.

Ollie moves through her day, preparing the spa for the upcoming weekend. Around five o'clock, she's discussing staffing with the pool manager when she receives the anticipated call from Sergio. She steps outside the pool gate to speak to him in private.

"We have a problem," Sergio says in a concerned tone. "Alexander has disappeared."

Ollie grips the phone. "What do you mean he's disappeared?"

"Detective Pratt sent two officers to bring him in for questioning. He's not at his house. The next-door neighbor saw him loading suitcases into his car when he went out to get the newspaper at dawn this morning. We think someone within the police department may have tipped Alexander off." Sergio lets out an audible breath. "I'm sure there's a logical explanation. He probably went somewhere on vacation."

"Or he's on his way to Virginia to finish off the job," Ollie mutters.

"Detective Pratt doesn't think you have anything to worry about. He's checking into Alexander's whereabouts. He promised to call as soon as he knows more."

"Great. I'll try not to panic. As if that's possible. Let me know when you hear from him." Ollie ends the call before Sergio can respond. Alexander killed their parents. By now, Karl Keller will have informed Alexander of Ollie's decision not to disclaim her inheritance. Regardless of what Detective Pratt thinks, there's a very real possibility her brother is on his way to Virginia. She considers contacting Martin in security, to advise him of the potential threat. But there's no point in alarming anyone until she knows if the threat is real.

Ollie manages to stay busy throughout the evening. Cecily is the first to arrive for the meeting with several pizzas and a cooler filled with craft beer from a new local brewery. "Courtesy of Parker." She opens the cooler and removes two cans of beer, handing one to Ollie. "And compliments of the brewery. They are hoping we'll add their brand to our menu. Parker wants our feedback."

Ollie forces a smile as she accepts the beer. "In that case, I'll be happy to give it to him."

After a busy day, none of the staff have time to go home and change, and they show up for the meeting in their work attire.

They roll up pants legs and sit on the edge of the hot springs with feet dangling in the water.

Stella calls the meeting to order. "Thank you all for coming on such short notice." Dark circles rim her blue eyes, and she holds her broken arm close to her body, like a bird protecting a wounded wing. But her spirits appear high. "I won't keep you long. I've been out of the loop this week and wanted to touch base with you before the weekend. If you don't mind, I'd like a report from everyone about preparations." She shifts toward Presley, who is sitting next to her. "Why don't you start? And we'll go around in a circle."

"Sure! We're in great shape. Emma and Amelia have everything buttoned up tight. The bride is a sweetheart to work with."

Everyone nods their agreement.

"Cecily," Stella prompts.

"We're getting there." Cecily snickers. "Poor Fiona's moving van broke down and she was delayed in returning from Atlanta. But she's getting settled in her apartment tonight and she'll be at work early in the morning. I'm not worried, though. She's incredibly organized. She's got everything under control."

Stella's gaze shifts to Lucy. "Welcome back," she says with a genuine smile. "How are things in the wine shop?"

"We, too, are in great shape," Lucy says. "The bride's father has a few wealthy wine enthusiast friends. We are organizing a tasting for Saturday afternoon before the ceremony. Holly has done most of the work. She's a marvel. She's expressed an interest in studying to become a sommelier. I could certainly use an assistant."

Stella says, "As fast as the inn is growing, I think that's an excellent idea. I'll leave it to you to speak to Parker and Holly about the details."

"Will do." Pink dots appear on Lucy's cheeks, which Ollie interprets as gratitude for Stella's vote of confidence in her.

When it's Ollie's turn, she reports, "I met with the bride this morning. All systems are a go for the bridesmaid's spa party on Saturday."

"Excellent." Stella looks from Ollie to Rita. "Lastly, how are reservations looking this weekend?"

"We're busting at the seams as usual. Most of the rooms are reserved for the wedding party. Jack can't build the family wing soon enough."

Stella laughs. "I'll remind you of that when we're dealing with construction noise this fall." She lifts two worn leather-bound books from the pool deck beside her. "With Cecily's help, I located two more of my great-grandmother's journals. I've struggled in deciding how much to tell you about what I learned. At the risk of betraying my great-grandmother, I feel we have much to learn from my family's past."

Ollie's mind wanders as Stella goes on about her great-grandmother's refusal to allow access into the hot springs. She checks her phone, but there's no word yet from Sergio. Why hasn't he called or texted? Does this mean the police can't find Alexander? How hard are they even looking? A creepy feeling someone is watching her sends shivers down her spine. She dismisses the feeling as paranoia. Her imagination is getting the best of her again. She'll be glad when this meeting is adjourned, so she can go home to the safety of her apartment.

Laughter jerks Ollie back to the present.

Stella is saying, "I believe the mineral water heals on some level. I've seen it myself with Jazz's sprained ankle. I've decided to add a third soaking tub in the spa. This treatment room will be available by appointment to people of all ages who are critically ill. Being a guest at the inn is not a requirement for access, and we will not charge them for this service."

"That's incredibly generous of you, Stella." With a twinkle in her green eyes, Cecily adds, "Then again, I'm not surprised. This is vintage Stella. Always thinking of other people."

Stella smiles. "I'm glad you approve. We'll proceed with caution, so as to avoid being mobbed again. I don't plan to advertise the service. We'll let word spread on its own." She gets to her feet. "Thank you all for joining me. My headache is returning with a vengeance. You won't see much of me this weekend. I trust you have everything under control. But do not hesitate to call if you need me."

Everyone stands at once, and with murmurs of chatter, they begin gathering up their trash and migrating through the gate. Ollie is turning out lights and preparing to lock up when a dark figure emerges from the shower area. A hand clamps over her mouth, preventing her from screaming.

Ollie feels a cold object pressed against her temple. "If you breathe a word, I'll shoot you dead." Even though he's whispering, she would know her brother's voice anywhere.

Lucy comes barreling through the gate. "Ollie, I forgot my phone." She stops dead in her tracks when she sees Alexander. "What's going on?"

Ollie screams, "Run," but her words are muffled by Alexander's hand.

Alexander trains the gun on Lucy. "Close and lock the gate."

Lucy does as he asks. "If it's money you want, I can get it for you."

"It's money I want, all right." He tightens his grip on Ollie's mouth. "But my sister, here, is the one who's going to give it to me."

"I don't have any money," she screams, more muffled words.

"I can't understand you, Ollie. I'm going to remove my hand from your mouth, so we can talk quietly. If you do as I say, neither you nor your friend will get hurt. Do you understand?"

With eyes wide, Ollie nods her head.

Alexander removes his hand. "I have some papers for you to sign. I suggest we go up to your office for privacy."

Ollie's gaze connects with Lucy's. "Let her go. This is between you and me."

"She's my hostage. If you don't do what I say, I will put a bullet in her head." Alexander shoves Ollie away and grabs hold of Lucy, his arm around her neck.

Ollie stumbles and falls to her knees. When she looks up, her brother is standing over her, the gun aimed at her face. "You're pathetic," he snarls. "Get up!"

She scrambles to her feet.

He motions her to the gate. "Now, lead the way to your office."

"The keys are in my pocket," she says.

He jabs the gun at her. "Then get them out. But no funny stuff."

Fishing the keys out of her pocket, she leads them out of the gate to the building's side entrance. When she moves toward the elevator, Alexander says, "Take the stairs. I'm not stupid, Ollie. I'm aware of the video camera in the elevator."

But he doesn't know about the live surveillance camera hidden in her office and panic button under her desk. When Stella designed the wellness center, she made certain the security was state of the art.

Ollie changes directions and heads for the stairs.

Alexander, with arm around Lucy's neck and gun pointed at Ollie's back, follows her up two flights of stairs and down the hall to her office. Locking the door behind them, Alexander opens and closes cabinets until he locates a silk scarf Ollie wore to work on one of the last cold days of spring.

He throws the scarf at Ollie. "Tie her hands behind her back. And tie it tight or I'll make you do it again."

Alexander keeps the gun trained on Ollie while she winds

the scarf around Lucy's wrists. Brandishing his gun, he directs Lucy to sit down on the love seat and Ollie to go behind the desk. "The sooner you sign these papers, the sooner I'm outta here."

Ollie sits down in her chair and rolls it beneath the desk, kneeing the panic button without Alexander realizing it. She prays she hit it hard enough. If not, she and Lucy are screwed. She's never seen the wild look in her brother's eyes. He killed their parents. There's nothing stopping him from killing her as well.

He slaps a white business-size envelope on the desk in front of her. "Sign these. And be quick about it."

She removes the folded sheets. "What am I signing?"

"One is a document disclaiming your inheritance. The other is your affidavit, stating you witnessed your ex-husband setting the fire that killed our parents."

A chill travels down Ollie's spine. The security staff better get here soon.

31

PRESLEY

C hris is sound asleep in his bed when Presley arrives back at the cottage from the meeting. She's no sooner put on her pajamas and crawled into bed than her phone shrills on the night table with an emergency alert.

Presley grabs her phone as Chris appears in the doorway. "What was that noise?"

"An emergency alert. The resort is on lockdown. I'm not sure why." Her feet hit the hardwood floor as she clicks on Martin's number.

When he answers on the third ring, she blurts, "Is this lockdown for real?"

"We're assuming so until proven otherwise. We're investigating. I'll call you back when I know more."

Pocketing her phone, she looks over at her brother whose face is twisted in concern. "It may be a false alarm. But we should be prepared just in case. Let's check all the windows and doors to make certain everything is locked."

After securing the cottage, Presley and Chris each grab a knife from the butcher block in the kitchen and crouch down behind the row of maternity dresses in the master bedroom closet. Martin calls ten minutes later. "The panic alarm went off in Ollie's office. As best we can tell from the live surveillance cameras, a gunman is holding Ollie and Lucy hostage."

Presley gasps. "What? Why? I don't understand. I was just with all of them a short while ago. We were meeting with Stella at the hot springs. Lucy and Rita were among the first to leave."

Martin says, "I don't have any answers yet, Presley. We've contacted the local authorities. They're bringing in a SWAT team. Stay sheltered until further notice."

"I'm at the cottage with Chris, Lucy's son. We're in close proximity to the wellness center. Should we move to a safer location?"

"Not yet. Sit tight. If the situation deteriorates, I'll send in some men to evacuate Cottage Row," Martin says, and ends the call.

"What is it?" Chris says. "Has something happened to my mom?"

Presley can see the whites of her brother's terrified eyes in the darkness. She repeats what she learned from Martin. "Don't worry. Local police are sending in a SWAT team. Your mom will be fine.

"But what if she's not?" he says in a tone verging on hysteria. "I saw her earlier today. She invited Amy and me to dinner. I said some horrible things to her. What if I never see her again? What if I never get a chance to tell her I'm sorry?" Dim light shines through the door slats, illuminating his tear-streaked face.

Presley pulls him in for a hug. "Shh! You'll get a chance. Your mama will be fine." She wracks her brain for a way to distract him. "Why don't you text Amy? If word of the situation leaks out, she'll be worried about you."

"But what if word doesn't leak out. I don't want to worry her unnecessarily."

"Good point. Keep checking your phone in case Amy texts you." Presley pulls down extra pillows and blankets from the closet's top shelf. "We might as well get comfortable. Looks like we may be here awhile."

They huddle close together with a blanket covering them. Chris rests his head on Presley's shoulder. "I should've given her another chance."

"You'll have that chance. Don't worry." She kisses his hair. "I never told you about my adoptive mom. Renee was one of the most renowned country music producers of all time. For decades, she represented the top names in the industry. She wined and dined the stars, hosted elaborate parties at our home. As a child, I loved to watch the florists and caterers set up for the parties."

Sniffling, Chris asks, "Is that how you became interested in event planning?"

"Exactly." Presley's mind travels back to the lavish floral arrangements and displays of food at parties past. "I learned from the best. No one entertains like that anymore."

"That's cool. How did your mom . . . Renee die?"

"She drank herself to death," Presley says and Chris's breath hitches.

"You mean, she was an alcoholic?"

"A raging alcoholic. A highly functioning one, though. Most people think she died from liver cancer. Only those closest to her know the truth. She died from cirrhosis of the liver."

"How did she hide her addiction?"

"She had a hollow leg. It took a lot of booze for her to get drunk. She usually waited until she came home from a party or until the last guest left our house before hitting the sauce hard. Regardless of how much she drank at night, Mom always started her day at dawn. She kept a cache of prescription pills that helped her through the worst hangovers."

"That's awful, Presley. I'm sorry." Chris's tone is genuinely sincere. "Was your dad okay with this?"

"My adoptive father died when I was a young child, and Mom never remarried. As far as I know, she never even had a boyfriend. It was my responsibility to clean up after her. The spilled drinks and vomit. She often passed out with lit cigarettes in her mouth. I saved her life countless times. She ruined more than one Thanksgiving and Christmas by getting drunk."

"Why didn't she go to rehab?"

"I begged her often to seek treatment. She had the money to afford the most exclusive programs. But she refused. She worried word of her addiction would get out and destroy her career."

Presley thinks back over the most difficult times, during her junior and senior years in high school. "I grew to resent her. By the time I left for college, I could barely stand the sight of her. I was older than you before I realized she couldn't help herself. The disease controlled her life."

"Just like Mom's mental disorder, or depression, or whatever, is controlling her life," Chris says.

"A wise woman, namely your aunt Rita, told me the other day that she'll keep giving your mom chances until there are no chances left to give."

A long moment of silence fills the closet. "Aunt Rita's been through the worst with Mom. If she can forgive her, so can I."

"I'm trying to be better about judging others," Presley says, thinking of her husband and how she's struggling every day to remain optimistic about their marriage.

"Amy says we shouldn't assume how other people feel until we walk in their shoes."

Presley nudges her brother. "Amy is a smart girl. She's a keeper."

"I think so too." Even though she can't see his face, Presley hears the grin in Chris's tone.

32

OLLIE

Ollie needs to buy herself some time. She takes several deep breaths as she collects her thoughts. She's being held at gunpoint by a lunatic. But that lunatic is her baby brother. Even though he's six years younger, he's always tried to bully her. Ollie has never let him get away with it before. If she can help it, she won't let him get away with it now. In her experience, bullies will push you around until you stand up to them.

Ollie risks a glance at Lucy who is somehow managing to keep a straight face as she struggles to free her hands. Although Ollie had wrapped the scarf around Lucy's wrists several times, she tied the knot loosely.

Ollie focuses on the papers in front of her, tapping her ink pen on the desk as she reads.

"What're you doing?" Alexander demands.

"I'm reading. Duh. I never sign anything before reading it first."

He kicks her chair. "Hurry up."

She tosses the pen on her desk. "Nope." She swivels her chair to face him, glaring past the gun in his hand to his face.

"Not until I get some answers." She softens her tone. "Why'd you do it, Alex? Why'd you kill our parents?"

"I wanted to make some changes, to bring the winery into the twenty-first century. But Dad refused to listen to my ideas." A hint of regret crosses his face, but it's soon replaced with anger and hatred.

Ollie says, "Our traditional approach instilled confidence in our ability to produce the best wines. Our customers enjoyed stepping back in time when they walked through the door. They appreciated and expected our old school ways. With that said, there were some things we needed to do to make ourselves more current. Why didn't you come to me with your suggestions? We could've worked together to make these things happen. You didn't have to kill our parents."

Alexander's dark eyes are black pits of rage. "Not just our parents, Ollie. You were meant to die in that fire."

Ollie is on her feet, the gun forgotten. "What about Mom? She had nothing to do with the business."

He shrugs. "She got in the way."

Out of the corner of her eye, Ollie sees Lucy reaching for the bronze statue of Aegle, the Greek goddess of radiant good health.

Ollie snatches up the papers from the desk. "I refuse to sign these." She tears the papers in half. "You'll have to shoot me to get my inheritance. But then you won't be able to spend it in jail."

"I have no intention of going to jail." He raises the gun, preparing to fire.

"I wouldn't do that if I were you. Do you see the painting on the wall behind me?" Ollie aims a thumb over her shoulder.

His gaze shifts slightly left. "What about it?"

"That's Stella's great-grandfather. He established Hope

Springs Farm back in the 1920s. Notice anything unusual about his right eye?"

Alexander squints. "No."

A smug smile appears on Ollie's lips. "His eyeball is a live-streaming video camera, monitored around the clock by our security team. And you just confessed to killing our parents."

"You're lying." Alexander grabs Ollie's arm and manhandles her over to the painting.

As they pass the sofa, Ollie gives Lucy a nod, and Lucy comes at Alexander from behind, cracking him over the head with the bronze statue. He collapses to the floor, taking Ollie with him. The gun slips from his grasp and drops to the carpet two feet above their heads with a clunk. Ollie is attempting to slide from beneath her brother's deadweight when he comes alive. He spots the gun, and they wrestle for it, clawing and biting as though they are children again. Ollie grabs his testicles and grips them hard until he screams out in pain.

Lucy scrambles for the gun, and with shaking hands, she aims it at him. "Don't move!"

Ollie gets to her feet and takes the gun from Lucy. "Go for help," she orders, and Lucy flees the office.

Ollie points the gun at her brother. "Interesting turn of events."

Alexander snorts. "You won't shoot me. You're too afraid."

"I've never been afraid of you, you little punk." She positions the gun and shoots a hole in the carpet inches from his head.

Recoiling, he shrieks, "You crazy bitch."

"Next time I won't miss."

The door bangs open and police officers file into the room. Within seconds, Alexander is frisked, handcuffed, and taken away.

Martin arrives on the scene. He removes the gun from Ollie's hands and embraces her in a bear hug. Her body begins to tremble, and he shushes in her hair. "It's okay, now. You're safe."

He leads her out of the office, to the elevator, and outside to the pool deck where Lucy is standing with a female police officer, a blanket draped around her shivering body. Breaking free of Martin, Ollie rushes over to Lucy. "You saved my life. I'm so sorry you got dragged into that."

To Ollie's surprise, Lucy presses her lips into a smile. "Most excitement I've had in a

while."

A white security truck parks near the pool gate, and Chris and Presley emerge. Chris throws himself into Lucy's arms. "I'm sorry for the things I said earlier. I love you. I don't know what I'd do without you. Please, don't ever leave me." He draws away to look at her. "Are you okay? You didn't get hurt, did you?"

Lucy cups his face. "I'm fine, son."

Ollie places a hand on his shoulder. "Your mom's a hero. She saved both our lives."

Chris's gray eyes pop as he looks from Ollie to Lucy. "You did?"

"Ollie's exaggerating," Lucy says. "It was a team effort."

"What happened?" Presley asks.

A knowing look passes between Lucy and Ollie. "My brother was the shooter," Ollie admits. "He started the fire that killed my parents. He intended for me to die as well. He came here to finish the job."

Presley furrows her brow. "That's awful. I'm so sorry. Thank goodness you're okay. But how did Lucy get involved? She left the hot springs ahead of me."

"She forgot her phone. When she came back for it, Alexander was holding a gun on me," Ollie says and recounts the events of the evening.

"Go, Mom!" Chris says when Ollie gets to the part where Lucy knocks Alexander over the head with a brass statue.

"I'm just glad everyone is okay," Lucy says.

The fear she's been holding back overcomes her, and Ollie breaks into tears, her body trembling. "I'm so sorry, Lucy. You could've been killed. You all could've been killed because of me."

Presley takes Ollie in her arms. "Not because of you, Ollie. Because of your brother. And he's in custody now. We are not responsible for the sins of our fathers or mothers or brothers. Only the sins of our own."

33

STELLA

Rita and Lucy throw a going-off-to-college bash for Emma and Chris on a Sunday afternoon in late August. They invite half the staff as well as family and other friends, including Jazz. Jack and I offer to pick up Ollie on the way. I'm worried about her. She hasn't been herself since the incident with her brother.

Jazz begs to ride shotgun, and Jack gives in, as he often does on short drive. When we stop for Ollie, she climbs into the back seat with me. She looks gorgeous in a white linen tunic and white leggings with her dark hair piled messily on top of her head. There's a sadness in her aquamarine eyes, and I worry she's been crying.

When Jazz and Jack begin singing loudly and off key to country music in the front seat, I place a hand on Ollie's arm. "Are you okay?"

She sucks in an unsteady breath. "I will be. Alexander's trial is set for mid-September. He'll remain in jail until that time."

"That's excellent news. You must be relieved."

"I don't know what I am, honestly. My emotions are conflicted." A sad smile tugs at her lips. "Jazz shared the name of her therapist."

"That kid is eight going on twenty," I say with a little laugh. "Have you seen Dr. Grant yet?"

Ollie nods. "A couple of times. My first sessions have been productive."

"I totally understand if you need to take some time off."

Ollie appears alarmed. "Not at all. Work is the one constant in my life, my motivation to get up in the mornings. I love my job, Stella. The last thing I need is time off."

"Good. Because I don't know what I'd do without you." I give her arm a squeeze. "My door is always open if you ever need to talk. And you're welcome to stay with us anytime, if you're feeling down and don't want to be alone. I have plenty of spare bedrooms."

"Thanks, Stella. I appreciate your concern," Ollie says, her voice tight and eyes wet with unshed tears.

Ollie goes silent, and I assume she's composing herself during the remainder of the ride to Rita's house.

Jazz insists on carrying the gifts she helped me pick out for the graduates—cotton throw blankets bearing the inn's logo for their dorm rooms. We follow the sound of music around to the backyard, which is decked out for the garden party with bulb lights strung across the patio. A long table is covered in hot pink linens with bouquets of fat zinnias in bright colors running down the center. Parker is stationed at a makeshift bar, mixing drinks and pouring a pale green concoction from a pitcher.

Jazz runs off to deliver her gifts, and Ollie excuses herself to powder her nose. When Jack goes to the bar for drinks, I make my way over to Presley who is chatting with her grandparents, Rita and Lucy's parents. Even though I've met Sam and Carolyn Townsend numerous times, I'm once again struck by the uncanny resemblance between Presley and her grandmother.

I greet everyone, including Emma's younger-by-one-year sister, Abigail. My gaze lands on Emma. "So, this is it, huh? Are you all packed and ready?"

Emma grins. "You know it! Mom, Abby, and I are heading out at the crack of dawn tomorrow. Chris doesn't leave until later in the week."

"We loved having you this summer. You're pleasant to be around and enormously resourceful. At any point in the future, if you want to work with us at Hope Springs Farm, you've got yourself a job."

"Thanks for the vote of confidence, Stella. But I'm like Presley." Emma loops her arm through her cousin's. "Hope Springs is too small for me. I'm gonna live in LA."

I smile, more to myself than Emma. I once thought big cities were the only place to live. Now I wouldn't trade my small town for anything.

When Emma launches into an animated monologue about parties for the rich and famous, I turn to Presley. "What have you decided? Are you planning to stay in town until the baby comes?"

"I've been meaning to talk to you about that," Presley says, and we separate ourselves from the others. "I don't want to talk about Everett. I might cry and ruin the party. But things aren't going well between us. I haven't heard from him since he was here in July."

"Oh honey. I'm so sorry." I reach out and tuck a stray strand of auburn hair behind her ear.

She swats my hand away. "Don't be nice to me right now, Stella. I can't handle it. I'll burst into tears and ruin the party for the kids."

"In that case . . ." I give her my best bitch face, and we both laugh.

"I never dreamed I'd have a baby at age thirty. But here we are." She rubs her belly. "I love this little one more than life itself. We don't need Everett. We'll figure things out on our own. My mother's disease forced me to grow up at a young age. I've always been self-sufficient. And I'll teach my child to be the same."

"Relying on others who love you isn't a weakness, Presley."

"I know that." She holds her chin high. "And I need my family and friends more than ever right now. Which is why I'd like to rent the caretaker's cottage if the offer still stands."

"The cottage is all yours for as long as you wanna stay." A lightbulb goes off in my head. The solution makes so much sense, I don't know why I haven't thought of it before. "Actually, I'd like to hire you to be the interim caretaker."

Presley's brow creases. "You don't have to create a job for me. Although, if you need me, I'd like to continue planning events with Amelia."

Taking Presley by the hand, I drag her farther away from the others. "Actually, I'm in desperate need of a caretaker, a second in command. And you would be the perfect person. I'm pregnant." I press my finger to my lips. "Don't tell anyone. I'm keeping it a secret until I reach the second trimester. But I feel awful. Morning sickness all day long."

"So that's why I haven't seen much of you lately." Presley's gray eyes are bright. "I want to squeal right now, I'm so excited for you. And for me. We're gonna be mamas together."

My mind spins. "I'm serious, though. Will you be my caretaker? I realize you'll need time off when the baby comes."

"Not too much time. I'm hoping to get a nanny."

"I plan to do the same. I can't see either of us being happy as stay-at-home moms." I lean back against the fence. "With Emma leaving, Amelia will need an assistant. We're looking to hire a second full-time event planner. Ideally, you'll oversee all of the events. You'll be busy doing both jobs, but I'll pay you well. And you'll live rent-free at the cottage."

Presley wraps her arms around herself. "I just got chill bumps. I'm totally up for the challenge. I haven't been this excited about anything in a long time."

"Me too." My shoulders slump as I exhale a deep breath. "I can't tell you how relieved I am. Now I can sleep all day and not feel guilty. Which is all I've been doing when I'm not puking my guts up."

Presley hugs me. "It'll get better soon."

Nearby laughter gets our attention. Brian is talking animatedly, and Rita and Lucy are swiping at happy tears. "I wonder what's so funny," Presley says, and we cross the patio to join them.

"I'm glad to see everyone is having a good time," Presley says.

"Brian is trying to set me up with a goofball," Lucy says, and the sisters burst into more laughter.

Presley and I exchange a look, as though they've lost their minds. I look over at my uncle. "Care to explain?"

Brian chuckles. "Andrew is a friend of mine. He recently divorced his wife. He's a successful attorney, a rabid pit bull in the courtroom. He's a bit of a goofball, but in a good way."

Rita straightens. "Brian was telling us funny stories about him."

Lucy presses her lips thin, as though fighting back more laughter. "In all seriousness, Brian, thank you for thinking of me. But I'm not ready to date. Maybe in a few months. For now, I want to spend time with my son." Her gaze shifts to Presley. "And my daughter."

There's not a dry eye in the group when Presley takes Lucy into her arms. Lucy finally appears to be getting her life in order.

I break away from them and go in search of Jack. We mingle until Rita calls us to the table for dinner. She delivers a touching speech about how much her daughter means to her and how much she'll miss her when she's gone to college. Abigail, Lucy, and Rita do a skit about Emma and Chris that has the whole table in stitches.

Parker cooks the hamburgers to perfection, one of the few meals I've been able to keep down in weeks. I watch Cecily and Parker while I devour the meal. The two are oblivious to others around them, lost in their own little world. Cecily's green eyes sparkle and her face is rosy as she listens intently to him talk. I never saw her smitten like this with Lyle. I'm happy for her. At the same time, I worry it's too soon after her breakup, and I don't want to see her get hurt.

After strawberry shortcake for dessert, I pull her aside. "What's going on with you and Parker?"

She places her hand on her heart. "I swear. We're friends without benefits. I must say, though, I have to control myself to keep from jumping his bones. But I'm waiting. For both our sakes, I want to make certain I'm over Lyle."

"Wait a minute." Taking a step back, I give her the once-over. "Who are you? And what'd you do with my impulsive friend Cecily?"

"Ha ha." Her face turns serious. "I'm trying, Stella. He's so wonderful. I don't want to screw up my chances with him. I never felt like this about Lyle."

"I noticed. You're actually beaming."

She touches her fingers to her face. "Really? I loved Lyle. But in a different way. Lyle and I viewed the world through two very different lenses. Parker and I have the same values, the same goals and ambitions. It's almost too good to be real. We're on the same page about almost everything."

"Just be careful."

"Trust me, I am. For now, we're just hanging out, getting to know each other."

"That's important. I'm happy for you, Cecily," I say, giving her a hug.

After cleanup, when the others settle in for after-dinner drinks on the terrace, Jack and I bid everyone goodnight and retrieve Jazz from the sofa in the living room where she's fallen asleep. When we arrive home, I help Jazz up the stairs, leaving Jack to let Angel out and lock up. After tucking her into bed, I retire to my room and change into my pajamas. I'm standing at the window, staring out at the inn, when Jack comes up a few minutes later.

Standing behind me, he says, "You're a million miles away. What're you thinking?"

"I'm worried about Presley and Everett. Their marriage is in trouble. His newfound fame is presenting challenges. Do you think love is enough to make marriages last?"

"Sometimes. But not always. In order to weather the worst storms, it helps if husbands and wives share similar beliefs and a vision for the future. Lucky for us, you and I see eye to eye about most things."

"I agree." I turn to face him. "Cecily figured out the hard way that she and Lyle were on opposite ends of the spectrum concerning fundamental issues."

"At least she realized it before making a colossal mistake," Jack says.

"True. I hope Presley and Everett are just going through a rough patch. But I'm worried they don't have the glue to keep it together."

"Who knows after their whirlwind engagement and wedding," Jack says with a chuckle.

"True. They didn't really think through either."

Jack kisses the end of my nose. "You're gonna be an awesome mama."

"That's a nice thing to say. You're gonna be an awesome dad too."

"I'm serious, Stella. You're already a great mother hen to your other chickens. Not only to Jazz, but to Cecily and Presley and Ollie as well. You're an excellent leader. You exert the right combination of sternness, empathy, and sincerity."

"I do feel like their mother sometimes." I rest my head on Jack's chest. "But mostly they feel like my sisters. I've never had friends like them. They mean the world to me. Trouble has a way of following those chickens around. And I sense there is more on the horizon. I will do everything in my power to protect them."

ALSO BY ASHLEY FARLEY

Boots and Bedlam

Lowcountry Stranger

Her Sister's Shoes

Magnolia Series

Beyond the Garden

Magnolia Nights

Scottie's Adventures

Breaking the Story

Merry Mary

ACKNOWLEDGMENTS

I'm grateful for many people who helped make this novel possible. Foremost, to my editor, Patricia Peters, for her patience and advice and for making my work stronger without changing my voice. A great big heartfelt thank-you to my trusted beta readers—Alison Fauls, Anne Wolters, Laura Glenn, Jan Klein, Lisa Hudson, Lori Walton, Kathy Sinclair, and Jenelle Rodenbaugh. A special thank you to my behind-the-scenes, go-to girl, Kate Rock, for all the many things you do to manage my social media so effectively.

I am blessed to have many supportive people in my life who offer the encouragement I need to continue the pursuit of my writing career. I owe an enormous debt of gratitude to my advanced review team, the lovely ladies of Georgia's Porch, for their enthusiasm for and commitment to my work. To Leslie Rising at Levy's for being my local bookshop. Love and thanks to my family—my mother, Joanne; my husband, Ted; and my amazing kiddos, Cameron and Ned.

Most of all, I'm grateful to my wonderful readers for their love of women's fiction. I love hearing from you. Feel free to shoot me an email at ashleyhfarley@gmail.com or stop by my website at ashleyfarley.com for more information about my characters and upcoming releases. Don't forget to sign up for my newsletter. Your subscription will grant you exclusive content, sneak previews, and special giveaways.

ABOUT THE AUTHOR

Ashley Farley writes books about women for women. Her characters are mothers, daughters, sisters, and wives facing real-life issues. Her bestselling Sweeney Sisters series has touched the lives of many.

Ashley is a wife and mother of two young adult children. While she's lived in Richmond, Virginia for the past 21 years, a piece of her heart remains in the salty marshes of the South Carolina Lowcountry, where she still calls home. Through the eyes of her characters, she captures the moss-draped trees, delectable cuisine, and kindhearted folk with lazy drawls that make the area so unique.

Ashley loves to hear from her readers. Visit Ashley's Website @ashleyfarley.com

Get free exclusive content by signing up for her newsletter @ ashleyfarley.com/newsletter-signup/

facebook.com/ashleywfarley

twitter.com/AshleyWFarley

instagram.com/ashleyfarleyauthor

CPSIA information can be obtained
at www.ICGtesting.com
Printed in the USA
FSHW010547211021
85595FS